FAMILY PACK

KALI METIS

RUNNING WILD

RUNNING WILD PRESS

FAMILY PACK

Published in North America and Europe by Running Wild Press.

Visit Running Wild Press at www.runningwildpublishing.com Educators, librarians, book clubs (as well as the eternally curious), go to ww.runningwild-publishing.com for teaching tools.

ISBN (pbk) 978-1-960018-87-8

ISBN (ebook) 978-1-960018-42-7

They had been told that she would be the cure to their ongoing war.
She would be their revolution.
But revolutions don't always happen as expected.

1

THE TRANSFORMATION BACK

Not all revolutions end how you'd expect them to. Some seemingly never truly end. They just take detours. Damn, I hope this is a detour.

The last we spoke, I had returned from Chago's crazy plan to take over the human race through a world war via the United Nations. Even as I write that, I cannot believe it was real. But it was. At the very last minute, The Lycanthrope Society, also known as TLS, came to my rescue, right when Chago was about to chop my head off. Instead they chopped off his. At least I think they did. I kind of blacked out at the last minute.

Not that I came out of it unscathed.

Not even close.

Instead, they had to fast track me to the emergency room to have me looked over and treated. Although I had passed out in the ambulance from the screaming pain - my muscles felt like they had been torn from my bones, my mind on fire with an inconceivable migraine from the mental battle with Chago which caused me to only see clouds of darkness, and my body covered in tears from the physical stand off of werewolf to werewolf. I jolted awake in a secret TLS location raging forward, my mind still in battle with the nearly immortal killer, Chago. Four caregivers held me down as a doctor injected me with a painkiller that, after a few more moments of me battling to get away, finally caused me to pass out. When I awoke again, it was in a high security patient's room, my mind still drowsy from the drugs and my body numbed by whatever they had given me to help encourage my wounds to heal. That said, the simple act of moving my head or lifting my arm brought forth the kind of muscular pain similar to what an athlete must feel after completing a marathon. Holy smokes.

All of this said, another good thing about my bloodline is that descendants of Ulf and Freya tend to heal rather quickly, so I was able to return home to Javier relatively fast. Remember, he was still in the hospital being treated after that wicked attack by a druggie. At least that's what we thought at the time. Luckily, I was healthy enough to be released the night before Javier was permitted to leave the hospital. I was there beside the wheelchair when the orderly wheeled him out to the car.

I drove him home with orders to make sure he rested and didn't do anything crazy. He had taken a rather serious hit when the supposed drug addict, later to be revealed to be a descendant of a different lycanthrope bloodline, Rebecca Lovegrove, had forced her way into the emergency room where Javier worked and demanded drugs only to be stopped by the nefarious efforts of Paul, the ER doctor who had recruited Javier to work the overnight shift with him.

I still don't know why Paul insisted Javier work the overnight shift with him, or why he pushed the override button which prevented Javier from getting into the restricted medicine cabinet. I had assumed he admired Javier and wanted him to be by his side for the challenging cases they find in the emergency room, but I'm not so sure.

I mean, in terms of Rebecca's appearance and his wicked actions, I can guess that Rebecca had been told to come in and make a scene. Which kind of makes sense considering she was aligned to Chago and The Righteous Group (TRG).

But I made a lot of assumptions with that. It was a side effect of my newly discovered lycanthrope condition to have an overactive mind racing for explanations, conclusions, and, simultaneously, assumptions. So, I assumed that Chago already knew who Javier was and that we lived together and that he knew who I was. Just the thought of that gives me chills.

And, if putting a scare into me and shaking my confidence was Rebecca's goal, then she definitely achieved it. She would actually be considered an overachiever. But Paul's actions, I still don't know why he thought that was appropriate. And the paranoid part of my brain has some scenarios, but I just cannot entertain them.

Anyway, on our way home, Javier placed his hand on my leg, and that simple act - that touch - was something I truly needed. I needed the feel of *us* after the events of the last several weeks, even if the touch was something as small and simple as his hand on my thigh. I smiled at this gesture, eager to get him home and I daydreamed about simply snuggling with my fiance and doing all that I could to help him heal. That's when I noticed his hand was lightly shaking. Not dramatically, but the kind of shake someone would normally experience after muscles have been overexerted after hours of exercise.

He had been looking out the window, checking out the neighborhood as we drove through, and at first he didn't notice it. Then, as if in an afterthought, he looked down, quizzically, and then looked at me.

"Must be the medication," he said and then gave a small smile.

I placed my hand on top of his and lightly squeezed, just

enough to demonstrate an acknowledgement of his comment and returned my hand to the steering wheel of our gray Mazda as we neared our apartment complex, a four-story modern building with a tan exterior and underground parking lot. It had been built the year before we moved in. Originally the parking lot for a next door elementary school, East Camden Elementary, it had been built to address a perceived lack of housing in the area. Believe me, we were happy to move into such a modern place for such a great rental price so soon out of college for Javier and pastry school for me.

At the time, I didn't believe this shaking could be the result of my sharing my own blood and performing the transformation ritual on him. Mind you, I didn't elect to make him into a werewolf haphazardly. I did it to save his life. If my guess had been correct at the time, then he wouldn't have begun his own transformation until years from then.

Hell, I hadn't begun my own shaking, one of the initial signs of the change, until my late twenties so it didn't make sense for him to begin so soon after the ritual had been performed.

At least that's what I thought.

I spent the next few weeks of homebound bliss caring for Javier. We had a daily routine rooted in me making sure he healed from his wounds.

During the day, I worked as the head specialty baker at *Bizcocheria,* which had been my second home even before I had graduated from school. I simply reveled in sifting the flour, folding the eggs, measuring the vanilla extract, cinnamon, cardamom and other spices so they were just so. The scent of the rising dough was ecstasy supplemented by the feel of the raw pastry dough between my fingers as I kneaded it in preparation to be formed, rolled, and cut. The flavored frostings, lavenders and chocolates and coconuts and lemons were specialties spread on top of specialties. I couldn't believe how lucky I was to have such an amazing role and to work for Margarite. She owned the business, and had welcomed me into her kitchen, treating me as a member of her family.

But I had family concerns of my own, so at noon, I would hand the production over to Alfina, Margarite's cousin, grab my car keys, and run home to check on Javier. I'd tiptoe into our small two bedroom apartment in the Eastern part of Camden that we had shared since graduating from school. We had moved into that apartment to be close enough to our respective sets of parents. We were both very close to our families and wanted to be able to see and visit them whenever we wanted while still maintaining our own private relationship and intimacy to feel like we were on our own.

I entered our bedroom. Javier miraculously had his favorite throw blanket with his favorite comic book character, Grim-Jack, across the foot of our bed was a true giveaway that she had visited.

At home, I would quietly enter our bedroom where Javier, usually wrapped up in his favorite throw blanket and his latest copy of the GrimJack comic (his favorite) close by, would greet me. I didn't think about it then, but I could never catch him asleep. He was always alert when he greeted me, impossible to sneak up on or ever be quiet enough to catch him napping. He shifted his way up in bed, as he readied for me to give him a kiss and his medication.

Then I curled into bed with him, enthralled by the feel of him, his warmth, and his natural musky, sweet smell. He wrapped his arms around my shoulders and asked how my day had been so far as I nestled my head on his chest.

I lay on my side, cupping his cheek in my hand, pulling his face towards mine so we could gaze deeply into each other as a sense of really seeing each other tightened our embrace. I always got lost in those moments. We gently kissed and then I ran my hands through his hair, before sitting up and maneuvering his body to massage his back and leg muscles.

Once I knew he would be okay, at least until I returned from work, I gave him another kiss and I made my way back to finish out the day.

That had become our midday ritual since he had been released from the hospital.

Then, after returning back to the cafe, as always, Alfina would wipe her hands on her apron and give me a high five as she headed out the door. She typically brought her lunch and ate it at nearby Whitman Park.

She and I were constantly enmeshed in special orders we needed to finish for an evening gathering in Rittenhouse Square, Philadelphia. Catering gigs we were offered as a result of our treats from the United Nations affair we had catered.

Yes, that's right. Although it had resulted in a bloody battle with the leader of a werewolf faction who tried to take over humankind getting his head chopped off, our little family bakery had been pummeled with catering requests from those who had reveled in the undoctored treats - the ones without the "special" ingredients meant to wage a battle against werewolves.

Alfina was a private person, and I didn't ever feel a need to fill her in on the more dramatic events of my day. I was just glad she was happy and let me care for my fiance while we knocked out orders. Heck, whatever worked, ya know?

And it was an absolutely wonderful set up. I figured that as soon as Javier was ready to return to work, and Margarite had plenty of catering orders to last several months, then we would be all set. Thankfully she had forgotten about the work I had missed earlier in the year. I knew from my conversations with

Birger that I needed to return to Sweden to finish or rather start my training.

Heck, after I'd found out about my lineage, I had heard about the importance of training with Birger so many times, I figured I should make it a priority. Even though part of me - that overactive mind again - questioned if this was truly a priority, considering Chago was no longer around.

And that's when the real shit hit the fan.

About ten days after Javier had been released, I headed home from the bakery around 5:30. I wanted to be sure to get home in time to make us dinner and ensure that Javier had everything he needed. I made a pit stop at my mom's and left some special treats for her and Papa. And, of course, I wanted to check on them to make sure they were okay. I knew that the loss of my brother Daniel was hard on them, especially on Papa, even though he never said anything, so that made my visits, even if only for five minutes, much more important.

I hugged them both and asked if they were okay; I knew they wouldn't tell me the full truth. I could see in Mama Olivia's eyes that she didn't believe me when I said I was fine. I saw her note my bruises.

"Luna," she said, "your smile. It's not the same as before."

I shrugged and politely changed the subject. "Javier is well enough now, so we will come over on Sunday. After church, okay? I'll bring treats, ok?"

She nodded and Papa smiled.

Before the assault, Javier and I would go over for brunch after my parents finished church - it was a nod to when Daniel and I were kids and the events had the equivalent of a banquet meal after giving thanks. In those days, neighborhood families would stop by and bring their own familial specialities to share.

Those moments were ones that really made us and our neighbors, a community - a family.

With that promise, I headed home, cognizant of the day's sun as it retreated and the moon encroached upon the day.

Once home, I always tiptoed into our bedroom, not wanting to disturb Javier if he was asleep. Admittedly, as the days passed, he was more often up in bed and reading or watching television when I arrived. His face brightened the moment he saw me.

He joked, "When do I get my engagement ring?"

I laughed. "Soon, soon," I waved away his comment as if it was in the air before me and a simple swipe would take care of it.

He patted the space next to him in the bed, inviting me to join him. He asked about my day at work. I placed my hand in his and told him about my day and brought him up to date on my parents and the latest with Margarite and some of our regulars who were old friends from the 'hood. He told me how his mama had stopped by and how she invited us to visit as soon as he was ready. He gave me a side glance as if to say that he wasn't quite there yet, but soon.

We kissed during breaks in the conversation. I reminded him about his medication. I got up and made sure he had what he needed before I made us a quick dinner of leftovers. This time, crockpot chicken stew made with a whole boneless chicken, carrots, potatoes, and celery. I always made dumplings with Bisquick, a tradition from when we were kids and his mama had made chicken stew with Bisquick dumplings as a special treat on Fridays.

Only after he had been fed, and I knew he was not in pain and asleep, did I go into the living room, hit the Zoom button on my laptop, and reach out to Birger.

We had planned out my eventual return trip to Sweden,

and I wanted to be sure I got as much done as I could in as little time as I could. It felt like much of our conversations were actually negotiations for me to do whatever I could remotely so I didn't need to leave Javier. It seemed like just about every request that varied from the standard way of doing things required permission from The Lycanthropic Society's board of directors.

Kind of nutso if you asked me. Total overkill, but whatever.

I stayed on with him until I could barely keep my eyes open and then snuggled into bed alongside Javier. I woke up from a deep sleep by the sound of quacking ducks, my iphone's alarm. The sound of ducks made me laugh. I hopped up, kissed him on the forehead and lips, got his meds, made a quick breakfast of toast with peanut butter and bananas, then hopped in the shower and drove to the bakery. Thankfully, Margarite was still in the habit of stopping off and picking us up cafe con leches so that helped to perk me up and get through the day.

At least that's what typically went down. I had the same, basic routine every day, same bliss at the bakery, same snuggling at lunchtime, same high five upon my return, same quick side trip but this time to check on his parents, same return home, same convo with Birger, same euphoric exhaustion as I crawled into bed.

And then, I woke up in a corner of the parking lot of our apartment building. A far corner in a darkened section farthest from the exit. My clothes torn to shreds. My body was covered in dirt and grime and other fluids I couldn't and honestly didn't want to identify. With care, I moved my arms and legs to check how damaged I was. I had the definite tell-tale signs of a wicked fight. I slowly stood up. I swear every muscle ached. And then I noticed the slashes across my forearms like I had shielded myself from a blow. What the hell had happened? Had I been in a fight and if so, with whom?

The moonlight shone through the entry to the underground parking area, telling me that we had not gotten to the morning yet. As fast as I could hobble, I made my way back to our apartment. Thank god we were only on the second floor so I didn't have too many flights to go and thank goodness we kept a spare key in a hidden lockbox otherwise I would have had to wake Javier to get my ass back inside. The last thing I wanted to do was explain why I was covered in shit, with slashes across my forearms (I hadn't checked the rest of me yet), bruised, and out in the middle of the night. Questions I couldn't answer. Well, at least not fully. And the answers I could give him, I knew he wouldn't like or wouldn't believe.

I made sure to clean up as best I could and cover up the injuries. I didn't want him to question me while I prepped for the day. That said he looked at me really oddly as I ran around to get him what he needed. Then, before I could make it out the door he asked, "Are you okay? What's going on?" He didn't look accusatory or upset, but rather perplexed like this was a mystery he wanted to solve.

I smiled. "I'm fine. Just running late. I'll call you later." I hurriedly kissed him on the forehead, fully knowing that he leaned in for a smooch on the lips. I knew that I wouldn't be able to fake like everything was okay if we kissed more intimately, so I stuck to something less incriminating and rushed out the door. Thankfully my car was in the normal parking spot, so at least that didn't get impacted. I texted Birger to warn him that we had to talk. I didn't go into details since I didn't have a chance to check our apartment for more listening devices like what I had found before. And I definitely didn't want to risk someone overhearing that convo. Shit. If someone had been listening, what the hell had they heard?

I made it to the bakery in record time, eager to get back into the swing of things. Definitely distracted from all that the events of the last few hours implied.

I was able to hide the scrapes, cuts, and bruises which thankfully had already healed quite a bit, a benefit of being a direct descendant of Freya and Ulf. So, Margarite didn't notice it. Plus I think she had lots of other business-related things on her mind. Alfina didn't say anything though I honestly think she did notice. We work so closely together that I would be surprised if she didn't, but I digress.

I thought about skipping my typical visit home at lunch hour but didn't want to chance it. Plus I figured I could send Birger a more detailed message through our secure chat via my laptop which would at least give him time to prep something, anything, for our call that night.

I grabbed some of Javier's favorite treats and let Margarite know that I would be back after lunch. I totally didn't expect to find in our apartment what waited for me. As I unlocked the door and called out my standard greeting, I peeked around the corner of the hall to find Javier as he kneeled in front of the bed, in his hands a ring box.

Holy shit.

I rushed over to him, doing my best to keep from crying in joy and surprise, covering my mouth with my hands until I kneeled in front of him and captured him in an embrace.

"I love you, Luna. I've loved you since the first time I saw you in third grade. Will you marry me?" he whispered in my ear. His voice soft, his tone pure.

I leaned in and kissed him deeply on the lips. He needed to know, so, with all of my body, I said yes. I pulled back and looked him in his eyes and cupped my hands around his to where we were both holding the ring box.

"I love you with all of my heart and soul, Javier Josef Rodriguez. I'd be honored to be your wife."

He moved my hands from his and opened the ring box. He removed a small plain gold band with a round cut diamond in its center and placed it on my ring finger.

He looked up at me and smiled with a snarky look. "I decided to stop waiting for you to get me my ring, so I bought you one instead."

I laughed out loud. I could see the twinkle in his eyes as he playfully said these words.

"Damn good thing. Otherwise, I could have forgotten," I laughed.

We kissed again. This time a joyful embrace that filled my soul and replenished my spirit.

I looked up at the clock and realized the time. "Oh shit. I have to go." I pecked him on the cheek and apologized. "I can't chance pissing Margarite off," I said.

He nodded in acknowledgement. He knew I had truly risked a lot to take so much time off and that I was worried that Margarite would fire me. We had talked about it several times. I helped him back up from the floor and as I guided him to our bed. He waved me off.

"I'm good. Go on back to work. I'll see you tonight."

Surprisingly, he didn't need a cane to get back up. Instead of our bedroom, he drifted to our living room and picked up one of his favorite editions of *Scalped*. I brought over his meds and a glass of water. He dutifully took them, glanced at my newest bit of jewelry then as he pronounced our unity, he kissed me on the hand.

"I'll be fine," he said. "I'll see you tonight."

With his acknowledgement, I made him a quick tuna sandwich with eggs, relish, mustard, and Miracle Whip with a side of Doritos and returned to the bakery.

. . .

That night, I waited until I was absolutely sure that Javier was asleep before I checked on whether or not our place was bugged. And of course, goddamnit, I found two listening devices. This time, I nearly crushed them, too pissed off to care whether whomever was spying on us actually knew that I had found the devices.

I felt my other-self wanting to come forward out of my anger. The passion that came with the fury caused my animalistic self to surface. I realized I simply couldn't allow my bestial-self to come out. I needed to calm down and take control of my emotions. I took deep breaths and practiced yoga breathing to help me re-center. Within my mind's eye, I saw my other-self calm back down and return to its place of safety.

In that moment of calm, I knew I simply couldn't allow it out until I had retained as much control over my bestial self and all of its various forms at all times as possible. If I didn't know that I had full and complete power over it then everything—every move, every countermove, every thought—would be too much of a risk.

I looked towards our bedroom and sadness came over me. I could not hurt Javier. I couldn't harm our families.

I gazed upon my engagement ring for a few moments and wondered what I should do next. I absolutely needed answers, even more than before.

Then, emotionally re-centered, I used some techniques that Birger had taught me to keep the listening devices intact while I disabled their ability to hear our conversations. With conviction, I made my standard call to Birger.

Before he had the chance to say hey, I blurted out, "I thought Freya's spell meant I could control my changing. All the time. Not just when I'm awake."

"Hello to you, too," he said in an atypical sarcastic tone. He must have been around me too long.

"I can't keep ... you know." I made hand motions to represent the changing. "I can't have people here seeing me in the ... ya KNOW." I emphasized the "KNOW" part in case he didn't truly follow my references. "Plus I don't know what's happening." I paused. "I can't risk hurting anyone," I whispered. The passion in my voice gave away my deep concerns.

He looked at me quizzically. That's when I realized I hadn't actually explained what had happened the night before. I had assumed he somehow knew. I took a deep breath and walked him through what I could recall from the last 24 hours - dirt, grime, injuries, and all. When I finished, he sat for a moment and then asked, "Why do you think you are changing?" He said this completely straight faced. I nearly fell over.

"If I knew that, don't you think I would have told you already?" I huffed. I tried hard not to be frustrated, but the more I thought about what I woke up to that morning, the greater the fear and the increased hesitancy to sleep since I had no idea what I would wake up to tomorrow morning.

My expression must have given me away because he immediately replied. "I'll need to do some research." This time with greater seriousness. "The only time I've heard of this happening was when there was a break in a tight bond between two lycanthropes. The closest would have been Daniel, and since Daniel was never trained and had never gone through the full ceremony, it's doubtful. Plus you're from the same blood, but not of the same blood, meaning Daniel didn't make you a Lycanthrope."

"What you're saying is that if the person who made me a lycanthrope had died then it's more likely that I'd be experiencing this, right?"

"I've never heard of a full blood who has gone through Freya's ceremony having these difficulties. That said," he paused for a second and collected his thoughts. "'I've never had someone go through the ceremony and not immediately be trained."

"You're saying my eagerness to get home to my family caused this?" I probably said this with a little too much annoyance and sarcasm but ... oh well.

"It's possible," he shrugged. "Let me look into it. This may take me a few days. I'll message you as soon as I have something to share."

"Great," I said flatly.

"In the meantime, may I suggest you figure out how to get back here? Since the only known way I can think of to correct this is to go through the full ceremony, but have it conducted by a full blood. And not leave in a hurry before it is completed. You'll need to return."

"I thought I was some rarity. One of the last ones? Who the hell could perform the ritual?"

"Me."

2
BIRGER, HISTORIAN

*Only when you lose all that you have loved do you realize the
importance of keeping them alive.*
Even if it's simply in the pages of a book.

T hat is how I arrived here, a few hundred years ago. My
brother and I had been taken from our natural home and
launched into a world that we could have never understood
until we were in it—and even then it was questionable. And
with those learnings, which I will provide later, we grew to
understand all that we were meant to do.

Some would say that I am not ancient enough. Some say I
do not have enough learning or wisdom to be of value. That
there is much more I need to understand before I can truly be
considered of any note.

I am aware that there are others who have lived much
longer than I. With each passing day, it seems that number

dwindles, yet there are others who are present and make themselves known from time-to-time.

I have been around long enough to know pain and to understand the importance of each and every moment that has passed. Remaining present in the actions of the day is vital because the learnings within those moments will assist in future events. These are things I must teach Luna in order for her to reach her full potential—control her reactionary tendencies—to fulfill her prophecy. For her to become all that she is meant to become, I must take the teachings from the last several hundred years and those scripts from well before then and get her to understand, no, to *embody*, the ways of The Lycanthrope Society and all that we are meant to be.

It had been predicted that one day a Lycanthrope would be born who could unify the warring factions. Those factions have been at war since well before the ones who are currently in the leadership roles had even been born. They may believe that they are the originators of these tribes, but that is far from the truth.

Until they open their minds to understand the natural and true state of the world which has always included humans and all other species, they will battle ad infinitum.

I was put on this earth to be the historian of these factions and to guard the records I've inherited from past chroniclers and those from the line of Hiwa. I was also put on this planet to protect and wait for prophecies foretold hundreds and in some cases thousands of years ago.

For in these predictions, the one who comes forth to unite our worlds will lose all in the process. And in that loss, she would find her true meaning before she understood the totality of what we may gain from her sacrifices and actions.

INTERLUDE 1

BIRGER

O ur beginnings were not of note. My brother, Ulf, and I had been born to parents not of means. They had left us at the doorstep of the first Christian Church in Birka. A modest building of stone and wood, it resided next to a Norse place of worship deep in the woods.

Barely out of our toddler years, I do not remember when our parents abandoned us at the church door. We were also unaware of the significance of our parents' choice to leave us with the Christians. They could have easily left us with the Norse worshippers or at the Temple Uppsala.

The first memory I have is of my brother and me was being instructed by the Monk Ansgar, but he had recently moved on and put us in the keeping of his student, a recruit named Monk Árni. I can still see Arni's flowing gowns as he stood godlike over us.

Árni had barely spoken to us previously. Considered rejects, throw aways, very few of the church acknowledged us. Even at the Monk Ansgar's guidance, others typically walked by us without a word or glance. When instructed to oversee us upon Ansgar's departure, Árni snarled. At that moment, I had chosen not to focus on his response. Ulf seemed fearful.

That night when we had finished our evening prayer and were guided to our straw beds, Ulf whispered to me in our backroom behind the horse stalls. "This is not good," he said. His voice barely audible. "We must go."

"Why?" I questioned. "We have all that we need."

"Not without Ansgar. Not without his protection."

I shifted under my woolen blanket. "You worry too much," I said.

"I do not trust this one." He did not have to say who he referenced. I knew.

"Give him time," I murmured.

Ulf looked uncertain, but then shook his head and agreed. With that we wished each other a good night.

And then the next morning, after we had finished our morning meal of stale bread and yogurt, Árni demanded we follow him. "You must earn your keep!" He bellowed. His commanding voice and insistence surprised me. Until this point, we had been cared for by Ansgar who fed us and taught us. Yes, he had us sweep the church and pray before the cross, but his commandments were nothing like the fiery demands of Monk Arni.

In shock, we must have paused too long for his liking, and he pulled Ulf and myself up by our hair and drug us across the dirt floor before the altar and stated, "Kneel!"

To this command, we had no difficulty. In pure terror, we kneeled before the cross and put our hands in prayer as we had witnessed churchgoers do many times before. He shoved our heads down into the dirt.

"You must show proper respect," he stated. I knew better than to look at my brother to see his reaction. "You shall repeat," Arni began and then went forward in prayer with nary a pause to give us a moment to restate his words of worship. As I cowered, my focus was purely on Arni's voice. I wanted to be sure that I repeated exactly what he said in the same cadence that he used. I did not want to give him any reason to be angered further.

For a second, I swore I heard Ulf replace the word, "God" with the word "Odin". I do not know if he did so with malice or to be playful, although playfulness in this moment would surprise me.

Arni stopped in mid-verse. The room filled with silence. I heard my heartbeat through my chest. Through the corner of my eye, I saw my brother's head suddenly slammed into the dirt. Then I felt Arni's breath as he leaned down over me, listening for something to incriminate me. I felt his breath against my skin. Smelled the anger as it rose from each pore. He sniffed as if something in the air would reveal a non-believer. Without a word, he moved onto my brother. His own breathing had become that of a beast. Somewhere inside he had to have known that even that slight change in prayer—the acknowl-edgement of another belief system within this area—would cause him pain. And yet he still rebelled with that deviation in the prayer.

Arni's face was an inch or closer to my brother. He sniffed. I uncontrollably shook with fear and anxiety. I swear I heard a growl before he grabbed Ulf by the back of his neck and declared, "You. You shall do the bidding of the true God!"

He then forced Ulf up from his kneeling position and into a back room. I heard my brother's cries, heard his calls for help. Heard his body slam against the wooden walls, tossed across the room to the hard-packed, dirt floors. I prayed to whatever god would listen to me to help him. Save him.

I whispered a prayer to the Monk Ansgar to come and help my brother. He may not have treated us as his own, but he never beat us. He may have had us act as his personal servants, but he fed us. He did not do *this*. Never this.

I have no idea how much time had passed, but eventually, Arni returned from the backroom and commanded me to get up. His voice without emotion. His stance dictatorial. Obediently, I did so and without question I performed the chores he then prescribed. He did not mention nor reference his violent exchange with my brother.

As I cleaned out the horse stalls, I reflected on the time with Ansgar and missed his readings from the Bible as if they were bedtime stories. I missed him allowing us to greet the churchgoers, even if they treated us as pets of the church. They looked at us with blank eyes. They petted us on our heads as they entered and placed gifts in our open palms. Ansgar had guided us that all gifts were spiritual gifts to the church and should be treated as such. With that guidance we gave them to him. I wondered where he had gone and if we could go with him; I longed for those earlier times.

When Arni called for me, I shuddered with fear, an automatic response based on his past actions. I knew not to ask what had happened to my brother, even though all I wanted to do was find him and help him. But Arni kept me busy all through the rest of the day and into the night. He did not allow me to rest or even take an evening meal.

"This is how you are to show your true faith," he said to me. "You must earn the true God's love and protection." And with those words, he finally allowed me to return to our simple room behind the stalls. The evening had fallen. My stomach was empty, but it had closed upon itself due to the anxiety of the day so even though I had not eaten since breakfast and the work had been harsh, I could not fathom eating a single bite. I simply wanted to find my brother.

When I entered our room, I had hoped he would be there.

Instead I found both our beds empty. I searched throughout the building in search of him and could not find him. With tears, I was ready to give up. I assumed the monk had beaten him with such fervor that Ulf was no longer with us. The thought was both real and surreal since we had been together for as long as I knew.

I searched all the rooms and passages until I came upon a small alcove just off of one of the stalls. And that's where I found the entry. A hidden door in the dirt floor behind the altar. By this time the monks had returned to their own rooms so no one was around to observe my seeming misbehavior. My brother had to be down there. It was the only place which remained.

I lifted the wooden door to find it covered an opening within the dirt floor. Within was a wooden ladder which led down into pitch darkness. I could not wait to find a light, I needed to know if he was there. I climbed down the ladder and felt as if the pitch enveloped me, making me a part of it. I lost my normal senses within the darkness. I whispered my brother's name in the hopes that he would hear me, too afraid to speak at a normal volume in case my voice gave away my rebellion to the point of being found.

"Ulf, please." I quietly begged. "It is me. Birger." I waited a moment and felt around the pitch. I carefully made my way farther into the space, one small step at a time. My foot knocked against something soft. I reached down and felt another's garment.

"Ulf?"

To that a slow, quiet moan replied.

"Ulf, are you okay?" I knew the answer to this question. Of course he was not okay. How could he be when he was tossed into the bowels of this space.

"Leave," he whispered.

"No, I need to know." I reached down and could feel the wounds on his skin. I could only imagine the depth of the beating he had taken.

"You must go," he said. His voice husky with exhaustion. "You cannot be here."

"I will not leave you," I declared. "I will not allow this." My instincts told me that Arni had tossed my brother in these nether regions as if he had already been declared that of the otherworld. Later my instincts would be confirmed. In this moment, I only knew that the one person who had been with me throughout my life was in dire pain and needed help.

"You must leave me," he repeated. "I will be fine."

"Not like this," I could feel his wounds, the inflammation. He jerked away from me.

"I will find a way. I will leave. I will be fine," he said. "For now, I need you to go."

"But ..."

"Trust me, Birger. You are my brother. We are of the same blood. The same heart. I will find a way out of here and then I will return for you."

"How?"

"Go." This was a statement. Not a request. Not an inquiry. With this word and his tone, I knew that I needed to obey him. I needed to trust.

I did as he asked and returned to our modest space. The next morning Monk Arni returned for me and immediately had me prepare the church for the upcoming service. As I wiped down the pews and washed the altar, I overheard a more junior monk arguing with Arni.

"But they will find them."

"Good," Arni replied. "They need to understand the power of our true god. They need to know that we cannot be ignored."

"But this is not the way," the other monk replied. "Only pagans treat other people like this. Treat them as sacrifices. We do not give of the flesh at the altar."

"We are not giving human sacrifices. We are simply reinforcing our power by demonstrating our physical might which is reflective of our spiritual might."

I looked up from my work and saw the questioning stare of the junior monk. Arni seemingly ignored him, too lost in his own words to hear what the other monk tried to tell him.

"This is how it shall and will be done," Arni stated and walked away from the junior monk.

As I indulged in the breakfast of bread and yogurt that the same junior monk had provided me while Monk Arni was preoccupied, preparing for the day's services, I witnessed the junior monk disappear into the hidden passage with a bag of food and a torch.

Once I was sure he had made it fully down the ladder, I snuck over, reopened the wooden door in the floor, and looked down. Within that limited illumination, I saw what he had referenced to Arni.

Ulf was not alone.

In that pit beneath the altar were multiple bodies in various states of beating. Some looked near dead if not already gone. Ulf looked up to see me. Our gazes locked and I gasped. This could not be the way, I thought. This simply could not be right.

Behind me I heard footsteps so I rushed away from the hidden door and returned to my chores. I swore that I would find a way to save him.

Before the service, as was the custom that Ansgar had initiated, I stood at the entry to the church before service with my palms opened to receive the spiritual offerings from the parishioners . They smiled and granted a coin and then patted my head. Some asked where my brother might be. I gently ignored their question, too afraid that anything I might say would reveal what I knew. Instead I looked away.

I was directed to take service like the others, but in the back of the church, sitting on the floor. Arni felt I had not earned the right to sit with the villagers, those who had been baptized in the nearby lake. "Once you have sworn to the true god, then you will be allowed to take service with the others, but not before."

I did not question. I simply obeyed. At the end of the baptismal service, I cleaned and scrubbed, as I had been directed. Monk Arni had returned to his quarters to prepare for the next day's services and to reinitiate Ansgar's efforts to bring villagers to the Christian faith by visiting neighboring nearby towns and preaching his faith.

I looked out of the window and I saw the junior monk speaking to another. One I had observed at the Norse services in previous nights. They were somewhat hidden underneath a cluster of birch trees. I considered where Monk Arni's room was, I doubted he could see them conspire. The junior monk animated in their discussion. He waved his arms with passion and motioned towards the church. The Norseman's face changed from one of curious listening to being enthralled in the conversation, and then, to fury. He nodded in acknowledgement of the man's words and they separated. The junior monk returned to the church through a rear entrance that only those of lesser status typically used. I am sure he did this not to be seen.

When I looked back up, the Norseman had gone.

. . .

That night, I had retired to our room. I had pocketed coins in preparation for our escape. I simply could not live this life anymore. I could not stand the way that we were treated. Just as I readied to retrieve my brother, the evening darkness deepened. I made my way outside and saw the neighboring Norsemen conducting a midnight ceremony. Their voices chanted in unison in a language I did not understand. Here and there I noted the names of their gods Odin and Tyr.

Their chanting grew in tone and repetition. The sound of the drum used in service grew in intensity. I felt their fervor, their might. Suddenly, the torches that lit their place of worship gave away their true intent. They headed to the church in which their bloodlust was as evident as their need for retribution in each and every movement.

I ran from the church and hid in the neighboring forest. Far enough not to be taken, but close enough to observe their actions.

They took their torches to the chambers of the monks who subsequently ran from their place of rest. As each monk ran in terror and screamed for their god to save them, they were ravaged with arrows from archers and beheaded by swordsmen. I nearly vomited from the bloodiness, the savageness of the executions. The scent of the burning, the sounds of destruction nearly overwhelmed.

The cries.

Dear God.

The cries haunted me for centuries.

I ran more deeply into the forest, afraid that they would note that I was missed since Ulf and I had become mainstays. I did not know where to go. I slept under a cluster of spruce trees and hoped that in my rest something divine would reveal itself.

I prayed for my brother. I did not know if the attackers would find the hidden door nor what they might do with those they found inside. I only knew that those were most likely the final moments of my only sibling.

With that acknowledgement, I cried myself to sleep.

The next morning, I returned to the place of worship only to find that the Christian church had been burned to the ground and lined up, as if in pews, were the remains of the bloody, disembodied, mutilated monks,

I found the remains of Arni and could not help but smirk. Since the horrible treatment he had forced upon others, this seemed like an apt death. I did not find signs of my brother nor of the junior monk.

I hoped this was a good sign.

I searched the ashen remains of the structure to find any remnants of them. I found the formerly hidden space, the ladder still intact. With the sunlight behind me, I was able to look within and see nothing. No signs of remains. No remnants of others. I prayed that somehow they had escaped this cruel and bestial death. This additional punishment for what I would never be quite sure. And with that confirmation that my brother was not among the remains, I began my trek to where I did not know.

I only knew it had to be away.

3
LUNA - QUESTIONS, MORE QUESTIONS

I swear I didn't know what to say when Birger laid that one on me. He's a direct descendant of Freya and Ulf too? Holy shit?!? I mean the way he and Bo talked about me and Daniel, I would have thought that they hadn't heard or seen another descendant in decades. After the initial shock wore off, I asked Birger for more details like how and what did it make us? Were we cousins? Is he my uncle? Did he know my parents? Who were they? Why did they give me and Daniel up?

After I had pummeled him with questions, he simply nodded in acknowledgement and politely said, "Luna, I need to go. I will talk to you about everything in greater detail as soon as you get here."

I must have had a what-the-hell look on my face because he continued with, "We need to get you back so we can perform the ceremony together. You need training."

I don't think I ever heard Birger get frustrated, but his annoyance definitely leaked through his last words.

It became pretty clear that he used the details of my family background and the truth of my parents as enticements to get me back to Sweden, which I understand. I don't like it, but I understand it.

I got off our call and immediately opened my browser to do more research on my family line and Birger's family line and see if I could find anything that even inferred a solution to my current physical problems.

I know he said that I simply needed to redo Freya's transformation spell and have him drive it, but I didn't feel like I had the time to wait for that. I knew I couldn't get back to Sweden the next day. I had too many responsibilities here. But I couldn't risk what my uncontrolled changing implied. I couldn't put so many at risk. I mean, I understand that I had no proof that when I changed I caused someone else harm, but I couldn't help worrying about it. I guess I was just afraid that I would unintentionally cause others harm.

My bruises and cuts were definitely proof that someone or something tried to cause me harm, and that fact alone kept me up at night.

The more I surfed, the less I found. Most of what I found on the internet referenced fairy tales. I had no idea there were so many variations to the werewolf and shapeshifter mythologies. I think every country has its own version. Lots of stuff made up for movies, which is cool but not what I was looking for. Not that it wasn't entertaining because it damn well was. But it didn't help my current situation.

I surfed the Ancestry.com community boards, rootsweb.com, ancquest.com, genforum.com, iaf.gov and a ton of others to see if there was even a hint of The Lycanthrope Society or The Righteous Group. I even posted on some of these boards questions like, "Are you a member of TRG or TLS? Please reach out." Or "Are you a descendant of Ulf and Freya?" Something that gave just enough information to get someone's attention but not enough for someone to get mad.

Or stalky.

Well, hopefully.

In the middle of my searches, daybreak came and I felt like I had barely started my investigation. There had to be more. There had to be a better way.

I had even brought out Daniel's old computer to see if there was something I may have missed in his notes. Other than a few more references to ancestral community boards and some sites on the Norse, the Vikings, and the Berka, I didn't find a whole lot that was useful.

I made my way to the kitchen and boiled water for some rather intense French press coffee by using double the ground beans than what I was used to. It was like I chugged extra strength espresso. Who knew there was such a thing?

I looked in on Javier to make sure he was okay. Curled under our burgundy comforter and snuggled atop our cotton pillows, he was still fast asleep, thank goodness. I swear I heard him lightly snoring. Again, a good thing. The less he was aware of, the better.

I took this opportunity to hop in the shower for a quick hot one and hopefully rejuvenate from the spray and cleanup before I set up everything for my *novio* fiance.

When I pulled off my shirt, I noticed that the injuries from the night before were nearly fully healed. *Holy shit. Now that's amazing.* At least I had some solace in that fact. One less thing I had to try and hide from my significant other. I must admit, I really got tired of this. We never had secrets before so this felt like a pile-on. One I was ready to toss aside.

I allowed the water spray to relax my muscles and rejuvenate my body. The scent of Irish Spring soap, Javier's favorite, perked me back up. I jumped out of the shower and quickly dried off before I tossed on the nearest t-shirt and dark blue stretch jeans. The more comfy the better.

Next thing I knew, Javier called for me. I found him in the living room, still a little slow and he looked lost. When he saw me he said, "Where were you? Are you okay?"

"I'm fine," I dismissed. I figured acting like nothing was wrong was the right move.

"You never came to bed last night. I could tell by your pillow—"

That statement told me that he wouldn't accept a dismissal of his concerns, so I went over to him and hugged him. I placed my hands against his back and rubbed them up and down in the hopes that it would calm him.

"I'm fine," I whispered. My breath gently caressed his ear. "I just had a bunch of stuff I wanted to look up last night. No biggie." I said these words with soothing and care while I pulled back and led him over to our Oyster gray overstuffed IKEA couch. Although he had clearly healed quite a bit since we first brought him home, I wanted to be sure that he didn't overexert himself. As I held his hand, I sat on his side on our sofa.

He looked over at Daniel's open AppleBook. "I thought all of that was done."

"Well," I paused. "Kind of." I looked down at the floor. This was not the conversation I wanted to have with him at dawn after a full night of no sleep.

"What does 'kind of' mean?" He clearly didn't want to hear what I was about to tell him but I had to. I sighed.

"I'm going to need to go back to Sweden."

"Why?" he asked. I could hear the concern in his voice. Not anger but more like he thought we had resolved everything with Daniel and had put those mysteries behind us. My father had taken care of Daniel's burial and celebration of life. This allowed me time to grieve a bit more. Otherwise, I would have obsessed over the details of the funeral and gathering. With those final moments achieved, it allowed all of us to officially close our gates of mourning. I think much of our families had allowed themselves to mourn and then move on. Not to forget, but to continue with their lives.

Including Javier and me.

"I have some more work to do there." I couldn't look at him. I wasn't sure how I would respond if we made eye contact. I was afraid I'd blab about all of the work I'd been doing. Or break down crying about waking up in the middle of the night covered in crap and scrapes. I was definitely working off of caffeine and adrenaline, so I couldn't risk it. Just the thought made my stomach turn sour.

"Work? What do you mean, 'work.' *Ay Dios mio*. What the hell is going on, Luna? You never stay up all night."

Should I have told him that I did it for his own good? To keep from transforming into something that may hurt him? Should I have told him that I needed to do this for our future? For our families? Based on his initial reaction, this was not the time. Maybe soon, but not now.

"There are a few more things I need to resolve," I said quietly and calmly and then sighed.

He interrupted, "A few more things?' What is that supposed to mean?"

"I'm sorry, Javier. I know this is difficult, which is why I've been putting it off."

"I'll come with you," he declared, his stance grounded and strong.

"No," I stated.

"You cannot keep going there alone."

How should I have explained that I was not alone? That I minimally had Birger and Bo in the far away country and possibly an entire tribe of people there? I had a full library of family history to explore, learn, and understand. And there's a deep part of me that needed to know. After I had spent the majority of my life knowing that my brother and I had been rejected by our own parents for reasons I still needed to discover, and then suddenly we found out that we were part of an ancient family line with what some might consider magical powers?

I mean, *damn*!

It was like all of my childhood prayers had been answered in one Ancestry.com community board post. If I spoke to Javier with that level of candidness then he would want to know the details and I just was not ready to share. I was not even sure I fully believed and understood everything that had happened in the last few months. Plus a part of me was still afraid to reveal all of this to him. Afraid of how he might respond.

I looked up at him. "I promise I will take you with me. Just not now." I almost made a joke out of it—*We will go there together on our honeymoon and get our Birka on!*—but immediately thought better of it. His dead stare stopped me before I could let out a chuckle.

He quietly sat and simmered in vexation as evidenced by him eyeing me. I knew that look. It was the "I'm checking on you to see what your next move is going to be," look.

We had been together long enough that I could nearly predict his reactions. Not totally, but nearly. That said, I could not leave him like this. The last thing I wanted was for him to feel alone and definitely *not* like I was leaving him. We had been through too much.

"I love you, Jay. I've loved you since I first met you when we were in Dudley Grange Park and you and your friends came to my rescue. I knew, in that moment, that you were the kind of man I could be with forever. I just ... " I shook my head. "I need to do this part alone."

I placed my hand on his leg and he deeply looked into my eyes as if he tried to observe my soul. I then let out a breath I hadn't realized I had been holding in. I wanted to continue, but I honestly did not know what else to say.

Sometimes silence is the best healer.

"Fine," he said. "I don't want to but … fine," he murmured.

I kissed him on his semi-chapped lips and we paused for a long embrace. Damn I needed that. I needed his touch, his feel, I needed us. In that moment, I considered changing my stance and asking him to come with me to Sweden. But a bigger part of me was too afraid of what Birger might reveal on this trip. I just couldn't risk having Javier along before I had a better understanding of what was about to go down. I had no idea what Birger had to teach me and I just could not risk getting those answers with the potential loss of the one man I have always loved.

I must admit, after that all-nighter with few answers and the morning "coming to Jesus" talk—as Daniel used to call it—my workday sucked. I really had a hard time staying awake. Even with the cafe con leche that Margarite brought over on top of the coffee I had chugged at home. It definitely hyped me up for a little bit, but it kept wearing off. I grabbed another one just to try to keep the caffeine rush going, but dammit this was hard. I even went to the bathroom and tossed cold water on my face and did jumping jacks. Anything to get my adrenaline going and perk me up a little bit. Alfina looked at me like I was insane. I doubt anyone thought I was 100 percent normal considering my gift to predict our customers' favorite treats.

At lunch I jogged around the block to get my heart rate up and then headed home to check on Javier. That felt like the longest short-drive of my entire life. I could not wait to get home. I ran up the steps of our apartment building to keep from passing out.

I found him in the living room watching one of our old favorite movies, *Back to the Future*. He was still huffy after our morning conversation and he did not even turn to look at me when I came in. That said, I was able to get him to laugh a little bit when I served him a hamburger with the ketchup in the shape of a smiley face.

Surprisingly, when I gathered his afternoon pills, he waved them off. "I don't need those anymore," he said and then he motioned to the bottle of painkillers. "I'm good. No need for the big guns." He must have been healing even faster than I had expected. He didn't look nearly as sluggish as before. In fact, his movements were even closer to his normal motions.

"Are you sure?" I asked.

He nodded in affirmation. "I'm thinking of heading back to work soon. Maybe in the next day or so."

"Will they let you?" I asked. I honestly had no idea. "Isn't there a minimum amount of time you have to be rested?"

"I'll call and see what they say. I'm sure if I check out okay they'll let me back early."

I looked at him quizzically. This felt wrong. "You were shot, Jay."

He shrugged. "So?"

"It's only been a few days."

"I'll be fine," he said.

This definitely felt wrong. "I'll leave the painkillers here. Just in case you change your mind," I said as I put them on the coffee table next to our couch. I kissed him and reluctantly returned to the bakery.

I barely made it through the rest of my day. I did my best to get absolutely as much done as I could before heading back home. I worked with my assistant, Eddie, to get different batches of batter together so they could sit overnight and set before we got to work again in the morning. We even pulled together extra batches so they could be used while I was away.

Proudly, I lined up the bowls of dough and wiped my brow as I closed the industrial sized refrigerator. I guided Alfina to the recipes and cooking instructions so she could find them while I was away.

Margarite, who typically worked the front counter during the day and handled business stuff in her small office in the back, had finished up the last of her errands for the day and had closed shop. After she locked the front door, she came over to me. "Looks like you've gotten a lot done today," she motioned to the ice box.

"We've had lots of great orders lately. We even prepped the recipes for tomorrow's batches."

She nodded.

"We should be all set for the next few weeks, actually. I've been training Alfina on how to handle some of the special requests and our standards."

Margarite laughed, "You sound like you're going some-where," she smirked.

"Well ..."

"Oh come on, Luna!" she exclaimed. "What in the world could be going on now?" she asked.

I couldn't make eye contact. "I just have a few more things ..." I trailed off.

She looked at me as if she didn't hear me correctly and then sat on a stool next to the backroom table. "Time off? For what?" she asked.

"I have some more family stuff I need to take care of." I paused. "Not a lot. Just a few small things."

She looked at me questioningly. She had always stated that family came first and treated us like extended family, but her response made it clear that I definitely pushed my boundaries. "We are just a small family bakery," she said. "You aren't the only baker here." At first I thought she said this with attitude. And then, she seemed to search her mental notes for how to continue. "Alfina and I can take over for you while you're gone. But people expect you," she said.

"I understand—" I began.

"You have become synonymous with us." She interrupted. Not in a judgmental way but more so like she tried to figure some things out. "I guess if we need to, I can call Mama and bring her back to help out in the back."

To her credit, she definitely pondered how she could support me in this. She could have rejected me and told me to get out. And honestly, I would not have blamed her. This was a lot to ask of her and her family. I stayed silent, not wanting to interrupt her train of thought. She rubbed her eyes. "Tell me, Luna. Are you going to need to do this regularly? Do we need to change how we are running the shop?"

I knew what she meant. Did they need to bring on another baker? Did I need to move to part time? Did she need to let me go?

"I think we'll be okay," I said. "After this time, I don't think I'll need to take more time off for a while. It's just that..." I looked up at her. I knew she wouldn't understand, or at least I didn't think she would, but I didn't know how else to say this. "This has become something I need to do."

She paused. She looked down at the mixing table. I could tell she tried to figure out how significant this was.

"A while, huh?" She looked me up and down, as if she wanted to see if she could believe me. Which I understood considering all that had gone down in the last few months. She only had access to whatever I chose to tell her, so I am sure she wondered how much of this was bullshit and how much was real.

She absentmindedly wiped her hands on her apron. "Okay, my friend. Just let me know when you are ready and we'll figure it out."

In a rush, I hugged her and thanked her. I had always loved her like a sister. She's the reason I was able to pursue my love of making pastries and she's the only reason I was able to go to one of the best pastry schools on the East Coast. She had always been such an incredible supporter of me. I just didn't know what to do with myself. I was near tears with gratitude. "This means more than you can know," I said. "I'll do whatever you need to set things up so nothing is disturbed while I'm away."

And I meant every word. I simply could not imagine putting her or the bakery at risk, even if it meant my life.

"Fine, fine," she waved me off. "Now go take care of *your* novio."

That night, I returned home and things with Javier seemed to have settled down. He was more responsive to me, more engaged. He also seemed more mobile, a definite plus. He wasn't kidding when he said he felt better. Although he still moved slowly, he was definitely moving at a pace closer to normal. Looked like things here were settling down so my trip to Sweden was actually feasible. Although I still questioned if he should go back to work so fast, everything felt right for me to head out to take care of my family issues.

Once Javier was in bed, I reached out to Birger to see if he had any more answers. I could tell the moment his face appeared on the video chat that he did not.

"I am still trying," he admitted. "I have a lot of records to go through."

I told him about all of the message boards I had found and the different groups I had left notes for. At first he looked concerned, like I may have made a mistake in reaching out, but when I explained what kinds of messages I left and the vagueness in the questions I posed, he calmed down.

I then walked him through all of the inroads and agreements I'd made towards getting back to Sweden. "Now that is great news," he said. "I know it is tough, Luna. We are asking a lot of you, but it is truly the only way I know of to be sure that your abilities have been reset and your control has been returned." He paused for a moment and then continued, "And there truly is much, much more that you need to learn."

Yeah, I got that. "I understand," I told him.

"Luna," it felt like he looked directly at me. "I know you probably want to try this on your own ... reset your abilities without me. And I understand that. But ..."

He paused for an eternity.

"I cannot promise that this will work without my guidance," he said. "And to be honest, I am worried because the last time someone's powers were not controllable... Well, at least the last time I am aware of ... was over 2000 years ago and that was with your great, great, great ... Freya."

"Okay," I did not know what else to say because, admittedly, I had seriously considered simply redoing the spell without his help. I mean, hell ... I did it on my own the first time, why not do it on my own again?

"And I know it is tempting to do it on your own, but I do not know what will happen."

"What does that mean?" I asked. I mean, *seriously*. He seemed to have answers to nearly everything up until this point, so he could not leave me hanging like this.

"We need to get you a plane ticket and we need to get you

back here. Hopefully in the next few days. In the meantime, I will keep researching what our ancestors have done."

"So you're saying you don't have a real answer."

"I am saying that you need to get back here."

The moment I got off the call with him, I restarted surfing for answers. Hell, Birger didn't need to be the only one to search for a solution. Just because it sounded like he was a billion years old did not make him right.

I don't remember falling asleep. The last I remembered, I was going through Daniel's digital folders, hoping I had missed something of note. Something that could lead me to a solution that didn't demand I go to Sweden.

Next thing I was aware of was waking up in the schoolyard across the way at East Camden Elementary school. The half moon was still bright in the night sky. I checked my appendages for indications of a fight. No overt signs, but definite scrapes and the beginnings of bruising. I moved my limbs to see if I had any pains. Nothing of significance. I felt my chest, shoulders, neck and face. Definite soreness like I had fallen or taken a blow, but nothing like I had the previous night. Well, at least I hadn't been in a battle. I don't think I'd been in battle. That part was good. But something definitely had gone down.

Of course, I had to wonder what brought me to this exact spot, but I had to deal with my number one concern—I needed to get back to my apartment. That sounds weird, right, but think about it. The last anyone from my "normal" life knew, I had been at home and getting ready for bed with my fiance. With that context, then really nothing else mattered. I needed to keep my "normal" world under the belief that I was 100%

human and there was absolutely nothing weird going on in my life.

I guessed—hoped—since I had changed once in the night, then I would not change again, so I joyfully returned, eager to lay next to my man. It had been too long since I could comfortably curl up against him and enjoy his embrace that just the thought made me lighthearted.

I got up from the awkward spot in the schoolyard, walked over to the apartment building parking garage, and made my way up the first flight of steps, seeing nothing of consequence, and then turned the corner for the second flight.

Not thinking that I had a reason to rush, I slowly made my way over to our apartment entry. The pale blue door stood closed with a note on it.

Not paying attention to the note, I was more so obsessed with the old cheap black piece of luggage that had seemingly been thrown haphazardly into the hallway.

Doing my best to shrug off that little bit of a scene, I headed to our standard lockbox where we kept our spare key. I tried the passcode for what felt like it took endless attempts until I was able to open it.

And it was empty.

That couldn't be right, I thought. I could have sworn I had put the spare key back there. I returned to our front door and saw that the note had been addressed to me. In a scrawl that resembled Javier's but had seemed to have been written in a rushed manner, I opened it to find this:

Luna,

I don't know what is going on, but I cannot live this way. I cannot live with your partial truths. Your convenient misrepresentations. I especially cannot stand whatever it is that you have become.

You are not the Luna I've known for nearly my entire life.

You are not the wonderful kind girl I grew up with and dreamed of marrying.

Whatever it is you are, I don't want anymore.

J.

My legs buckled as I read the letter. I collapsed on top of the luggage, unable to process what he had written. Less than two days ago, he had proposed to me. He had pushed aside all of my fears and doubts about getting married, about truly giving my heart to another, and yet here I was with the most devastating rejection letter I had ever seen or even heard of. I couldn't even fathom crying. All I wanted to do was sink into the depths of the earth and be enveloped in it.

I knocked on the door in the hopes that he would answer to no avail. Not knowing what else to do, I pulled together the luggage and huffed it to my parent's home.

Meekly, I asked if I could stay for a few nights. Without question, Mama Olivia and Papa took me back, even in these wee hours of the morning. They let me stay in my old bedroom which had been converted into a sewing and crocheting room for Mama Olivia. Two hobbies she had always fiddled with, but only in retirement dove into.

I laid down onto the guest bed next to her sewing machine and box of crochet needles and yarn and begged for sleep to take me. Maybe something would come to me in dreams. An answer, perhaps, or at least a temporary reprieve from this nightmare.

Speaking of nightmares, oh boy did I have one.

A werewolf, straight up werewolf with nearly pitch black matted fur and glowing yellow-green eyes and bare teeth hovered over me in a thick fog. Like something out of an old Lon Cheney movie. With a deep growl, he sunk his long curved and sharp claws into my pajamas. The kind of knit sky blue pajamas I wore when I was a kid with clouds and all.

He pinned me to the earthen ground. His bestial scent overpowered me. I opened my mouth to cry out and nothing happened. I tried to break free, but it was as if an invisible barrier far stronger than even his grip kept me down. I shook and tried to shove him off of me, I even tried to knee him in the you-know-where and my legs simply didn't move—couldn't move.

You'll need to make a choice. A phantom voice spoke through the swirling fog. The werewolf glared at me, and I swear his eyes glowed a little more with each syllable.

The choice will not only change your life. but the world as you know it.

I tried to say, "Isn't that a bit melodramatic?" Yes, I own that this was clearly my defense mechanism coming forward. Humor tended to be a great leveler, but the words still refused to come. I felt my entire body fill with sorrow.

I just want my life back.

I want to be normal.

The werewolf snarled in a way that was more like a laugh. With his entire body, he seemed to chortle at my thoughts and then howled. His face contorted with a devious grin. He touched his nose against mine and then dug his paws in even deeper, his claws broke my skin. I knew this was a warning but all I wanted was to be home. The pain shot up my arms and legs. I opened my mouth to scream and again my tries were useless.

It then treated me like I was the pedestal that it stood on and with a mighty howl dove forward like he was going to devour me.

. . .

I woke up, drenched in sweat, the need to dive out of the beast's way still prominent. My whole body shook from the adrenaline. I could feel him jumping on me and had the desperate need to get out of the way.

I pulled up my shirt sleeves to find claw marks still seeping with blood.

Shit.

I sat up in bed and took a few deep breaths to calm down. I looked out the window to see neighborhood kids heading to school. The coolness of the autumn day came through the partially opened window. It helped me reset myself. What the hell did that dream mean?

I heard Mama Olivia call for me.

"Luna, baby. Come downstairs for breakfast." From the sound of her voice, I guessed that, just like when Daniel and I were kids, she stood at the bottom of the two story wooden staircase and called up to me. It must have been later than I thought. I checked the time and tossed on the nearest clothes I could find. As I ran down the steps, I was greeted with the aroma of bread toasted in butter and her own special cafe con leche. As expected, she stood at the bottom of the steps in her oversized multicolored housecoat, black stretch pants, and fluffy pink morning slippers. This had become her favorite outfit since retiring. I didn't blame her, it must have been incredibly comfortable.

"Hola, Mami," I kissed her on the cheek. She handed me the toasted bread wrapped in napkins.

"*Que bueno?*"

I grabbed the breakfast and thanked her. "*Si, bueno.*" I could feel her uncertainty in my reply. I took a step back to really look at my adopted mama. "I love you, Mami. I promise I'll be fine." And hugged her with a full body hug.

She smiled in a way only a mama can smile when she's acknowledging her child's response but doesn't quite believe it.

"*Donde esta Papi?*" I asked. I hadn't seen dad since the previous day. Mama had greeted me when I arrived last night which was strange for Dad. Normally, he was on top of stuff like midnight visitors. Not that it happened frequently, but any bit of weirdness in the typically daily routine was handled by him.

She shrugged. "*Dormido,*" she said. "It's still early for him."

I unrolled the napkin and was greeted by the incredible aroma of butter, toast, and cinnamon.

She placed her hand on my shoulder. "*Mija,* are you sure you're okay?" she asked.

I couldn't meet her gaze. I felt like I would cry if I did. Instead I simply said, "I just need to figure things out." I took a bite from the toast and let the flavors give me comfort. She had a magical way of grilling bread that I swear I couldn't replicate.

I thanked her as I bolted out the door.

Thankfully Margarite was running late so she didn't notice my own tardiness. I quickly got to work, eager to get as much done as I could. I couldn't stop trying to figure out what had caused Javier to kick me out, reject me? What happened? What did he see? What did I do? I almost went to check on him over lunch, but then thought better of it. Margarite questioned why I didn't do my standard run home.

"He's doing much better now," I told her. Which was not a lie. Heck, for all I knew, he had gone to work today.

She perked up, truly happy at the news. "Good, good. Maybe he can come in soon and say hi?" she asked.

"Sure," I replied and then changed the subject to some-

45

thing less potentially heartbreaking like the tostadas we needed to prepare for an upcoming catered breakfast gathering.

That night, I came home to Mama Olivia and her homemade tostones, fried plantains, pollo guisado, and empanadillas. If anyone ever questioned where my love of homemade foods came from, this would be a great starting point. Papa sat grumpily at the head of the table. Per his traditional stance, he quietly ate while Mama Olivia served us. She truly got a lot of joy out of feeding us. When Papa sat back from the table and then got up and kissed her on the cheek, I could see her beam with delight.

Taking Papa's cue, I didn't make small talk during dinner. I just dove in and relished the meal. One I always daydreamed about whenever I was stressed. It truly was a comfort. Mama Olivia started to make conversation and then she must have thought better of it. I'm sure they had already had conversations about what had brought me to them at 2 AM with a suitcase in tow and ripped up clothes. I was also sure that even if she had stopped herself from bringing things up at the dinner table, she would revisit the questions that loomed over us once Papa had gotten out of earshot.

"*Mi hija,* come help me clear the table." She waved me into the kitchen. They hadn't updated a single thing in the house since Daniel and I were little. This was one place in the entire world I never wanted to change. I dutifully followed Mama and picked up a dish rag.

"You can pack some of this for your work tomorrow," she motioned to the pots and pans on the old white iron stove. "Grab the plasticware out of the cabinet and make a few meals for you this week."

Just as when I was a child, I dutifully pulled together packages to take into work for lunch and even made a few for my *parientes* in anticipation that they may want some of their own bits of loveliness during the week too.

"Papi loves the tostones," I said. "So I put double in his lunch boxes."

Mami got ready to argue. I'm sure she wanted to tell me how he doesn't need lunch and blah blah blah, but she stopped herself, stood back, and then watched as I packaged the lunches and put them in the refrigerator.

She shook her head and then with her hand on her chin said, "You do us all proud, niña." She smiled.

"I just want to be sure we all have for the week." I brushed off her compliment, really not sure what putting together some lunches had to do with making them proud.

"Come," she waved me over to the sink. "Help me with the dishes." She handed me a scrubbing brush and a plate and motioned to get to work. Without looking up, she asked, "Are you going to tell me what happened?"

I sighed. I really didn't want to. I wanted all of this nightmare to go away and for my fiancé to come back and not be afraid of me. At least that's how I interpreted it.

"I don't know," I said. "One minute I was in our apartment sleeping and the next minute I was out of the place and with my luggage packed."

"Damn. What you did must have been pretty stellar."

I laughed. "Yeah. Epic even."

"Well, Javier is a reasonable boy. I wouldn't be surprised if he shows up here to apologize." She whisked the bones from Papa's plate into the trash can beside her.

"I would," I mumbled.

"You don't give yourself enough credit, Luna. That boy has been with you through things others wouldn't know what to do with. He truly loves you."

She reached over and hugged me. The soap suds covered my hands and arms.

"I hope so, Mama. I hope so." I curled my head into her shoulder, thankful for this reprieve, no matter how small, from the world I'd experienced lately.

That night I debated over visiting Javier. I knew he was upset with me, but I have no idea ... okay that's an exaggeration ... I could guess why. I just wished he'd given me a chance to talk it through with him.

I convinced myself to curl back into bed and then revisit the broader conversation with him the next day. I tried my best not to stay awake. But I just couldn't stop imagining whatever it was that got him to react in such a huge manner. He'd literally never gotten upset or mad at me like this before. Never.

And that's when it hit. I thought it was another weird dream. I was in the middle of a field and being swirled with a dense fog that licked my arms and caressed my face. It swirled around me as if to tell me that I was welcomed there. I felt my limbs shake. A light vibration and then it seemed to morph into a more insistent variant. I looked at my hands and saw my fingers elongate from the knuckles and the nails thicken and lengthen and curl. In the middle of it I felt my back arch and it felt like my chest was going to hurl through my t-shirt.

"No," I insisted. "Not here. No."

Each word seemed to act as a trigger for the transformation to continue with greater intensity.

"No, this cannot be happening. Why is this happening?"

And that's when I physically burst through the transformation and found myself in the backyard of my parents' home, on the grass, erupting through my pajamas, the seams ripping through. I looked down to find my arms, legs, and chest in mid transformation.

"NO!"

I demanded as if my command would somehow affect the transformation. Somehow cause me to regain control, and then I realized that I had no idea what time it was or where my parents were or what I'd done in the middle of the changings.

Shit.

When I regained control of my body, I started for the back door so I could quickly get back inside, clean myself up, and hope they hadn't noticed anything. But that's when I realized my pajamas were covered in blood. I couldn't tell if it was human or animal and honestly, at that moment, I didn't care. I only knew that I could not risk causing them harm. I needed to get myself away from my parents.

I transferred my belongings from the cheap black piece of luggage, tossed them in an overnight bag, and got the hell out of there.

4

BIRGER...LIBRARIAN

It had begun simple enough. The queen of Denmark, Thyra, at the time, had been in discussions with the ruling factions of neighboring countries. All had agreed there was benefit in joining forces, acting as a united power. They agreed that together their influence could span continents. She had met with the ruling parties of the Norwegians, the Swedes, and the British. By the end of the week, only the Danes, Norwegians, and Swedes remained. The Brits had decided to move on, independent of this ruling party.

She had voiced a concern about the Germanic presence across the countries and that this presence did not desire what would benefit all parties, but rather, what would only benefit Otto I, the German ruler of the time.

Otto I objected. He said this was not true. He reiterated that he always sought what would benefit the masses and part of that meant that he worked to put as much of Europe under his control as possible.

He did not need to state that he sought to rule all of Europe; that was evident in his overtaking of Italy, Saxony, and all of Germany. And his battalions continued to hover and influence neighboring countries.

This did not put the queen at ease. Instead, it forced her to form what some might call an underground faction among the rulers. So that they would continue to keep one another engaged and informed for there were others who sought greater power as well, and the queen convinced the other rulers that the only way they would be able to retain their lands was to secretly join forces.

The queen had evidence that other factions were at play in many of the battles that had become synonymous with Otto I. In the process of forming her coalition, she had discovered groups that Otto did not have control over. She brought forward witnesses, trusted advisors to her court who were able to speak about transformations from human form to that of a bestial type which would occur before Otto and his men went into battle.

She convinced them enough that they agreed to meet under every full moon to discuss their next plans to keep their homelands intact. The fear of being taken over by Otto I was prominent and for good reason since his actions spoke louder than his statements.

Although the queen had not witnessed the changing from humans of her court to beasts of another type, she had been told of the dramatic metamorphosis of more than one group within her own party. This telling had been so passionate and urgent that she became determined to witness this transmorphism herself.

Under a full moon, she waited at the top of an overlook where her battalion had headed off Otto's most recent attempt at a bombardment. Atop that hill and under the bright moonlight, the clear night sky gave her a wondrous view of the rolling valleys below.

Late into the night and nearing the early morn, she waited, searching the rolling plains for signs of these creatures that her court members had spoken so intensely about. She neared giving up when across the plain she saw the glimmer of movement that had not been there a moment prior. She focused on that one area of the plains, determined to witness what her trusted advisors had seen.

Under the starlight she saw the movement as the sources of motion brayed and howled, hunted, and clawed the grassy plains in search of what she did not know. What she did know was that these creatures were not of the human-kind.

They were lycanthropes.

And that is when the queen's true influence began.

INTERLUDE 2

(800 AD) BIRGER AND ULF

I do not remember when our mother left us on the orphanage's doorstep. Based on what I was told, she had waited until a Sunday and after church service to put us there. Admittedly, in retrospect, she was quite young, even for that time. I would be surprised if she had been older than sixteen. A bit of a scandal perhaps. I vaguely remember her gentle caress as she placed us on the step, a soft smile, eyes of sadness, and then she was gone.

My brother, Ulf, did not say much at the time. Although he is the older of us, he tended to be a man of few words. I am guessing he was preoccupied with our mother's behavior since we had been shuffled around a bit. I had a difficult time keeping track of who we were left with and for what purpose. Sometimes it was for a day, other times a week. Other times longer. At one point I thought we were going to remain with a great uncle whom our mother had said she trusted.

"He will guide you," she had said. "He will be your best mentor."

She had behaved like she was going to leave us there,

meaning move on without us, but then in the middle of the night, she woke us from our makeshift cots in a backroom of our great uncle's residence, dressed us in a hurry, and took us back out on the road. Again, we did not know any difference. For all we knew, all children shuffled the countryside with their mamas in search of what felt like a permanent home.

When Ulf asked mama why we were leaving, she simply nodded, put her hands to our backs, and encouraged us forward down the winding dirt path into the hills. That lack of acknowledgement told us more than any verbal answer.

Since our father had long prior disappeared, and, to be fair, I do not know if he literally disappeared or if our mother made sure we were difficult to find, but either way, we had been on our own with our mother for as long as I could remember. She made no attempt to hide the fact that our world consisted of the three of us. No matter how frequently we asked for our papa or inquired as to the location of our grandparents or other extended family; our mother's answer was, "Not today." At the time I did not quite understand what that meant. I simply knew that it meant we were not to see those family members on that day.

Our mother, truly a child, had taken us with her across the landscape in various degrees of begging. I had thought it was normal for us to sleep on the sand packed earth under a star filled sky. Only when we had been given an actual bed did I realize that the circumstances in which we had been sired were unusual.

I remember the night she had wrapped us in blankets and placed us in front of the gated door, in anticipation of what, at the time, I did not know. I only remember reaching for her and her gently reaching out and shushing me as if I had interrupted midnight storytime. I had reached for her, my small pre-pubescent hands eager for the touch of our gentle mother. And when

I asked where we were to go next, she simply smiled and said, "Soon."

With that one final word came the last touch, the last caress I would ever experience from my mother; that Ulf would ever know as being the touch of our blood, our kin. And with that touch, she turned and disappeared down the road into the moonlight.

I do not believe we saw her again, at least not in a manner in which we recognized her as our mama.

I do not know what you have heard of orphanages from this period. They were somewhat unusual. I do not know if it is because children were rarely left for others to care for or if few accepted the responsibility to care for parentless children, but either way, most children were left at workhouses or with family who may or may not have treated the abandoned children as if they came from the same blood. In many cases families chose to behave as if the children were from another family line and put them to work in the fields or mines. From what I understand, we were lucky in that we were saved by one who saw something in us that others did not recognize.

We had been in the care and guidance of the militaristic regime of an orphanage. One we did not question. It was simple enough: get up, make our beds, clean the room, and then clean every space that we encountered from the moment we woke until we went to bed. Unusual, but effective. My brother would complain under his breath how they never truly cared for us and how the orphanage was more about capitalism than it was about caring for those who were in need.

I did not question, I simply listened as we made paths

through the hallways, bathrooms, and beds. I watched as other children questioned and fought and found themselves in a world of pain—isolated in remote rooms with limited ability to access others outside of our small living area. I saw others escape through the kindness of third parties who seemed like princesses and princes coming to save my brethren.

I simply observed and at night took mental notes of what had occurred in the previous days to help my brother and me plan the most beneficial exit.

Routinely, we performed our standard chores and ensured that the space had been spick and span until one day a woman of unknown origin had made her way into the remote space and conducted discussions with our instructors. As she made her way out of our temporary home, I followed. She took a path off of the main road, cane in hand. For an unknown period of time, I did my best to stay out of eyesight for fear that she would see me and tell me to turn back. Sure to be close enough to track her by sound, I continued forward. I started to worry as the sun went down that she had decided on a random path forward and that we would reach wherever she was headed before the moon's rise.

Not knowing or understanding where she headed nor her intentions, I continued in the wake of her footsteps until I reached a large oaken door.

Upon getting to this spot, I rapped my knuckles on the door three times and awaited a response. Truly, I did not know why I was there nor what benefit I had to gain from this, but I knew that in this moment it was where I was meant to be.

Within seconds, the woman I had tailed through the countryside widely opened the door. "Come in," she said and waved her hand with a grandiose gesture.

Meekly, I followed her inside. The cottage walls were lined

with bottles and containers of a variety of sizes and shapes. Some seemed to be lit from behind with a soft glow.

"Come," she motioned towards a chair next to a firepit at the farthest end of the room. Awash with the oranges, reds, and yellows of a blazing fire, the heat of the room emanated from that one spot. "You came quite a ways."

As I sat in the chair across from her, she handed me a metal cup filled with a warm fluid. I sniffed it, unsure if this was something I should ingest or simply hold onto.

"It is okay," she said. "It will help warm you after the long hike." She motioned for me to drink from the cup and I did. I cannot describe its flavor. It was as if the cup held a warmth and comfort in its center that then transferred into my stomach and spread through my limbs with each sip.

"Magic," I whispered as if the word made it true.

"Do you know why you are here?" she asked what seemed to be an odd question at the moment. Especially considering I truly had no idea why. Just that there was something about her that quietly encouraged me to be near her.

I nodded that I did not and took another pull from the goblet.

"Get comfortable," she encouraged. "For it is time that you learn of your origins. Your family."

5

LUNA

"I cannot do this. I cannot wait any longer. I need to get the hell out of here," I said. Birger had picked up on the first ring.

"Where are you?"

"I can't wait. This needs to end now," I had taken off in the middle of the night. Covered in blood and with what seemed to be injuries from yet another battle, I got the hell away from my parents' place. Hell, I went as far away from other people as I could. Headed north and made my way to the most remote spot of the Ramapo Forest. I sought out a camping ground that we had frequented when we were teenagers. A spot that was so remote it felt like the least likely place to find others.

As I approached it, I realized that it may have been abandoned. The wooden cabin had no electricity and the bare floors were dusted with dirt. It smelled like abandonment and emptiness. I tossed my overnight bag in the empty room and washed up at the nearest stream, the cool water bitter against my wounds.

Once I had settled in, I checked my phone to find that I

needed to seek out a spot a little less remote so I could call Birger. It had only been one night, but it felt as if it had been far too long since I had checked in with him. Several miles down the forested mountain, I found a picnic area where I was just barely able to catch a signal.

"Luna, where are you? What's going on?"

"Get me that ticket," I demanded. "I have no idea what is going on, I just know that I need to get back." Based on the state I kept finding myself in, my bet was that someone was a bit pissed at me. Had someone aligned to Chago or The Righteous Group sought me out? Was that what was happening at all hours of the night? Was there some way that someone had figured out how to trigger the changing? As if that thought brought my animal senses forward, I sensed someone approaching me, but when I looked around the picnic area I didn't see anyone.

"Please," I begged Birger. "Please just get me that ticket." And without another bit of hesitation, I hung up and fled.

I made my way back to the campground. If someone was following me and wanted to hash it out, then I wanted to be sure that we were as far away from others as possible. Who knows what would trigger my shifting.

I didn't know who was following me around, but someone had been. I figured, *fuck it*, if someone had come after me then I wanted to be sure we were somewhere to really bang it out.

I made my way into the log cabin and hid behind the door. I heard footsteps approaching, the movements hesitant. Just as I heard the stalker enter the cabin, I jumped him from behind, put him in a chokehold and knocked him out.

"Alright, fucker!" I exclaimed as he went down.

And that's when I saw who it was.

"Oh shit, J.!" I dragged him to the corner of the room and propped him up on my blanket to get him in a comfortable position. I ran to the stream and soaked a shirt in the water and then brought it back to wipe down his brow and bring him back to consciousness.

As he awakened, I asked, "What are you doing here? Are you okay?"

He seemed like he didn't know where he was. "What's going on?" he asked.

I gently wiped his face again with the cool damp cloth. "We're in Rapano State Park. You were following me."

He propped himself up. "Your parents guessed I could find you here."

"But what are you doing here?"

He brushed off the dust from the dirt floor and rubbed the back of his neck. "We need to talk."

6

BIRGER

The Queen Gyrid had convinced the underground leaders of the lycanthropic families to come together. They met for several nights in deep discussion regarding how to proceed against Otto I and how to ensure that they regained their power.

In an odd move, the leaders agreed that they would legally remain separate and instead form an underground community entitled The Lycanthropic Group. They did not want Otto to be made aware of their agreements. They had seen how he had retaliated against those he perceived as threats and they would rather remain neutral against the human leader. They agreed with the queen that King Otto I should remain in power, at least on the surface.

Queen Gyrid and her peers did not care if Otto thought that he ruled all of Europe. Instead, they preferred that he continue to believe that he was the sovereign. They understood the frequency in which the monarch traveled, and saw that as enabling Queen Gyrid and these leading factions to retain the true power.

They continued to meet under each full moon, and quite quickly it became clear that the absolute monarch, the true ruler of both domestic and foreign policy, was the queen.

INTERLUDE 3

(800'S AD)

The Seeress continued in her telling. I simply sat and listened.

"Your papa, Johan, had been a well-known warrior. He was a favorite of the King. When he had first met your mama, she was barely of age and he had immediately been enrapt with her presence. She had been the youngest of the Duke of Smartly. The favorite duke of the King. Unfortunately, the duke did not find value in his youngest pairing with the King's favorite warrior and insisted that he stay away from her. Little did he know that she, too, was fascinated with the captain and had begun to secretly sneak out to visit with him in the middle of the night.

"Convinced that this was true love, they conspired to run away together. At that time, she did not realize that Johan was of the King's special warrior faction. She simply knew that whenever they were mentioned by her father, he glowed about the battles they had won, but had gone out of his way to keep his daughters away from them. This confused your mama since his daughters who were of age could have done well to marry a celebrated soldier. Instead her papa vehemently demanded that they all stayed as far away from this special faction and encouraged them to speak only to those whom he backed.

"And that is when she took off in the early morning hours and met up with your father in a neighboring town. They were married in secret by a nobleman and then began their journey together. Your papa had gotten agreement from the King, Harald Bluetooth I, to lead a new faction, in secret, across the countryside. The King had valued him too much to let him go, however, while knowing this marriage was not something the Duke would have cared for, the King agreed to release him. Harald also understood that this was the best way to keep an eye on your mama and ensure that both his most valuable soldier and your mama stayed safe.

"Knowing no different, your papa would leave for battles and simply tell your mama that he would return shortly. She learned to wait for him patiently. When he would return, she ensured that their home was spotless, a fresh meal was waiting for him, and they would celebrate their reunion. She did not question why he seemed to return unscarred, nor that he never seemed to be severely injured. She simply assumed that this was indicative of him being such an excellent warrior.

"Within months, your mama realized she had become pregnant with your brother. When she told Johan the news, he was overjoyed. He had always dreamed of having a family. That said, he realized that the time had come for him to be transparent with your mama. He sat her down and explained the nature of the special faction. And why the King valued them so.

"They were lycanthropes. Werewolves. Shapeshifters.

"Unsure of how to respond, she simply listened. When he was done explaining this to her, she was a bit surprised. You see, she had been raised to believe that she would be able to bear a child with only another human. The Duke had been quite clear in his views against Lycanthropes, how they were subhumans and meant to serve. Now her father's biases against her love made more sense. She looked down at her belly as she absorbed all that her husband revealed. He placed his hand on her stomach and with a soft and warm smile, told her how blessed they were to be granted such a wonderful gift. She could see in her husband's eyes, his true joy.

"After a few moments, and a bit in shock considering all she had been raised to believe, she asked, 'What does this mean for our child?'

"In truth, your papa was not sure. He had not known his own parents. He only knew that he had been gifted, like the other lycanthropic warriors, to the King.

"But the King knew.

"Once Johan had revealed the upcoming joyous news to the King, he was informed that he would need to give up his children to the royal court so that they would fulfill their destiny.

"Your father argued. He said he wanted his children to have normal lives and make their own decisions. To make their own choices. He did not want his children to have the same fate as he did. But the King demanded.

'You cannot change what they are,' he said. 'This is their destiny.'

"Johan pondered how he could keep his family together. After much discussion, he and his wife came up with several alternatives including going into hiding and taking their children away. But that was not a viable option for either of them since they wanted to ensure their family stayed together. Another choice, again one they did not love but at least meant they could raise their children and keep their family together, came forward.

KALI METIS

"Johan returned to the King and asked, 'If my child stays with my battalion, can he remain with my wife and me?'

"The King contemplated this. 'There is truly no need for your child to be trained until his transformation begins. If he stays with your battalion, then he can still live with you.'

"The King's decision set Johan at ease. He could finally have the family he had always dreamed of.

"Your mama gave birth to your brother. Within moments of the birth, she had declared that she would do anything for her newborn. This declaration made your papa wildly happy. For the only remaining question he had in his mind was whether or not your mama would remain. You see, he knew from his own experiences and from the experiences of those within the battalion that it was unusual for shapeshifters who were found among the people to remain with their families. And in truth, most families seemed to give up their children without argument. At least that was your papa's perception. He also knew of your grandfather, the Duke's storytelling and beliefs regarding shapeshifters, and feared what that influence would have on your mama. This said, even though your mama looked on to your brother with questions and uncertainty, she continued to love him, care for him, and grew to look upon him with a depth of caring that Johan had never seen before.

"Your papa's other worry was that your mama would reject him. Instead, she declared, 'All that we have been through, become, and all that we have fought for, only reinforces my love for you.'

"Again, with a joy he did not know previously, your mama accepted him into her heart and embrace.

"Not too long afterwards, she had gotten pregnant with you. This said, your papa had not informed your mother of the deal with the King. Although they had discussed the possibili-

66

ties, after so much trauma, he feared that this may break her heart so he avoided the conversation for as long as he could.

"When your papa traveled on the King's behalf, the King sent a nursemaid who had raised other warrior children to check on your mama. That nursemaid, not understanding that your mama had not been informed of your pending future, began discussing the coming months and years with your mama as if she understood until finally your mama questioned, "I am sorry but I do not understand."

'They will be taken into the King's service in the coming years.' She looked on at the sleeping children. 'You are blessed to have them for so long,' she stated.

"Your mama looked on in confusion. The nursemaid continued, 'Since they will most likely be taken by the age of five to begin their training. You are given a rare gift.'

'Gift? What are you talking about. They are my children,' your mama said.

"Confused, the nursemaid revealed what the King had told her of the agreement between the King and your papa.

"In a panic, thinking she would lose her children, your mama did not know what to do. Should she stay and take the chance that her sons would become part of this elite warrior group and take the chance that she may not only lose her husband but also her children in battle? Based on what the nursemaid described, it sounded like she may lose you even sooner and that the King's true intent was to take you away well before puberty, so that she would never see you again.

"She calmed herself and thanked the nursemaid for her guidance. She then spent several nights in internal debate about what to do. She had given up everything for her love and her family. And here the King threatened to take it all from her in one simple move.

"She weighed her choices and finally she packed you and

your brother and took off before your father returned. She figured that if she could get her children in hiding and out of the purview of your father and the King, then they would not be able to take them."

"I don't understand," I said to the Seeress. "Then why did she leave us?"

The Seeress stirred what was in the pot over the burning fire and remained quiet in contemplation.

"She had taken you both across the country. For months she had done all she could to at least keep you and your brother with her. She had traveled from town to town begging in order to feed you and to find shelter. She took odd jobs to allow her to give you minimally what you needed. At times, she cried in the middle of the night, fearful of what might happen next. She prayed that some miracle may happen to allow her to have all that she had dreamed of again. Her love, her life, her family.

"Again, she pondered what she should do next. What did she most desire? Looking upon you both, she knew she wanted you to have a good life, and in that downtrodden state she also knew that she could not give you the life that she wished for you.

"So, a time came when she simply felt exhausted—physically, mentally, and emotionally. At this point she was convinced she did not know what to do or how to raise you and your brother. She needed to find someone who could assist. Someone who could give you a good life and this is when she sought out someone she felt could grant you a beautiful life. This is when she left you with the priest."

Frustrated, I asked, "Why are you telling me this? She betrayed us," I said in a fluster. None of what the Seeress shared made sense. How could she haphazardly give us away like packages of no value.

The Seeress must have felt my anger as I tried to keep it

under control for she turned to me and said, "you and your brother have a clear destiny. On the surface it may seem like imprisonment, subjugation, but it is much more." She took a deep breath and sighed. "Birger, you are destined to be one of the King's warriors. Once you are of age, you must join the King's men."

"She reached out and took the cup from me. "You must return to the orphanage," she said. "You must remain there until the day comes when your transformations begin."

Even more lost after all that she had shared, I continued to ask, "why?"

"Because this is truly the one way that you both will be able to fulfill your destiny."

Confused, I wanted to scream from the rooftops. I wanted to create havoc. I wanted to do all that I could to release my resentment, bitterness, and sadness. None of what she had shared truly explained why my mama would go through so much only to give us away. At least, at that point in my life, I did not understand. I craved my mother's touch. I dreamed of my father's caring. I saw them in my dreams as if they continued to look over me and my brother. So these words, this history of how we were left with such a cruel and abusive man only contradicted what I felt whenever I saw our family together.

All of this said, I did as the Seeress had commanded. I did not have many other options and I wanted to be sure to share all that she had told me with my brother. Upon my return, I shared the stories with him. Not sure how he may respond, he listened and then asked, "When will we return?"

Somewhat relieved that his response was one of inquiry and curiosity, I responded, "Tomorrow, my brother. Tomorrow."

That night I dreamed of our family, of our parents. I saw us together, our parents held our hands as we walked the beaches nearby, felt the wind, and laughed in the sunlight. When I awoke, it felt as though all of this was real which made my eagerness to revisit the Seeress even greater.

We had hurried to finish our chores before the priest could come up with more for us to accomplish, we hurried off to the Seeress's cottage. She did not seem surprised when I knocked on her door. Instead, she opened it widely and waved us in.

"Come, come," she said with a smile and a warmth I had not anticipated. "I was expecting you both."

After granting us a treat of homemade porridge and fresh milk which allowed our typically empty and growling stomachs to be full and warm and comfortable, she continued her tales from the day before.

She eagerly told us our parents and the history of the Lycanthropes and how they were heavily interwoven with the Nordics. She shared how our papa led a society of shapeshifters whose goal was to not disrupt human society and instead intended to create their own paths, their own truths, their own futures. This had been considered unusual given his allegiance to the King. Our papa, she told us, had done all that the King had asked for in the belief that by doing so, he would have the family he had always dreamed of.

When he had returned home to find that our mama had left, he cried out in pain. In one fell swoop, he had lost anything and everything that had meant anything to him.

He searched the neighboring lands to no avail. He inquired with all he could think of with no success. He returned to the King and demanded that the royal assist him in finding his family. This is when the King revealed his true colors. In so many words, he informed our papa that this was meant to be and that our father needed to refocus on his upcoming battle. The King, ignorantly so, thought that if he could get Johan to simply refocus, then he would forget about his family, about his true love, and return to the role he was truly good at and to the function that our papa had been meant to fulfill.

Aghast, our papa left the King's chamber fully aware that he would never get the assistance he needed from the King.

Our papa continued his inquiries as to the location of our mama and us. No matter where he went, he leveraged his contacts, to discover all that he could. In deep sadness, he was about to give up when another member of the battalion approached our papa.

"'I may be able to help you,'" she restated what the other warrior had said, and continued, "Your papa, curious but cautious, perked up.

"I do not know where she went, but I have heard of others who exist to help those who elect not to be among the King's servants." She allowed the last word to hang between them with a tinge of anger tainting it. "This group may be able to assist you in your search.

"And with that your papa simply said, 'Tell me more.'

7
LUNA'S

"Luna, you have to be honest with me," Javier said. "What is going on?"

"What do you mean?" I asked.

"Don't start. Don't play innocent. There is some seriously weird shit going on and I need to know what it is." He paused.

I wasn't sure how to answer this. There was so much going on that I just did not know how to explain.

"Look," he started. "When I went in for the check up, they said I had fully healed."

"That's great!" I said.

"It's not possible. There is no way I should have healed so fast. I know it, you know it. We all know it. But I need you to tell me what you know."

I started to play dumb and asked him why he assumed that I knew something was going on. Deep down, I wanted to tell him that he was wrong. But I just couldn't.

"I can tell by the way you've been acting that something else is up," he said. "And since you jetted from your parents, I'm assuming it's pretty big."

"But your note," I started.

"Note? What note?" Javier replied.

"You put a note on the door saying you were breaking off our engagement," I explained.

"What are you talking about?"

I sat across from him and put my hand on his leg. "I found a note with your signature on the door. So, I thought I was giving you what you wanted. I thought I was saving you," I said. And that's when I went into it. I explained about the trip to Sweden and what Daniel had discovered and our heritage and what had happened when we were attacked at the hospital and how he had nearly flatlined.

And what I did to help him survive.

He sat quietly and listened. His eyes to the ground. When I finished, he did not say a word. At least not for a little bit. I found myself nearly babbling onward about the United Nations and Chago and the rest of it but instead, I forced myself to remain silent.

"So we're monsters," he finally said.

"I wouldn't call us monsters. I mean, we're related to one of the most famous warriors of all time."

He got up from the floor and stood at the window. The night sky had taken over the day. Crickets sounded off with the rustling of leaves. "That's what's causing the shaking," he said. He looked down at his hands. "That's what I saw you turn into," he continued. "You had become a beast."

"I'm sorry." I didn't know what else to say. "I truly thought I was saving you."

"Why, Luna? Why did you do all of this?"

"At the time, I didn't think I had a choice. I thought I was going to lose you." We remained in silence for what felt like an eternity. The more I hoped he would look at me, talk to me, the quieter it became.

"I need to be alone for a while," he whispered.

"What does that mean?"

"I can't ..." he wiped his hands through his hair. "I can't deal with this ... with you." He finally turned to look at me. "I need time to think."

"I love you," I blurted out. "I'll do whatever you need." I could feel myself readying to cry. "I just don't want to lose you," I barely choked out.

"I love you too," he whispered. "I just can't ... I don't know what to do with all of this. And who wrote the note?"

"Let's find out together," I said softly.

He was quiet, but he nodded.

8

BIRGER'S

Queen Gyrid had been meeting in secret with the leaders of the Lycanthrope families for quite some time. These were the same ones who had been asking King Otto to provide them better representation. They no longer wanted to simply be at the whim of the King and his desire to rule the world. They no longer wanted to be in fear of whatever he may decide he wanted to do with them and their offspring. They wanted to live their lives in unity with the humans, in community, and they wanted to be assured that their offspring would have futures greater than that of warrior slaves.

The queen, the third wife of the monarch, agreed that they should be treated as peers. A decision based on the hierarchy of her husband's court and driven by all that she had witnessed growing up in a neighboring royal court as the youngest of her father's daughters. She leveraged this knowledge to the shapeshifters' benefit.

After much discussion, she convinced them to continue with their plans of building their own political and cultural epicenter in lieu of the King's commands. She advised them to erect it in some remote place. Some place where they would be able to live in peace without concern of retaliation. A location in which those who wished to could relocate their families and live in harmony—and in secret.

With her own following among the members of the high court, she leveraged her allies to assist them in identifying unclaimed farmland within an hour's distance of the castle. A clearing that enabled them to gather in the moonlight without repercussions and without fear of retaliation by the King or those who were closely aligned to his desires. For just as the King saw benefits to enslaving the lycanthropes, she saw just as much benefit to treating them as equals. A mentality her own mother and her mother's mother had taught Queen Gyrid and her siblings.

The queen assisted them in developing a plan to help ensure that their allegiances were not temporary but rather had the groundwork to last centuries. That meant they needed to record their verbal history and to come to political agreements across the familial tribes. She had witnessed first hand the benefits of changing from verbal alliances to written allegiances. She saw the dramatic shift among the rulers. It was as if simply putting these agreements in writing made each and every word real. So although the tribal leaders were at first hesitant, the Queen's eagerness and passion for the shift in approach had won them over.

She assisted them in identifying someone they would declare as the historical representative for all lycanthropes. This historian, Eddie, someone she had brought over from her home of origin, met with the family members and recorded the oral histories and traditions of each sect. This also assisted them in getting a better understanding of where the families overlapped and what their broader powers were. That historian had the rare knowledge of reading and writing, skills that during this time in history typically only those of the upper class and the church were taught. This same historian met with the Queen each day and reviewed all that he had recorded. This historian was one that the Queen had trusted. He knew her true origins and familial background. And understood the significance of these confidential actions. For Viking folklore would not be written down until more than 200 years later. So this gift of a written history meant the lycanthropes were actually more advanced than the Nordic humans.

Meanwhile, King Otto I had been planning on another quest in which he would take his favorite soldiers from the Lycanthropic Warriors and pursue his own long held dream. After having successfully unified Denmark and Norway—two countries that originally had warring tribes—King Otto I had become obsessed with what may be the benefits to himself, his people, and the greater continent, if he overtook England and France. Once conquered, he wanted to see what the benefits would be to unify these countries with his most recent wins of Denmark and Norway. Then to continue by overtaking Germany.

He hand selected a dozen or so of his favorites special warriors and commanded them to select their favorites among the troops. Once the team had been selected, the Vikings headed off with the intent of raiding, fighting, and winning.

On the day of their leaving and arguably a bit overconfident due to his most recent accomplishments, the King stood before his subjects and announced that he felt they would overtake these additional lands within a few weeks. This statement surprised the Queen considering the King had never made such an accomplishment in such a brief amount of time, but she also did not want to discourage him in his endeavors.

"Of course," she stated. "You shall bring forth lands that

have never known a central ruler. And they will come together with joy."

The King toasted his wife's statement and confident as to their abilities, he proudly placed her in charge during his travels. Their son, Sweyn Forkbeard, had barely reached the age of twelve and although Otto had been truly proud to have an offspring to continue forward with the bloodline, Sweyn was still too young to take over in his father's stead.

"I have no doubt that we will shortly return having expanded our lands."

The crowd cheered their ruler with glee.

The King beamed at his wife and his people's encouragement and eagerly announced that during his travels she would act as the monarch in his stead. Not wanting to tip off her true intentions, she auspiciously thanked him for his generosity and promised that she would do her best while he was away.

The Queen waved at him as he led his warriors off into the distance. She looked on with love, caring, and joyfulness. All of the emotions that were expected of a supportive queen.

In reality, she viewed him as a man she had married because it had been dictated by her father, a neighboring royal. At the time of their initial union, barely of marrying age and raised to be a political advantage to her parents, she did not see a disadvantage to marrying Otto. Instead, she saw this as the way things were meant to be. In summary, although she did not see anything wrong with the marriage nor her husband, she did not see anything right with them either.

She viewed his actions as being performed because he felt they were the right things for him to do and because he was the King. This meant that in his mind everyone had to do as he commanded. Again, because he was the King.

The longer she had been wed to Otto I, the more she observed how he treated his human subjects versus the shapeshifters. While humans were allowed to elect their own paths and their own futures, the lycanthropes' futures were dictated. While humans were encouraged to be educated and raise their children, the male lycanthropes were enslaved into the King's private special forces. Some women shapeshifters also joined the royal guard while others became a form of housemaid to the royal court while still others seemed to disappear when they reached puberty.

Because the King had voiced how the lycanthropes were his elite warriors and were given special training, she had assumed that he viewed them as being a race above all others.

With that and the King's gregarious verbose statements regarding the shapeshifters, she and others among their royal court thought the lycanthropes had been granted special treatment. That they were a level above humans. At least that's what she had assumed when she first joined the royal court.

Through observation and continuously witnessing the sadness perpetuated by the Lycanthropic members of the King's communities she began questioning her assumptions. She witnessed their mourning for their loved ones who had gone to battle for the King. At first she had thought that they had volunteered to be among the elite guard. So they should have been prepared for such repercussions. She assumed that the families viewed this as a point of pride similar to how she and her sisters had been raised to believe that being married off in a loveless marriage was for the advantage of their father to be considered an honor. That was until she realized that they had been taken by force to do the King's wishes.

At one point, after she had been wed to the King for a few years, she had gone on her ritual walk through the countryside. A practice she had begun when she was still within her father's grounds. She came upon a deeply distraught young woman by the side of the road who seemed to have been abandoned.

Wearing clothes covered in dirt and soot, her hair and body clearly needing a bath, she did not acknowledge the Queen. Instead, she continued weeping into her hands, lost in her own sadness.

The Queen quietly approached the young woman and sat next to her. "How may I help?" the Queen asked.

The young lady, not realizing the Queen was the Queen, babbled how her dearest to whom she had been betrothed had been taken away weeks prior never to be seen again.

The \Queen took the young woman into her arms and calmed her, hushing her and rocking her to a better place. Once the young woman had calmed, the Queen asked, "Where has he gone?"

As if the Queen had not spoken, the young woman continued that her older sister had been taken as well because she had been identified by one of the King's seers as a gifted member of the people. A person born to bring forth offspring to serve the court.

At first the Queen listened in quiet surprise. She had never heard of such a thing. Part of her wanted to tell the young woman that she clearly was wrong and must have misunderstood the purpose of her sister's capture. She asked the woman to reiterate what had happened to both the betrothed and her sibling. Once she had confirmed her original understanding of what the woman had relayed, the Queen promised to discover the truth of the disappearances.

Upon the Queen's return to the castle, she had inquired to one of the King's trusted court members regarding the whereabouts of the youth. He acted as if she had said something humorous and waved off her inquiry.

"Nothing for you to be concerned about," he snickered.

This caused her to continue her inquiries with other court members. When none gave her a direct answer, she continued

forward with Otto's most trusted servants. Not really antici-
pating she would be granted a direct answer, she decided that
this was something she needed to know.

No one overtly told her why the young man and young
woman had been taken, nor did they reveal where they had
gone, but some of the servants confirmed that the King had a
habit since long before he had officially become the King of
identifying the "best of the best" among those in his kingdom to
do his bidding. It was not so much what they said her husband
did, but rather how they looked when they relayed this
practice.

Looks of deep fear and concern.

This fear is what had originally caused her to perform a
deeper investigation of the true nature of what he had been
doing. She wanted to know who or what she had married.

In her investigations, she found that there were areas of the
castle which very few frequented. These were segments that
she had not visited as well. At one point, she found a corner of
the castle near the ancient jail cells that no one spoke of but
some of the servants who only served the King could be seen
going into. They were only seen in this section at random times
of the day or night. Never for any overt reason yet careful not to
be caught in their actions.

She elected to follow one whom she knew to be a true loyal-
ist. Deep into the night, the servant carried a candle barely
lighting his way with soft footsteps through the main halls of
the castle. The Queen, disguised in a black, hooded cloak and
wearing men's classic high boots, trailed the servant as he made
his way down curving halls and into the depths of the castle.
Finally reaching a jail cell door that appeared to divert into a
subset of the cells, but actually led to stairs that winded deep
underneath the castle into long forgotten caves.

In the echoes of their footsteps, this is where she found

dozens of young lycanthropic women chained to the floor and sparsely dressed in dresses of cotton. All were in various stages of alertness, clearly drugged in place.

The Queen hid behind a pillar and observed as the servant selected one of the women, chained her hands behind her back, and took her to a side room where males awaited for the breeding ritual to begin. The woman screamed and cried and fought against their actions to no avail.

Horrified at their treatment of the young woman and fearful of what else might be done in secret, she became determined to change their fate.

That night she could barely sleep, aghast that she had married such a beast, someone so horrific in his treatment of others. She awoke with greater determination to align herself to the shapeshifters and ensure that all of these wrongs of her husband had been made right.

As soon as Otto I had taken his guards to attack England and France, she had gained alignment of various members of the royal court and her servants to continue the work that she had been performing with the lycanthropic family heads. She used her gifts of persuasion for these humans of influence to change their allegiance with the King.

With this change in alignment and once she felt as though she could release the young women who were enslaved in the depths of the castle, she engaged her most trusted servants to remove the young women from the hollows of the underground dwellings and returned them to their families. Since the King had put her in charge, at least at first, those who were aligned to him did not question her overt rebellion against his policies.

The more she heard the shapeshifters' tales of being taken from their families at young ages and made to initiate their training, the more she knew her true path. The more she heard of their desperate fights, their near death experiences, and at times being left for dead in completely different countries, the more she knew that her husband was truly a monster.

Not before she had witnessed a mama being forced to give up her children at the command of her husband had she truly understood that all of the talk of the King regarding their value was simply to keep the shapeshifters under his control.

She gave the warriors who had remained behind an option of whether to stay with the special forces or to move on. To which, a surprising number stayed in the service of the King. Some of whom said that this was the only life they had ever known, something the Queen understood.

Having righted the treatment of the young women and young men, she then ensured that the Lycanthropic Society met on a regular basis. With these familial oral histories recorded and the unearthing of additional bloodlines, the Queen saw the King's latest quest as an opportunity to change the shapeshifters from being the King's playthings to formulating and reinforcing their own culture, acknowledging their history, and unifying the sects.

The first family lines to be united were based in Denmark and Norway. She was able to gain agreement among the heads of the families to unify and share the knowledge of how to control their gifts and the variations of their abilities. With the sharing of that knowledge, the groups were enabled to stop viewing their powers as problems and instead to view them as gifts.

Her son, Sweyn Forkbeard, quietly observed his mother's behavior and asked what he could do to assist. It turned out that he had questioned his father's choices for quite some time and was rather eager to help his mama in her desire to make shapeshifters and humans more equal. At first, unsure what to do and not sure she fully trusted her son's intent, she asked him to lead some of the efforts to provide food and shelter to shifters who had been left homeless. Something she had been inspired to support after meeting that one young woman so long ago and aware of similar initiatives for humans within his purview. The more tasks her son performed on behalf of The Lycanthropic Society, the more she grew to trust him. And the more she trusted him, the more she requested of him.

Many months had passed and the King had yet to return. Aware of the implication that he may not have been successful in his intentions, the Queen began to plan who would be the ruling party if anything happened to her. Classically, it would be her son, Sweyn Forkbeard, although he was barely of age since most monarchs of Norway went into power in their 30's and Sweyn had barely hit puberty. A part of her felt like she needed to do more for the leaders, both human and werewolf.

Meanwhile, also aware of the implications of the King not having returned, The Lycanthrope Society leaders, not wishing to overtake the ruling parties, but instead desiring to live in unity with humans, agreed for the Queen's son to be named the leader of Norway and Denmark as long as each family member received a seat on the royal court. After some contemplation, the Queen agreed.

She had several conversations with existing court members to explain the benefits to having the new court members. Some agreed. They saw the value of what she was proposing. Others vehemently disagreed. They did not see the value in changing the court. It had worked well for hundreds of years, there was no need to change things. With further discussions, they in fact declared this to be worthy of an uprising. With the words, "uprising", some court members looked around the royal court room and realized that based on the number of current members in support of the additional seats, the number of actual additional seats, and the number of court members in opposition to the new court structure, that they were outnumbered and should await the King's return.

Two years had passed and the ruling parties heard no word from the King and his platoon. This is when the Queen informed the royal court that she had not been of good health for quite some time and fearful that she may not be long for this life, she announced her desire to have her son, Sweyn Forkbeard, to be named the new monarch.

Within days, the Queen passed to the mourning and distraught of the lands. She had become well loved and admired by many. Even those who disagreed with her changes to benefit the lycanthropes agreed that all she had done was with the intent to benefit all.

For a little bit of time, everyone seemed to at least be neutral. No wars broke out. No fighting. Until, that is, Sweyn Forkbeard began to show his true intent in aligning to his mother.

To become the King.

Actually, to become more than the King.

Violently more.

INTERLUDE 4

(800'S AD)

The Seeress continued to share how our father had taken the direction of a fellow battalion member to seek out this secret society. One of the Lycanthropes who did not want to overtake the King, but simply desired to create a world where Lycanthropes and humans could live in unity. And with that purpose, they assisted those who peacefully went against the King's commands.

I looked over at my brother, Ulf, who seemed enwrapped in the Seeress' story. Admittedly, so was I. She shared that, "if you wish to be reunited with your family, then you must return to the King's battalion as soon as you are of age."

We knew, based on what she had said as much as what she hadn't, that there was much more she knew. I could also tell that at this time in our lives, she was not ready to share more. Still, I had to ask, "Is our father still with the King?"

With a slight smile, she nodded, "yes".

"And our mama?" my brother inquired.

Her expression changed to one of sadness. "That is for

another day," she said. And with those words, she told us it was time to return to the orphanage. Reluctantly, we did as we were instructed. Both of us deep in thought, we discussed what the Seeress had shared and what we thought it truly meant. Our conversations typically ended with both of us deciding that it was best for us to return for greater insights.

Meanwhile, upon our return to the orphanage, the priest made it clear that the purpose of our existence was to do his bidding and his expectation was that we would only be at his call. Neither Ulf nor myself found this to be compelling. If anything it actually acted as an impetus for us to do the exact opposite. We took every opportunity that arose to leave the compounds of the orphanage and seek out the Seeress.

We were aware of the priest's violent repercussions if we did not do as he commanded, so we became extremely careful in our activities and ensured that our cleaning was even more spotless and our chores were done with the utmost care and perfection so he had no reason to question our actions. For a while, this strategy was successful.

We visited with her on the sly and she taught us about our familial line. At first she drew images in the dirt with a simple stick, but then she chose to teach us how to read the Nordic runic alphabet. At this point, the King had ensured that only humans were taught how to read runes because of the perceived magical properties of each one. So the fact that she had gifted us with learning these symbols, and how to interpret them, was a rarity and something that would help us in our advancements. Her sharing this ability enabled us to better understand what was happening when the priest prepared his lessons and lectures. As well as what was occurring around us in the greater world. The more she taught us, the greater my hunger for knowledge grew.

Ulf also had a desire for knowledge, but there was something in his stance, in the way he sought it out that made me question his objectives, his purpose. It seemed like he secreted away every bit of information he could, compiling it, socking it away for a future intent.

He had created opportunities for us to leave the orphanage grounds without the priest's knowledge, so that we could spend as much time as possible with the Seeress. He found ways for us to clean the church grounds, perform every and any possible chore that the priest could think of before he requested it.

At this age, I truly followed my older brother with deep admiration. If he said jump, I asked how high. And this was only reinforced by the Seeress' guidance. In her tellings of our heritage and her insights into our parents and how we may be reunited with them, she made it clear that we should stay aligned to one another, look out for each other.

"For you will always have one another," she had said. "No matter what happens."

She told us of our family history of shapeshifters and what our mother had done and why she had abandoned us at the orphanage. All of this had felt surreal like the Seeress simply created these stories like they were some kind of fairy tales. Remember, we had not begun the changing yet, and we had no proof that this stranger, this witch, actually knew what she spoke of. But at this juncture we had no other guidance other than the priest and his goal was to keep us in his power.

"Be aware," she said. "Be ready for in the coming months your transformations will begin. You need to be prepared for what this will mean."

She had described the transformation to us and, of course, we listened on, completely enwrapped in each and every word. We had never heard of any such things.

She had forewarned of the beginning stages of the transformation and provided guidance as how to handle those first moments. Uncontrollable shaking? Brain fog? Loss of memories? Awakening in the middle of the night at random places with our clothes in shreds? It all sounded so unbelievable.

But of course, exactly as she had predicted, my brother's light shaking had begun a few months later. This truth, simply reinforced for us both that we needed to continue to follow her, listen to her, go to her for guidance since no one had been able to provide answers to the mysteries we were beginning to experience.

Ulf's shaking seemed to occur at random moments, and lasted for only brief periods of time, and then simply stopped as if it had never occurred. And yet, it began again at a different time with seemingly no trigger. Each instance lasting for varying lengths of time and to varying degrees of severity.

She continued in her distinct and detailed guidance.

On her final day of teachings, she said, "you must be prepared for there will come a day when your transformation will be completed. On that day, you will need to go to the King's special guards and begin your training."

After so many months of education and so many teachings, we both snickered at this guidance. Who would voluntarily go forward to be sacrificed in battle? We had gone through all of this and risked being punished by the priest in order to avoid pain and trauma, not seek it out.

"Only you will know when the time comes," she stated. She had a twinkle in her eye with those last words as if she knew we were already in the throes of the great transition, which, in reflection, would not have surprised me.

As predicted, only a few months later, what seemed to have been light shaking of my brother's limbs had progressed to something I do not know how to describe. We had completed another day of chores at the orphanage and performed the begging of the visiting parishioners to support the priest's most recent lecture.

Exhausted from a full day, we had retired to our modest backroom. We had been discussing when our next opportunity may be to head to the Seeress's cottage. Even though she had made it clear that our formal training had ended, this was when we would regale in her homemade treats— stews, and vegetables, and baked breads unlike our standard fare of leftover and tasteless porridge. After so many weeks of meager meals, sometimes without significant sustenance, we were more than ready to make our way to visit our benefactor.

I had curled up on my cot and had just closed my eyes when Ulf called out for me, his voice shaky and in panic. When I opened my eyes, I simply looked on in terror.

"Birger," he cried out. "Help ..."

I did not know what to say or do. I did my best to remember what the Seeress had instructed us to do, how to minimize the effects of the transformation. How to take control of the first full transfiguration. His body in full seizure, his teeth chattered, his limbs violently quaking. I barely believed what I saw. In the coldness of the night, my brother's hands seemed to elongate as his nails grew and twisted at a speed I did not fathom.

"Breathe," I guided. "Close your eyes and slowly breathe ..." I continued to walk him through what I remembered of the Seeress's guidance. "Focus on controlling your breathing."

He did as I guided. His shoulders seemed to broaden and his arms and legs lengthened and curled. "Breathe through this. Breathe through the pain. It will help you reduce the pain," I said, doing my best not to panic. "Focus on each part of your body as you feel it shifting."

His back arched and his legs reshaped to that of a beast. His golden blond hair elongated and grew at a rapid rate and in moments he was covered in thick golden hair.

His teeth lengthened and sharpened exactly as she had described and yet witnessing it still did not make it real. Neither did being present make it any easier to accept.

Once the metamorphosis completed, he lay dormant on our dirt encrusted floor, completely immobile.

Crickets chirped. Leaves rustled. The stillness was eerie.

"Ulf?" I said his name, uncertain if he would even recognize me. With the sound of my voice, he slowly got up on all fours and sniffed the air. His face fully changed into that of a wolf, the only reminder of the boy he was remained in his eyes, glistening and gleaming.

I knew my brother was still in there.

He pointed his nose upwards and sniffed as if he was in search of something. I stayed immobile, suddenly afraid this transfiguration may have altered more than my brother's body. Although I could see remnants of him, I wasn't sure how much of him had remained.

I was careful not to make any sudden moves, while he made his way to my cot and sniffed the air just inches from my face. In the darkness of the night, he behaved as if he could not see me, but instead acknowledged my presence through my scent. As he got closer to me, he let out a low growl, paused, and then bolted out of our door and into the woods.

Terrified, uncertainty froze my abilities to decide what to do next. Should I follow him into the woods and see where he went and what he did? Should I tell the priest of my brother's changing? Should I let him go? The priest most likely anticipated that both of us would be transforming, but that didn't help me decide what to do or help determine what his intentions for us were. The man had never shown parental concern for us unless it was to his advantage, and I did not want to know how he would view our changing to be his advantage.

I almost ran for the Seeress's cottage hoping she would be able to provide guidance. She had already done so much for us, and had truly provided a refuge from our challenging lives, yet, I could not make myself seek her out. The coming about of the future's she foretold may put her—and me—in danger.

Unsure how to progress, I forced myself to stay awake until dawn in the hopes that my brother would return. I watched the border of the forest, hoping to see his shape again. But I could not merely wait, and, not wanting the priest to find me in this precarious situation, I launched into a haphazard search for my sibling.

After what felt like an eternity with my instincts keeping me on edge, I happened upon him on the edge of a stream.

The first edges of daylight streamed through the treetops, highlighting the raging waters as they passed his unconscious body. Ulf was covered in scrapes, unconscious, and naked.

With care, I woke him. He clearly had no idea where we were nor what had transpired. Thankfully, when I offered my hand, he obediently took it and he followed me back to our meager place. I helped him clean up and find clothes, still early enough to be before the priest sought us out to begin our daily chores. Ulf moved with care as if his entire body ached from the previous night. I was dying to ask him what it felt like, what he remembered, what did he do in those missing hours. But I held myself back, aware that my curiosity had to wait and we needed to focus on getting him back to a somewhat normal state and out of any potential quandary with our overseer.

Again, I debated over telling the priest of my brother's transformation or if we should keep these latest events to ourselves. I was more so afraid of what the priest would do if he discovered my brother's alternate form. Although the Seeress had guided us to align with the King, she had not overtly stated what the priest's intentions may be once he understood, or rather had confirmation, that we had grown into out true nature —our true selves.

We agreed, we had to go back to the Seeress for guidance.

The cottage seemed nearly barren when we arrived. My brother tagged along behind me, and although alert and moving better as the sun warmed his body, he had spoken very little since I had found him by the stream. Before I could even tap on the door, she opened it and swiftly ushered us inside. We did not need to tell her what had occurred.

She knew.

She checked Ulf's vitals and gave him a drink that seemed to help him in his renewal. "Birger," she began. "Has yours begun?" She looked at me with an intense sense of concern.

I simply nodded. My changes had not begun In truth, I had questioned if the fact that our father had been a lycanthrope dictated that both of us were destined to become shapeshifters as well. As far as I knew, there was no proof that this was a dictate.

I began to infer this by starting with, "Who's to say ..." and shrugged.

She looked at me and smirked, "The time will come when you will need to make your own decisions."

"What does that mean?" I asked. Based on what I witnessed my brother go through, this was not something that he had a choice in. Instead, it seemed to be a mandate.

She motioned to my brother who had taken a spot near the fireplace. He reveled in the comfort of the fire and the cup of nourishment she had provided him. "You will see," she said. "Just as Ulf is discovering his path."

She patted his back and after a few moments of stoking the fire and seemingly in deep thought, she continued, "Ulf, you must go to the King's elite warriors. They will ensure you begin your training. They will look after you."

"Does this mean we will be forced to become one of the guards?" I questioned.

Offhandedly she said, "It means that this is how he will begin to fulfill his true destiny."

Ulf looked at her throughout our dialogue as if to absorb all she had said.

"Birger," she began. "You must stay with the priest for now. The time will come when you will need to create your own path. In the meantime, your brother must go to the elite guard. They are truly the only ones who can help him through this transformation."

Although I questioned the logic of this, we mostly did as she directed. I was not going to let Ulf travel alone. So, after an additional night at the orphanage, we decided to move forward together.

We made our way to the King's castle and the elite guard's entry. Upon reaching the special gate, we informed the guards that we were there to initiate our training.

"Training? What makes you believe you can simply arrive here and command to be trained?" one of the guards, an older gentleman who had clearly experienced more than we could imagine, stated in response.

"We are one of you," I said. I knew I had no proof that I was a shifter, but at this juncture I was not ready to leave my brother so I took the chance. We had been through too much together and the last thing I wanted to do was leave his side and be left alone with the priest.

In the waning daylight, before the high castle walls and wooden gates, the guards were clearly circumspect. "Show us," the head guard commanded.

With that command, Ulf demonstrated his abilities. To this

day, I am not sure how he knew the way to shift on command. Maybe it was the sheer need of the moment. Maybe it was a coincidence and he was about to change anyway. Maybe this was something he simply knew how to do instinctively. No matter, his action proved to the warriors his abilities.

I was accepted without any more proof than stating I was Ulf's brother, and thus began our initiation and training.

In retrospect, I do not know why they simply allowed me in. They truly had no reason to let me tag along. I had no means of proving my lineage. I guess they must have figured that we had to be related in order for us to arrive together. I could think of no other reason.

We were taken into the stone castle and guided down a barren hallway towards a central room where others congregated. Each wall had two doors leading to other rooms and halls. Those who were there looked at us with circumspect. I am sure they had not anticipated a teenager and a preteen to appear unexpectedly that day.

We had not planned on it, either.

The elder guard guided us to a storage room and introduced us to the overseer, a kind and forthright woman with salt and pepper hair, wizened skin, and a questioning but warm smile.

"They will need one of each," the elder guard stated.

"New blood," she replied. He nodded. "Always good to see the next generation join us." She searched through the closets and returned with a stack of clothing for each of us.

"I will show you to your spaces," the elder guard said.

He led us to one of the entries and down a hall which ended with a huge open room filled with cots. Much nicer bedding arrangements than the meager ones we had been accustomed to. He pointed us to two that seemed to be available.

"Dinner will be in an hour," he stated. "In the meantime, you will meet your instructors."

He then showed us to one of several training rooms and introduced us to the lead trainer, Svend. I would later discover that there were head trainers for different specialties and levels. Svend's purpose was to lead the sect that was tasked with working with those who were completely new. Those considered inept. Before we could truly be trained, they had to identify what we were good at and what our challenges were. Only after they had discovered our true talents and worked us a bit, could they truly begin our training.

Svend provided us with a daily agenda which consisted of morning exercises, afternoon classes, and evening drills. We were assigned chores to be completed as a part of our training.

Throughout this my brother remained silent. I began to worry about him since it was unusual for him not to speak for so long. I looked at him questioningly, and he quietly acknowledged me—a look on his face letting me know he was fine.

Thankfully the drills did not require transformations, but only, rather, our undivided attention. We were to perform specific exercises repeatedly to help train our bodies in proper movements.

The instructors were surprised when we demonstrated our ability to read during the afternoon classes. When Ulf was asked how he had learned to read and write, he finally spoke, "A governess."

What the Seeress had taught us had only been the beginning of what would turn out to be an intense, in-depth, and treacherous period.

Our initial days were exhausting, but satisfying and welcomed. For the first time in our lives, we were a part of something that made sense to me. I understood what the instructors shared with us. I valued their guidance. They guided us in the ways our bodies would transform and what we could do to prepare. Ulf, having undergone the process of transformation, obtained a deeper understanding while I still had to accept the pre-teen sense of not having reached puberty. I was envious of my brother's blossoming maturity, but at the same time, I was overwhelmed with pride as I watched him quickly, naturally respond to the tutelage of the guards, easily emulating the techniques of their skills.

In addition to the physical aspects of our training, they prepared us with spells and techniques to help us through those early days, weeks, and months. And they welcomed us.

I felt like we had finally found a safe place and enjoyed being among many, dozens even, who were of the same background. Yet, even though they clearly seemed to be open, honest, and to have taken us in as family, Ulf continued to remain silent.

I felt his sadness and circumspection seep from his pores. He did not trust them, which, considering our background, was not hard to understand.

I asked him what was wrong, and he simply shrugged. "Not where I wanted to be," he said.

I did not understand. "Where else?" I asked.

With my question, he behaved as if I had not spoken which, for my brother, typically meant he was not ready to share.

. . .

That night, he and a few other youth in our dorm, were taken away by a small squad of the training soldiers. I pretended like I slept with my head underneath the blanket and waited for their return. He finally did in the wee morning hours, looking beaten and sore. He limped and nursed wounds. The others were in similar states.

When I asked what had happened, he whispered, "training" and left it at that. If that was what more in-depth training entailed, then I did not want to be considered part of the elite guard.

After several months of being awakened in the dark of night and taken off to god-knew-where, he decided he had had enough. He awakened me and said, "It is time for us to leave." These were the most unsolicited words he had spoken since we had arrived.

Without question, I followed my brother's guidance.

He showed me through the sleeping quarters, down the hallway, past the primary training rooms, eating area, and out a side door. We made our way to the farthest wall surrounding the castle and climbed over it, jumping down to the other side. He motioned for me to remain quiet as he checked the area near us for guards. I directed his attention to the overnight guards standing nearby. With that, we headed in the opposite direction, towards a winding road which went into the depths of the forest.

Within a few hours, I realized he was returning us to the Seeress's cottage. Surprised, I asked him why.

"That is not where we belong," he said of the King's castle and left it at that.

In the midnight hour, without us having to knock on her door, she granted us entry. She looked disappointed to see us, but still took us in.

"You are not done," she said before he could utter a single word.

"We do not belong there," he replied.

She eyed him, letting him search her face to let his spirit discover his sought-after revelations.

"Come," she said. "We will find the answer."

9
LUNA'S

The flight to Stockholm took almost 14 hours including a layover in London. I had a window seat near the back for the first leg and an aisle seat closer to the front in my second leg from London to Sweden. I had not expected much. I just knew that I needed to get there—sooner rather than later.

I kept replaying my interaction with Javier in the log cabin in Ramapo Mountain State Park. After my initial oopsy of knocking him out (hell, I didn't know it was him), we had talked for what felt like hours with limited success. I had hoped he would forgive me. I hoped that he would accept what we had both become, even though I admit that I hadn't quite accepted this either. I understood his perspective, that he wasn't given a choice in being made into a shapeshifter. That I hid the fact that I was a werewolf from him. I get that. But at the time, I didn't know what else to do. Based on everything I knew, if I didn't perform the ceremony on him and give him an infusion of my blood then he would have died and I just couldn't do that. I just couldn't let him go.

And then there was the mystery of who wanted me away

from him enough to devise an elaborate break-up scheme with a note and a suitcase full of my clothes. Javier knew nothing about it. But someone knew everything about it. Someone wanted me out of the apartment, out of the relationship, and out on my own. But who?

I admit that I'm still trying to figure stuff out. Hell, if I knew everything then I wouldn't need to travel to Sweden, right?

Over the course of several hours, I did my best to convince Javier that we weren't beasts; we weren't monsters. I don't think I was successful, not based on how we left it. He didn't tell me to totally fuck off, but we definitely didn't finish our exchange in an intimate embrace. It was more like a sad farewell.

I spent the flights trying to figure out what I could have done to make it better. How could I have made everything right? The look on his face, pure grief, it's like he was heart-broken for whom and what we had been and what we had become. That look left me breathless.

I admit, I could have performed Freya's spell on him to take away his powers, but I was afraid to, considering I didn't and still don't know what the hell was going on with me. I figured that once I had the answers to that million dollar question then I could help him through this transformation or take it away. Whichever he preferred. We should still have plenty of time. I mean, he shouldn't truly begin his full changing, if that happens, for years from now. At least that's what I'm guessing. It's not like he's a full blood relation. If I understood all the stuff I had read up on it, he should have a few years before he goes through the equivalent of a shapeshifter's puberty.

I hope.

. . .

My call to Margarite at the bakery had been surprisingly brief. Because we had already set up batches of batter for the coming weeks and she had my assistant to help knock stuff out, all she asked of me was to keep her posted for when I thought I would return.

Birger had sent some documents to go over while on the flight. Stuff about the origins of The Lycanthrope Society and The Righteous Ones. He had said this may help me understand our background and provide glimmers of comprehension as to why certain things were happening, including this bizarreness with my shapeshifting.

Can I say how insanely thankful I am that I didn't transform while on the flight? I mean, seriously. I was terrified the entire way that at any minute I'd start shifting uncontrollably. Birger sent along a sleeping agent to help knock me out. He thought with the additional assistance from the drug that I wouldn't shift in my sleep. Although I appreciated the thought, the idea of getting any kind of shut eye scared the hell out of me. I just kept imagining myself waking up in mid flight and finding that I'd taken out the crew and half the people on the flight.

Now that would be a nightmare.

A nightmare I could risk.

By the time I landed in Stockholm, I hadn't slept in nearly 24 hours. Not the smartest move on my part but there truly seemed to be no viable choice.

When the pilot announced we were about to land, I couldn't have been more relieved. The view of the lands of Sweden were truly breathtaking as we landed. Tired-drunk, let's say I didn't quite walk in a straight line as I made my way off the plane and into the international airport.

Birger, dressed in his standard dark pants, white button down shirt, and with his hair slicked back, met me outside the customs area. The closer I came to him, the more concerned he looked. I tried to fake one of those "hey, it's awesome to see you!" smiles and gave him a big hug.

He pulled me away from him and asked, "Have you gotten any rest?" He held me at arms length and then reached down and took my luggage.

I started to respond and then realized I didn't really need to. Based on his reaction, he knew the second he saw me that I was dizzy-tired. He guided me through the airport's international terminal five, a one story metal and glass phenomenon, and towards the security checkpoint where guards were checking the bags of travelers departing Sweden to confirm no psychos got on any planes with uncontrollable needs to terrorize the world. I found that ironic, that I could have transformed and terrorized people without a bomb hidden in my shoes or my underwear.

We continued towards the exit. I was a few steps behind him, and he looked back intermittently as if he was checking to make sure I was still there. He waved me onward to SkyCity where all visitors parked. He moved with a swiftness and purpose that made it clear we would continue our discussion later.

"Did you find anything else out?" I took a shot and figured I'd start the conversation.

"You need rest," he countered. He took my luggage, loaded it into the rear of his car, and then unlocked the passenger side door for me. I barely moved in a straight line and definitely felt like I had somehow landed on another planet.

"I'll tell you what. I promise to sleep when we get to wher-ever I'm staying as long as you tell me what else you've found out." What made me think I had any stance to negotiate beats me, but it was worth a try.

He smirked. Clearly he had become accustomed to my ways of getting what I wanted. He closed the passenger side door and made his way to the driver's side.

Once he locked the door and started the engine, he replied, "I found one case of similar episodes."

"Great. Now what?"

He drove us down the freeway and away from the airport to the countryside.

"What you are experiencing is a kind of seizure. We believe it is triggered by a combination of stress and overexertion. Your great great great great uncle had similar episodes."

"Will reperforming the spell take care of it?" I asked.

He paused for a moment and then replied, "It should."

"That does not give me warm fuzzies. What does 'It should' mean?"

"It means that according to all of my research, redoing the control spell worked for him, but I believe that you will still need to complete your official training in order to give you overall control of your transformations."

"In other words, I can't just redo the spell and then jet."

He laughed. "Correct, Luna. You cannot do what you did the last time. I do not know what will happen if you do so. I cannot promise that you will be fine."

"You make it sound like if I leave like I did the last time then I'm at risk of an even bigger problem."

This time he did not reply. Instead, he kept his eyes on the road and slowly nodded.

After a moment, he said, "It is time we start."

10

BIRGER'S

S weyn suddenly found himself at the head of the throne with his mother's passing. Within months he had made it clear that although he had aligned to her changes in the ways in which those—meaning humans and those of other species— within their royal court were treated, he did not necessarily agree with her visions for the future. Secretly he had been meeting with the factions of the royal court who were also against the changes she had made. He had believed that only humans should be allowed to rule and to have certain rights. All others were subspecies and must obey humans.

In the ruse of celebrating his mother, King Sweyn had created a festival, The Festival of Gyrid. He invited the members of his court to spend three days in celebration of her with masses of food and drinks and music. All gleefully accepted and thrilled in the tidings. On the second night of the festival, the celebrators spent the night. Some had passed out in random spots of the castle while others made it back to their guest chambers after having nipped a bit more of the distilled beverages than they had anticipated—or needed.

With swiftness and in the dark of night, guards who aligned to his vision for the new Viking world captured the Lycanthropic members of the royal court and placed them in jail. Each was placed in chains per the new King's orders. Using the element of surprise to their advantage, the guards were able to capture the members with limited fuss. At the same time, they gathered the human court members who had aligned to the queen and gave them an option, "You may either demonstrate your allegiance to me or you will have the same fate as the shifters."

The first to acquiesce was the head of a small house who had only had his position for a few months. Hungry for power and not eager to lose all that he had worked for, he quickly agreed. The new King guided him to the cell in which the shapeshifters were held. He pointed to one of the imprisoned, handed the head of the house a freshly sharpened sword, and motioned for him to move forward.

The killing was swift, bloody, and vicious. The others looked on in horror, quickly understanding what King Sweyn's command meant for them. One-by-one, each head of the house who had been previously aligned to the queen were handed a sword and told to take the life of a Lycanthrope who had briefly been considered a peer. Many did so because they were afraid to lose their own life, not due to any true allegiance. While others had secretly never really been aligned to the queen. They only did so in order to keep their positions of power. The few who stated they could not, would not, take a life to simply take a life were held down by the guards as King Sweyn performed a similar act of bloody viciousness on them.

In the end, King Sweyn believed those remaining were truly aligned to him and would do his bidding. What he had not realized was that a court member who had led one of the Lycanthropic families had been given a heads up regarding the King's intentions. This member, along with several others had sent others from their houses to represent them during the celebration. Enabling them to take a moment of distinct disadvantage and turn it to a moment of advantage. This member, known by the name of Chago, had believed that Lycanthropes were not intended to be peers with humans but rather to rule over humans. He had been waiting for years and viewed this as an opportunity to overtake the ruling party and raise up the Lycanthropes to become The True Reign later to be called The Righteous Group.

INTERLUDE 5

(800'S AD)

The Seeress took us in and used her Runes to better understand the challenges my brother had and why he had driven us to run away.

She asked him questions during the process to better assess what the runes revealed. She had known from the previous predictions that my brother had been destined for something and that my future had been a bit more open. She had assumed that this meant he was to be a member of the guard, with no choice.

With the leading questions and additional tossing of the runes, she came to realize that although it may have partially been true, it was not fully the case.

"You are gifted," she said to Ulf. "You will be a member of the guard. You will lead the guards," she continued. "But there is more."

"I cannot do what they command," he said. "I do not believe in it."

She tossed the runes again and looked at him quizzically. "What transpired?" she asked.

With that he continued to explain what had happened in the nights when he and other newly transforming shapeshifters within the King's guard were taken.

"We were commanded to perform special actions," he vaguely said.

"Continue," she requested. When it was clear that he did not want to reveal more, she added, "please."

He described how at first, they were all taken to a special clearing in the midst of the forest where they were taught how to control their shifting and how to shift into other beings, other creatures.

"Yes, as you should," she interrupted.

Frustrated, he continued. "No," he said. "No one should be forced to shift into beings of fright and horror. No one should be made to become those creatures and then use their powers for harm." He blurted this out with a passion and force I had not witnessed before.

The Seeress sat across from him and with a look of concern asked him to continue.

"We are not simply of the wolf. Some can become many more beings."

She looked surprised. "Some?"

"Yes." When it became clear that he had her attention, he continued. "There are methods, spells that we can use. If we are from a certain breed then the spells will enable us to transition into other beings."

"Like?" I interjected. Now he really had my attention since this implied what my future held as well. To this juncture we had only been taught that we would be werewolves, and we, or at least I had only considered this one characteristic of our condition. But what my brother brought forward implied that what we had been taught was only true for a few and others had much more waiting for them.

"I have seen bears, birds of flight, panthers, and creatures I had never seen before," he elaborated. "Ones of myth." The last word he said with a quietness which I knew meant he did not want to continue and would not provide greater details.

"Why does this keep you away?" she asked. "If they are able to teach you, train you to do much more, then how is this bad?"

I looked at his arms that still showed the aftersigns of fights with light scarring. What he had said so far did not explain it. He caught me staring at the thick light pink ragged scars and touched them on each arm. He nodded towards me. "For reasons that my brother has already seen," he said. "To see who is the strongest and who has the greatest skills, we are taught the spells. We are then forced to fight."

He looked down at the ground in embarrassment, and continued, "Sometimes I remember the battles. Other times I awaken covered in proof of the fray." He paused for a moment as if remembering what had transpired. "Sometimes we survive and other times ..."

He did not need to say more. Based on his expression, he had killed others and had not known what had happened until after he had awakened to see the results of the foray.

He looked up at the Seeress. "I cannot do that again. I cannot kill simply to kill."

Her look towards him softened. As if she had suddenly realized and understood why this training was so critical and the reason he had so desperately needed to both run away and stay. "I see," she said. She tossed the runes again, and then as if for an additional confirmation, she tossed them again. With that, she continued. "The only way I know for you to gain full control of your abilities and to master your powers is to be trained by the elite guard. This is the only way you can learn how to ensure that you are aware during a battle and therefore have control of when you kill and when you do not."

He looked at her with deep concentration. I could tell that this was not the answer he had expected nor that he wanted.

"That is why at times I cannot remember and other times I can?" he asked.

She searched his expression. "Yes. Those times when you can remember are when you have more fully mastered the changing to that creature. If you do not remember then it means the spell, the transformation, worked but you need to master it."

I was eager to ask him what the battles were like. Were there times when some of his fellow classmates transformed and others did not? Were those who did not transform forced to fight in their human form? If he did not remember then how did he know that he was the one responsible for another's death? What happened when he remembered?

I held these questions within me simply because I could tell by his reactions that this was not the time. I also assumed that there would be a time in which I would discover these truths for myself. A time I was not looking forward to.

"Is there another way?" he asked her.

She tossed the runes again and then searched the firelight. Her eyes wandered the flickering flames.

"I wish I had a direct answer," she said. She looked at us with concern. "The only way I know of for both of you to be taught and to become skilled in your gifts is to become part of the King's elite guard."

My brother looked as if he had become sickened by her reply and I felt lost. Like this was a truth, a reality that I had not been prepared for. "There must be other ways," I said. "In the entire world, there is not a single person, a single means other than the one you have described?"

"Within our Viking world," she began. "The King has orga- nized it so that those who are taught are aligned to the elite guard. There are changings who are not trained and are not aligned to the King, but they often become destitute, alone. In ways beyond the physical. Ways I hope you never experience."

Ulf looked like he seriously considered this option. I had no real idea what he had undergone, but whatever it was, for him to truly contemplate destitution as an option was surprising.

"You may stay here," she said. "For now, while you decide."

"Can we stay here forever?" I asked. Hope leaking out through each word. I did not care for any of the alternatives she had brought forward. And based on what my brother had told us, the little he had shared, I was not sure that returning to the King's guard was truly a healthy, viable, nor smart choice.

"I too am in the service of others," she admitted. "And you must know that my time here will end soon," she said this with a bit of melancholy that I had not anticipated. She had always been the one we could go to for answers, for help, for a reprieve. For her overall stance to change from that of the confident guide to one of sorrow and turning inward, whomever she obeyed must have been one of significant power. "I must move on."

11
LUNA'S (2000S)

I'm not sure what I expected, though I had anticipated going back to the library where I had met Birger six months before. Instead, Birger drove us through the bright green and flourishing fields of Sweden.,. If anyone would have bet me where I would be on this day and all the stuff that happened in the last year, I would have lost that bet in spades.

Birger didn't really talk to me during the rest of the drive. In all honesty, I was kind of thankful for it. I mean, all I really wanted to do was go to sleep and with the latest news that my random shapeshifting was a form of seizure triggered through stress and exhaustion, well, it didn't relieve my anxiety in terms of what would happen between now and when I finally got fully rested, but at least I knew there was an out. Hell, I wouldn't be surprised if he showed me to a padded room and said, "Have fun!" and locked the door.

Thankfully, he didn't quite do that. Instead, he gave me a brief rundown of what I had to expect in the coming days.

"Our schedule for reperforming Freya's spell will be among the first priority," he said. "And then we will have a daily routine of physical and mental exercises which will be taught by instructors from TLS. The best of the best," he said with a grin.

I'm sure the smile was meant to ease my anxiety, but it actually caused a bit more. He seemed a little too happy or rather mischievous for the Birger I knew.

"Do not be concerned," he said as if he could read my mind. "None of this will occur until after we have ensured that you are fully rested and physically ready."

Although relieved at this statement, it left open questions like, "What does physically ready, mean?" and "None of what? I thought we were just going to perform the spell and then study or something?" But the way he said this, it sounded like we had a huge amount of work ahead of us.

I opted to focus on the last question, "What do we mean by physical and mental exercises?"

Of course, my timing for asking this question seemed to have been stellar because I asked it just as we drove up to the tiny cottage in the midst of a sheep field.

"We are here," he said and shut off the engine. He turned to me. "I will show you to your chambers while you are staying with us."

He retrieved my belongings and led me inside the intimate cottage filled with books, some hundreds of years old. All titles related to the Lycanthropic history, legends, and beliefs. I loved walking into the space even though it was a little claustrophobic with the aisles filled to the top with books and the limited walking space but the scent of book pages made the place feel welcoming. He guided me to the back and into an underground passage which must have been the size of the sheep field, it was that enormous. "What kind of fetish do you people have for hidden passages?" I sarcastically asked. "I mean, you seem to have them everywhere."

He raised an eyebrow and then simply continued forward down the poorly lit passageway, beyond multiple doors, and into an open room. It reminded me of something out of old *Mission Impossible* movies where the team members are locked up somewhere top secret for training. I kept imagining Tom Cruise popping out of a side room and ready for action.

When that didn't happen, I obediently, and a little in awe, continued to follow Birger to a room that I assumed would be where I would stay while I was there.

Decent sized, it easily contained a queen bed, an office desk and chair, a cabinet for clothes, a closet, and its own bathroom with shower. The walls were a plain eggshell white— no one had bothered to decorate it. Fully stocked with bathroom amenities such as white fluffy towels and toilet paper, this was nicer than some motel rooms I'd stayed in.

He placed my luggage on the bed. "I will leave you here to rest. When you are ready, simply go down the hallway and ask for me. I will come out to show you around."

He patted my shoulder. "There are several individuals who are eager to meet you, Luna," he said. "I know I have said this previously, but your line is quite rare." He smirked. "And your breadth of abilities, well ..." he trailed off. "We will see truly what they are."

"What does that mean?" I asked.

He headed to the door, "It means that once you are fully rested, I will show you around and your true training will begin shortly thereafter."

Just as he closed the door, he paused. "Luna, you brought those sleeping pills with you, yes?"

He referenced the pills he had sent to me for the flight. He had wanted me to take them on the airplane, but I was too afraid to do so without knowing what the hell was going on with me. I'm pretty sure he could tell that I hadn't touched them based on my exhausted state.

I pointed towards my bag. "Yup, they're right in there."

"Do me a favor," he began. "Take at least two before you lie down for the night." His look turned even more serious. "I want to return to find you in one piece. Not pieces."

12
10TH CENTURY BIRGER'S NOTES

The newly crowned, King Sweyn, ensured that the violent acts of dissention had been completed which included the murder or enslavement of lycanthrope advocates, and all remaining shapeshifters in the castle were placed back in chains and were being assessed for how they may best give service to the King. He leaned on his knowledge of his father's methods for assessing those beings, methods we will not go into detail at this time.

Even though Vikings did not necessarily have a robust written history, the previous King had ensured that a historian was on hand among his court with key information to be shared with his son. Admittedly, the court historian had not anticipated that his knowledge would be warranted so soon, but he also did not shy away when the new King Sweyn approached him for details of how the lands were run prior to his mother's reign.

After the initial visits with the historian and the reassessing of the court members and former members had begun, King Sweyn decided he had a visit to make.

In the wee hours of the morn, he made his way to the seaside. His mother's body had been prepared for a sea funeral. Her body had been preserved in such a way to allow the good people of the village to pay their respects. Placed within an open-faced coffin, her pale and oddly serene looking body had been surrounded by all of the objects she had adored in her life. As was the royal Viking custom, they would be set afire and join her in the afterlife once the official cremation ceremony occurred. The dock was oddly barren except for the pristine Viking ship originally used for celebrations and deemed the only appropriate vessel for Queen Gyrid's final resting place. King Sweyn walked the wooden plank to say his final wishes to his mother and also to report back to her regarding the activities of the previous 48 hours. He reveled in the opportunity to gloat about all that he had undone from her time in charge for he had secretly hated every moment that he had been forced to be of service to those of a race subservient not only to him, but to all humans. The ship's boards creaked with his footsteps while the ocean waves crashed against its side. The saltwater scent wafted in the morning air. He had anticipated the smells associated with a rotting corpse accompanied by the scents of her favorite flowers and foods beginning their decay and yet those smells of decomposition did not dominate the seaside air.

This should have been the first hint to the young King that something in his plans was amiss. Instead, he made a brief mental note of it and continued onward.

Expecting to see his mother within the deep mahogany coffin and her body wrapped in bejeweled fabrics prepped for visitors to pay their respects, Sweyn quietly approached the sarcophagus with his mind racing with the stories he eagerly anticipated sharing with his mother's spirit. The last words he anticipated that she would hear before she was set alight and before the ship would be released from the dock and sent off into the ocean. Enabling her spirit to be freed from the confines of her body and ready for her joyful afterlife with all of her favorite objects.

Yet what he found was a bit different. Her favorite jewels and clothes and objects of the court were all intact beside her coffin. They had been lined up and placed in positions of honor. The ship had been staged for the simple act of setting it aflame and then releasing it from the dock and into the deep ocean. All of this he found exactly as he had anticipated. Yet, the most critical component of the entire funeral had gone missing: Gyrid.

He called the guards who had been assigned to watch the dock and all activities along the dock and ship to ensure no one, other than the King, came aboard.

"Where has she gone?" he demanded as he directed them to the empty chamber.

Surprised, the guards simply began searching the ship for signs of her body or at least a hint of what may have happened to her remains. For they must be nearby. The King questioned if there had been any visitors or signs of grave robbers. To which the guards responded that there had not. And why take the body, but not the jewels?

The King had heard of legends of bodies gone missing only to return in alternate states of consciousness. Some pale creatures feeding off of the living. Others shifting into other dark beings of the night. Some feeding off of the happy spirits of others due to their own deep sadness. Of course, he did not believe in such mythology. And yet, as they continued their search on and near the burial ship with all reporting that they found no signs of foul play, he could not help but mentally assess if these stories of yesteryear had been based in some form of truth.

The King sat on the dock and waited for the warriors to

return from their assignments. He needed them to find her body or at least confirm that they had distinct evidence of her being present at some point and not have it seem as though she simply disappeared.

Instead, they returned only to report that they had not found her body and there were no signs of grave robbing or theft. For if this was done by grave robbers then it would have been most likely that they would have taken her valuable possessions since they would have a much higher resale value in the open market and it was unlikely that they would only take off with her body. The only other option they agreed upon was that a witch or some other magic performer may have taken the queen's remains for various spells.

Angered and perplexed, the King, concerned of how her disappearance may be interpreted by the people, found a homeless woman of similar size and stance and proceeded to take her to the nether plane with a brutal swiftness. He then guided those he trusted, a rare few, to embalm the body and put it in the place of honor in lieu of his mother's body. Knowing that he had at least ensured he had avoided a panic among the people, he returned to the castle to move forward with his already begun efforts of placing humans back in the place of righteousness and shapeshifters in the service of humans.

What his warriors did not tell him was that they found evidence of footprints leading away from the ship and into the neighboring swamp surrounded by thin reed like trees. Not eager to discover the meaning of this, they simply acknowledged the finding amongst themselves and moved on.

They were quite familiar with mythos among the Vikings of beings that returned from the dead to live off the living and were called Draugr. Modern Americans would be more familiar with this myth— more commonly known as vampires.

What the King had not realized was that his mother had been part of a long line of Draugr and that in order to initiate the changing, she had to be killed. Previous generations had been cremated rather quickly so their changing had been stopped due to perishing by fire and with only their ashes remaining. But with the act of having the queen on display for her villagers to pay their respects, this enabled her to have enough time for the natural transformation to begin.

As the warriors looked into the high reeds to see if they could get a glimpse of who or what had wandered into the muddy space, the eyes of the dead queen peered back at them. A wall of glowing fungi grew at a rapid pace, forming the passageway between the lands of the living and of the dead.

INTERLUDE 6

(800'S AD)

The Seeress allowed us to remain with her for several nights until the full moon had appeared. I am sure there was an assumption that with the full moon our changing would come, but alas that is only from fairytales and folklore. And besides, I had not reached the age of changing yet.

In reality, the moon's waxing and waning did not affect us nor our physical state at all. What it did do is note for the Seeress the seasons and that her time to move on had become imminent.

And with that confirmation, she packed her most sacred belongings and left us in her cottage as she set out to return to wherever she had originated.

I turned to Ulf.

"What shall we do?" I asked.

He paused, deep in thought. As I mentioned, I did not experience what he had experienced so I did not feel as though I had the right to make the decision. He was the elder of us, and I knew that he would make the choice that was best for both of us. He ran his hands up and down his arms, as if he was in search of markings. Even though a few days earlier he was covered in light scarring, now they seemed to have been fully healed.

He then met my gaze. "We will return," he said. "It is the only way."

"For what?" I asked. I truly did not understand.

"If all the Seeress has said is true, then we must learn what it means to be Lycanthropes, and we must learn what our powers are. Only then will we be able to live on our own and be our true selves," he said.

This made sense to me. Although neither one of us liked the idea of returning to the King's special guards, they held knowledge that we simply did not have access to unless we became one of them. At this juncture in our Viking heritage, Norwegians did not truly maintain written histories. We did have runes but they were not used in the manner of tracking historical events. Our culture at that point in history was dependent on the passing of knowledge through storytelling ... one generation after another. In part, this is how my own fascination and dedication to recording the events of our time and continuing this tradition through the centuries had begun, but I will go into greater detail regarding that at another time.

Later, we would discover that a written history had begun in small segments, but at this time our only true option had been to return to the royal special forces.

The next morn, Ulf and I packed our meager belongings and returned to the King's guards. We were immediately separated, Ulf had been quickly whisked away to a remote set of quarters. They had said it was because he needed to continue his more advanced training which was done with the smaller group of soldiers and elite trainers. I was guided back to my modest cot among the dozens in the open floor plan sleeping quarters.

I laid awake that night, praying that I would see him again. I prayed that he was alright, since based on the last time I had seen him return from an evening set of teachings, he was covered in blood and wounds. I had no idea how vicious the training would be for him.

The next morning, as I made my way down the hallway and towards my own set of training courses which covered topics like sword fighting, hand-to-hand combat, and how to best shadow your enemy, I saw my elder brother as he made his way through the hallway along with his peers. He would not make eye contact, but clearly he moved with a carefulness and awkwardness indicative of another night of special training. I wanted to run to him and ask him how he felt, what had occurred, and so much more. But I knew better than to leave my place in the haphazard line to class.

Several nights and days passed with limited to no interaction between us. I must admit, I wondered if they would kick me out since I had shown very limited signs of the initial stages of transformation. A little shaking, but nothing nearly as severe as my brother had demonstrated at the same age. But I knew better than to mention it. I would rather remain so that I was close to my brother rather than put myself in a position in which we may never see each other again.

And that is when I was called into the head trainer's office.

"The King has summoned you and Ulf," he stated. His stance was one of confidence and authority.

"Why?" I asked. I wanted to ask a dozen other questions but figured it was best to begin with the most simplistic.

"He has chosen you both for an upcoming initiative. One that requires certain skills."

"I do not understand," I replied. At least as far as I knew, I had not shown any remarkable skills. Why would the King call on me?

"You and your brother are to meet in the Western Wing of the castle, along with others who were specially selected, to begin your journey. You will be notified at that time as to the specifics."

He nodded to me as if that movement empowered me to leave.

And so I did.

The next morning, I dressed in a hurry and caught up to my brother in the hallway, on our way to the Western Wing.

He did not look at me. Instead he simply walked forward with a dominance in his stance, his head held high, his stride long, his eyes forward.

"Ulf," I called to him. "Ulf?" I reached out as if to touch his hand and he seemed to pull it subtly away.

"Not now," he whispered. "Soon."

When we reached the Western Wing of the castle, we were greeted by a commander standing on a platform, overseeing all who came into the space. He motioned us forward. A dozen or so warriors congregated around us. All of varying ages, ethnicities, and backgrounds. There were warriors there of legend, meaning that I had only ever heard of beings of such immense height, others with such jet black hair and still others with such dark skin and curly hair. It was clear that many had already been through several battles, based on their physical scarring, their stance, and the ways in which they greeted one another. For some, it was like they had been reunited with family members, while others stayed a bit more distant from their fellow shapeshifters. Ulf remained quiet and emotionless and so I did my best to emulate him.

The commander began, "you have been chosen by the King for an investigative mission. Mikael, Gudrun, Njal, and Ulf. You will lead the following packs." He then listed off the warriors names, one by one. Thankfully I had been placed within my brother's pack.

We made our way, as directed by the commander, onto a ship which then navigated for several days until reaching the shores of our objective location.

Obediently, I followed my brother and the other warriors along mountainsides and into terrain I had never envisioned.

Upon reaching a specific point, my brother guided us all to take our places, as we had been taught. Each warrior removed their primary clothing and was down to the bare minimum— the equivalent of today's underwear. He then commanded us to initiate our changing.

For me, this is when things truly became real. As he and the other shifters began their transformation, it was as if their spell engagement and shifting fast tracked my own changing. My body shook uncontrollably. I could feel my bones elongate and hear them cracking as they broke and bent with my initial shifting. I cried out, mostly in fear, even though I had seen my own brother go through this and I had helped him in his moment. I suppose because all others present were in the midst of their own transformations, there was no one truly there to help me in mine. At one point I blacked out and awoke in the center of the field, bloody and terrorized bodies blanketed the grounds. My own body was covered in blood. I checked my limbs and torso and confirmed that I did not have any severe wounds.

That said, however, the viciousness of the ravaged beings nearby horrified me.

Anxious to find my brother, I searched the faces of the unconscious and undoubtedly killed individuals and prayed that his body was not among them.

"Here," I heard a rough and scratchy voice. "Over here." I turned to find him near the end of the clearing. His body had been smeared with the blood of others. He had already dressed in his gear.

The more actively I moved, the more I realized that I had deep wounds which called out in pain with my motion. I hobbled my way to him and found several other fellow warriors congregating nearby. Of the dozens who had joined us on this quest, many had survived the exchange which, considering the casualties, surprised me.

As instructed I cleaned up and made my way to a campground where other factions of the King waited for us.

That night, we huddled next to fires that had been set and used for cooking, keeping us warm as we waited to return to our ships. Ulf turned to me. He had learned much during our time away from one another. More than just how to fight.

"If the King is in the middle of negotiations with another ruler and they are not coming to an agreement, then he will suggest a battle to be the deciding factor. Some rulers scoff and decline the suggestion. Others agree to the terms. What they may not realize is that the King will send his special forces for any battle where he knows that his own lands are on the line."

"Do all royals have a shapeshifting squad?" I asked.

"No, not the majority," he smirked. "Most only have human warriors whom they rely on. Which is perfect for most needs, but if there is something that the King feels as though he needs an advantage, well, that is when he sends us."

"Why do the other kings not know about us? Why do they not have their own shapeshifters?" I asked.

"Some know about us," he said. "At least based on what my instructors have said. Those are usually the ones who decline these offers. While still others seem to be overconfident with their own battalions and agree to the King's terms. While others have their own shapeshifting battalions of varying sizes and skills. Most of it depends on how their villages perceive shapeshifters."

A nearby warrior must have been listening to our conversation because he visibly shivered at that comment. Ulf looked over at him and lowered his voice, leaning in to me. "Some villagers believe that shapeshifters are evil. That we were born only to do harm, so some crucify the shapeshifters as soon as their true selves are discovered. Others believe that shifters are not meant to be among humans. Their people perform various cruel acts on shifters while still others simply abandon shapeshifters upon discovering them so that they never learn how to control their powers and end up abandoned, homeless, and destitute."

I looked around the burning fire and noted my fellow soldiers with their wizen looks and grave stances. "Is that where these soldiers came from?" I whispered.

"Some," he said. "I have heard rumors of others being bred."

"Bred?"

He looked around at the others, searching their faces. And then continued, "There are tales of Lycanthropes from different bloodlines being forced to propagate in order to ensure the strongest, most gifted are birthed."

I stared at him for a moment, unsure if I heard him correctly. "Forced to?"

"There are reasons we are who we are and why we ended up where we were. For now simply accept that we are where we are meant to be." He said this with a gravity that seeped into each word.

"Is that why I am at this battle? In your battalion?"

He shook his head. "No. One of the King's advisors had told the commander that based on our ancestry, you may need additional assistance in getting through your first changing." He looked me in the eyes. "And that the best way to do that was to have you go to battle with other shifters who were much stronger and in control of their gifts. I did not want that to happen as a part of a more volatile exchange. I wanted to be sure I was there in case you needed anything. I knew that this battle would be relatively painless compared to other potential battles because I knew, based on what the commander shared, that this would be against lesser skilled warriors," he said. "So I requested for you to join me."

With that last comment, one of the other leaders called out for us to prepare for another battle.

"At the point of midnight, we will return," he said. "If we are being called back to a skirmish," Ulf continued, "then that means the kings did not come to an agreement."

"How is that possible?" I asked. "The sheer amount of blood. The bodies ... how?" I did not know how to articulate what I was feeling. The royals not being able to declare a victor was inconceivable based on all that I saw though admittedly I had only seen a fraction of what had occurred.

Ulf tossed some leaves into the flames and watched as they sparked the firelight.

"We do not have much time," he turned to me. "I need to teach you a few basic spells to help you in your changing and to maintain control during the skirmish."

Still stunned and a bit in shock from the earlier engagement, I obediently followed my brother's lead. He showed me how to initiate the changing, how to better control the full transition, and provided guidance on what to do when or if I became aware while in the bestial form.

"Your awareness will come with time," he said. "Know that everyone is different. Some are aware from the first moment they transform into their beast selves, others gain awareness the more frequent that they transform, while others never gain awareness during that period."

"What about you?" I asked. "Do you know?"

He looked like he was experiencing something in another world, another dimension. His immediate awareness disappeared for a moment.

"Ulf?" I said softly and waved my hand before his face. He remained still, silent, not present. Just when I was about to get the commander for help, his consciousness returned.

"Birger, I need you to be careful," he said. "I do not know if you will have awareness. I only know that the training we have both been through in the last several months will naturally come forward no matter what our physical state."

With those words, the commander beckoned us all to take our places for the subsequent battle.

As my brother predicted, I did not remember the transformation. I barely saw our opponents across the field before we initiated our group transformation. Upon awakening, again, I laid in a field covered in blood with bodies strewn all around me. Some complete with their throats ripped out. Others with body parts missing only to be found hundreds of feet away. One of our enemy warriors, only a few feet away from me, was alive, though he moaned with each breath as if the act of breathing simply caused him pain. One of the captains came over to him, the captain in partial transformation, his arms the limbs of a wolf, his face partially transitioned with the bloody-fanged snout of a wolf, his eyes glowed with the hunger and elation of a recent kill.

The captain tilted his head back and let out a howl strewn with hunger and need. He then swiftly dove down and ripped out the half-dead soldier's throat. Terrified, I looked away, not wanting to see more. It was one thing to awaken after a battle and find myself covered in blood and surrounded by bodies and a completely different thing to witness this violent bloodshed firsthand.

I heard the half-man-half-beast rip apart and devour his victim. And with each bit of sound, I winced, my mind bringing to life the realities of the situation with great ferocity. I knew I should not feel such sympathy for the victims since we were there precisely to do what the other warrior was in the midst of doing—to defeat our opponents in battle.

But this was not my war. This was not my battle. These other creatures were here for similar reasons—someone in power had a disagreement with another person in power and had decided to send their strongest to battle in their stead. I understood that this was the nature of war and the nature of being a soldier, a Viking. I also understood that this was the only way we would be able to learn how to best control our physical forms.

But it did not stop me from wanting to run far, far away.

The commander guided us all to return to the docks. "Come!" he began, "Our ship awaits us." He motioned for us to follow him as if we were in line to board the vessel. Without looking up, I did as he commanded and went out of my way to not interact or have an exchange with another. I simply wanted to go back to my home.

Upon our return, I made my way off of the vessel and, head down, back to our barracks. The commander righteously announced our accomplishments, our winning of the war, to the royal family and their followers.

He pulled me aside and gloriously stated to the King, "He

has earned the right to be among the next tier." He patted me on the back and nodded. "A true warrior."

With that declaration, I was transitioned to the next level of training. I must admit, based on the commander's statement, I was still not aware of what I had done. I clearly regained consciousness after I had performed additional feats in the state of the werewolf. I winced at the thought of what I must have done to deserve such pomp.

No longer placed with my brother, I saw him only on occasion, typically in the hallway or in the dining hall. I had the greatest opportunity to interact with him when we were commanded to participate in an event. Although we were not assigned to the same team, we found opportunities to congregate on the sly to check on one another. His moments of being lost in his own thoughts seemed to be triggered at random, unpredictable times. I tried to identify some type of common trigger and the only thing that seemed to be the same with each one was that we were either on our way to a battle or in the midst of one. I am not sure how accurate that is, considering this was also the only times I saw him.

Meanwhile, my own awareness of transformations seeped into my dreams. When I awoke after a fight, I had the sense of what had occurred and I could see parts of it through a haze as if I had imagined it. Only when other warriors spoke about the battle did it become clear that what I thought I had imagined had actually occurred. With each engagement, the fragments of hazy memories grew until I remembered the full exchange. Again under the cover of a dream-state. It was as if I was in someone else's body and could not control what that person was doing. No matter what I did—whether I mentally commanded my arms to move a certain way or to walk or run—my body seemed to do whatever it wanted.

I slowly grew to trust my instructors at the castle and began asking for additional guidance. Once it was clear that what I thought was a dream was actually my conscious state while I had transformed, I approached my most favored teachers for additional guidance.

One of my instructors, Eric of the Fairhair Dynasty, taught me additional spells to help me through these periods. "You need not be fearful," he began. "Each of us transforms differently and matures at different rates, which is why we are here. We will help you in regaining and maintaining control no matter what physical state you may be in," he said. "Here," he handed me a booklet. "This contains spells that will help you in maintaining control."

"But how do I even know if I have lost consciousness?" I asked.

He smirked. "When you feel as though you are in a dream state, that is when you are most likely actually in an alternative state. You must force your consciousness so that you are actively engaged during these transformations."

I thumbed through the booklet and read the initial spells. They seemed straightforward enough, but I still did not feel as though he had truly answered my question. If I was in a dream state then how did I know I was in the dream state? How did I force consciousness?

Eric of the Fairhair Dynasty eyed me as I skimmed through his gift. He clearly noted my confusion.

"For everyone it is different," he said. "We all gain our control at different rates. Your time will come." He patted my shoulder. "You must have patience."

I felt like a teenager going through a growth spurt. "So if I acknowledge that I am in a new state then that will enable me to be present in the alternate state?" Admittedly, I feared what I did when I went into my other states, especially during training. Since it seemed like if I went into a different state while around other shapeshifters then I had a higher likelihood of engaging in violence. I was not afraid of fighting, but I did not like the idea of killing another without being aware of it. Something about that felt wrong.

"Fear not," he reiterated. "All of this is expected. It is just a natural part of gaining control and mastering our gifts."

I do not know if I was simply lucky in that I never killed a fellow soldier while in that dream state or if others did not inform me of the killings that I had performed. At least as far as I knew, I never killed someone without being conscious of it.

But others did. And that made the battlefield that much more dangerous.

Within months I began waking in the middle of the night drenched in sweat, my mind racing. All I could see in the dream state was my room transformed into a battlefield and warriors in the throes of a violent fight. I looked down to see my own hands in the form of sharp, wicked claws as they thrashed at enemies. I did my best to force consciousness, but with limited success. More often than not, I awakened in the midst of a scream. A scream I would try to hold inside not wanting to awaken my fellow classmates.

The occurrences of these presumed nightmares became so frequent that I feared going to sleep. I laid awake on my cot and stared at the ceiling, praying the morning light would come so that I could return to training and get as far away from them as possible.

Half asleep in the daylight, I continued my training and did my best to stay focused on the teachings. Whenever I was in transit between classes, I looked for my brother just to be sure that he was okay. And incredibly thankful whenever I saw him looking fit and well.

Eric, my head trainer pulled me aside, clearly aware of my

altered states and the challenges I experienced in gaining control of them.

"You must work through it," he said. "We all go through this at some point early in our maturity."

His words were meant to calm and help me through this period. In reality, they simply fell flat. I understood the intent, and what I was supposed to be doing, so I nodded obligingly. I saw him eye me as I continued onward. I am not quite sure what he expected of me in terms of a reaction. It felt like there was more, much more that he seemed to believe was due. Not sure how else to respond, I smiled slightly, nodded with a bit of uncertainty, and continued on to my next class.

His words did not make the nightmares go away. They did not cause my hallucinations to stop. I gained greater control of my shaking which caused some of my anxiety to decrease, but it always felt like there was much more that I was supposed to be doing. I sought out Ulf for he was the only person I thought I could truly trust and who would understand the anxiety I experienced.

I found him during our dining hour. The hall was full of students from all walks of life and all levels of skill. The instructors lined the edge of the room and acted as guardians. I made my way across the chow line and paused for a moment to greet him.

"Ulf," I said. "Meet me tonight, yes?"

He looked at me quizzically and then nodded in agreement. "Western Wing?" he asked.

I nodded.

Knowing I would finally be able to speak with him, I rejoined my class, elated at the thought of regrouping with the one person I could trust. The one person who would understand what I was going through.

Later that night, I waited for the rest of my class to lie down for the night and then made my way to the same location where we had first been reunited for my very first battle. My first experience of transforming. My coming of age. As I made my way to the central room, the empty halls echoed. The high ceilings and barren space only propagated the feeling of vastness and being alone. I prayed he would appear soon. For all of the spells, techniques, and trainings, none enabled me to overcome these moments of desperation and fear. Those moments of reliving the battles as they came to me in dreams or triggered at what felt like random moments.

I heard footsteps and I did all I could not to transform automatically in response to the presence of another lycanthrope. My flight or fight mechanism engaged with flashes of moments in battle, which typically happened when another came up from behind. Thankfully, rarely did someone come up from behind me, but in this moment my mind flashed an instance when we were in battle, and I had been attacked by an opponent from behind as he came after me in full beast mode. My transformation was automatic and immediate. Thankfully a part of my brain was aware that I was not in the midst of a fight and I was instead at our home base. This awareness, however, did not stop me from changing.

The next thing I knew I was in the dream state, partially transformed, and coming after my brother. He pivoted quickly and changed into a being I was not familiar with. Seemingly part bear, part wolf, part human, he grew to triple his human size. I changed into a being larger than I had previously experienced. A wolf-type creature similar to the one that my brother had become. Nothing close to Ulf, but at least twice my typical size.

He shoved me away, batting at me like I was some minor afterthought. I flew across the room and I slammed into the wall, my breath knocked out of me. I crumbled to the floor. My human self cried out in an attempt to force my bestial self to stop, to no longer attack. I felt at odds within my different forms and tried desperately to get my human self to regain control. I saw my own paws grow and the nails lengthen. In this dream state, my body leapt up and dove for him again. And again, he tossed me aside like a minor annoyance.

My body slammed to the floor, my head banged against the hardened flooring. Suddenly, the dream state disappeared, and I was back in my human form with my human consciousness. I suddenly seemed to be able to take control of my motions that one degree of separation from consciousness crumbled. I began to get up, my body sore from the skirmish, and I looked up to see Ulf coming after me.

"Stop, Ulf. It is me, Birger," I tried to call out. "Please, stop." I did my best to form these human words and instead they came forward like the grunts of a beast. I repeatedly tried, desperate for him to know that I was fully present.

But my voice, my normal human way of communicating did not return with my state of consciousness. His eyes glowed with a fierceness indicative of one about to retaliate. Unable to communicate to him, I did all that I could do—submit and pray that he would not destroy me.

With a growl and a swiftness I had never seen before, he pinned me to the wall. Aware that any sudden movement may be perceived as a counterattack, I decided to simply go limp and not fight his actions. I needed him not to perceive me as a threat. He started to go in for the kill, clearly he had become so enthralled in the moment that he was having difficulty controlling his actions as well. I ducked out of the way and barely missed his bite.

"Please," I thought. "Please, it is me. Your brother."

We continued in this manner for what felt like hours, but in reality, was probably closer to a couple of minutes. One thrash after another. One point and counterpoint, moment after moment.

Spent, we both laid across from one another in this barren space. Exhausted from the fight, we both naturally shifted back to our human selves. I watched as my brother transformed, aware of my own change. In the rags of what had been my night gear, I waited for my brother to return to his human form.

Once he had come to, he looked at me with sadness and doubt. He slowly sat up on the floor, across from me and acknowledged my presence. With his nod, I said, "I cannot do this anymore. I cannot risk it." The guilt and fear of what may happen next was overwhelming.

Originally, I had intended to talk to Ulf about ways in which I could get through the nightmares, the daymares, reliving these horrific moments. Assuming that since he had matured at a faster rate than I had, then he would have critical and vital tricks to regain control. But I had finally reached the point of physical control I had prayed for. The point in which I had full control of myself in the throes of a battle. But it was not enough. I was still at high risk of harming the one person in my life who meant more to me than myself. I was not willing to risk that.

"What are you talking about?" he said, clearly angry with me.

"I need to get away from this place. I cannot handle this," I felt like I was whining but I did not care anymore.

"No," he said. "You will never learn how to fully control—"

I interrupted him. "No. The only times I change is when I am around others like us. I cannot handle this, Ulf. I cannot hurt others like this."

He glared at me. He paused for a moment and did his best to regain his composure. "If you go, do not ever come back." He said this with a ferocity that shocked me. He had always been my protector; the elder brother. He had never rejected me like this before.

"Why would you say this?" I cried.

"I have given more than you will ever know to make sure that we both survive. If you leave, you are rejecting everything that I, the Seeress, and our mother meant for you to have. You will be rejecting all that anyone has ever done for us."

I gasped at him. This was not what I expected from him. I tried my best to respond with words of acceptance and of understanding. But at that point, it felt like there was an invisible barrier between me and the other warriors. No matter what I did, my simple will would not move forward. And with those final words of Ulf's and my last exchange with him being that of combatants, I opened my mouth to speak, yet found no words.

Silently, I got up from the barren floor, made my way to the rear exit, and I left. In my tattered clothes and with nothing of value, I simply exited the Western Wing. It felt as if I could go nowhere other than away—far, far away from the castle—never to see my brother again.

13
LUNA'S - 2000S

I'm not sure if the sleeping pills kept me from changing, but I can definitely say that they helped knock me out. Before they really kicked in, my mind raced with thoughts about Javier and the bakery and what I would do when I returned and if Javier would ever speak to me again and my parents and what I would tell them and was Birger for real when he kept talking about how "rare" I was and what did that mean and did Daniel really need to die and could we have avoided it and how much I missed him and then in the midst of that flood of thoughts and images and worries, it was like a wave of warm comfort rushed through me and the next thing I knew I awoke, not really sure where I was, but eventually realizing I was in the comfort of my room.

My eyes blurry, body cozy underneath the plain soft gray comforter, it took me a moment to focus. I placed my hand beside me, mindlessly searching for my love. I craved waking up next to Javier and feeling his warm body against mine. I wasn't sure how to react without him here. Without the knowledge that somewhere in the world he craved me too. The one thing super real was the knowledge that somewhere out there he wasn't sure if he wanted me knowing what he knows about me now. I felt an overpowering sadness and loss.

My body ached from the stress it had gone through in the previous days. With the realization and recollection of what had occurred, I got up and stretched to help alleviate at least some of the aches and pains.

I made my way to the bathroom and turned on the shower, hopped in, and enjoyed the steaming jets of water as their intensity massaged my aching muscles. I slowly washed up and then dried off, dressing in my favorite jeans and a white t-shirt. I kept myself busy by constantly checking my cell phone hoping I had messages waiting for me. I quickly realized doing so only made me sad and I really needed to focus on why I was there.

With that, I headed down the hallway, passed multiple closed doors that I assumed led to similar suites, and followed the enticing smells of cooked eggs and hot coffee. My stomach grumbled telling me it was definitely time to get my nosh on. I headed into the dining hall and found rows of tables with modest metal chairs. A buffet of breads, spreads, meats, cereals, muesli, eggs, and much more lined the far right wall. Across from that was a station of coffees, milks, and juices. I knew where I was headed first.

"Good to see you up so early," I heard from behind me. I turned to see a smiling Birger. "I see you easily found the dining area."

Birger then walked me through the rest of the chow hall and confirmed that this would be where we would take all of our meals while I was in town. I greedily piled up a plate of eggs and toast and devoured them as if I hadn't eaten in days. Birger silently drank his coffee and kept me company as I finished up my meal.

Once we were done, he showed me the trash and where to return my empty plates. "While you are here, we will have specific instructors who will guide you through the basics," he commented. He motioned me towards the exit and then guided me down the hallway. "You will have a full agenda with classes from the history of our kind through self defense methods, and specific spells that will assist you in controlling your gifts."

He nodded towards classrooms and introduced me to my instructors. Hilda, a muscular and friendly woman with long chestnut hair and gray-blue eyes, had been designated to teach fighting and defense techniques. "And more importantly how to leverage these methods when you are in your bestial states," Birger commented.

"You will enjoy our classes," Hilda commented. "I'm sure there will be a rather immediate benefit to them." She smirked. I am not sure I wanted to know what she referenced, but I was sure I was about to find out.

We continued down the hallway to another instructor—tall and lean with short jet hair. Birger nodded towards her. "This is Rune," he began. "She will be your guide for the spells, techniques, and methods that are more greatly aligned to the management of your physical states and to help you through any emotional or mental assistance you may require."

"I have heard much about you," Rune reached out her hand. "I've heard you're quite the natural."

I looked at Birger and then back at Rune. "Well, I'll have to take his word for it." I shrugged.

Based on the bit I had read from the materials Birger had provided previously, it sounded like I would find both series of courses critical in the upcoming days. Heck, it sounded like these classes were pretty critical for Birger too, or at least someone who went by the same name. I didn't have the balls to ask him outright if the Birger in the notes was a relative, so I waited for the right moment. The thought of him being the same dude was a little much. I mean that would mean the guy standing next to me who looked like he was maybe in his late twenties or early thirties was really born in the 8th century. And although I was getting used to similar stories among these shapeshifters, it didn't make the realities of it any less weird.

"Before we begin your official teachings, you and I will re-perform your initiation spell. We will do so within the next hour. That said, you will have one additional set of classes," Birger got a smile in his eyes with this one. "I will be teaching you about your familial history, the bloodlines and types of the shapeshifters including the Lycanthrope."

"You mean, there's more?"

14

BIRGER'S - 10TH CENTURY

Through the high reeds of the swampened lands came a soft luminescence that grew with a pulsing sensation into the late hours of the night. The glow formulated into the shape of a passageway, a doorway of sorts that guided visitors along the same path as the newly resurrected Queen Gyrid.

As one stepped through the darkened passage and into the pitch blackness, the entryway seemed to go on ad infinitum. It felt so infinite to the point that when a new traveler entered the space, the visitor commonly experienced a panic attack due to loss of sense of place and time. Right until the moment occurred in which he broke through the darkness and flew to the grounds of the alternate world. The world of only barren lands, midnight skies, and eternal smog that hovered over all— hiding true beings of the night.

The newly resurrected Queen Gyrid waited among the succulent reeds. She sat atop what was once an oak tree and through the centuries had transformed into a barren stub. She glared through the passageway at her son, fully aware of the tricks he had done, eager to return and show him exactly what pissing off his mother meant to him.

INTERLUDE 7

(800'S AD)

I walked along the trails that led away from the castle, preoccupied by the words of my brother, Ulf. "If you leave, do not return," he had declared only moments after we had battled one another in a few of our alternate forms. I could not believe that he didn't understand why this was so critical to me. Why it was so important that if we could not control our changings while we were around one another then we needed to be separated until we were able to ensure that our natures would not cause each other harm. I could not believe that he did not understand why my leaving was absolutely imperative. And yet he did not and could not understand.

I randomly walked through the forests in the general direction away from the castle. At one point I rested among the trees along the riverway, taking a break before continuing forward to find a new place to reside. I knew from the years of training and traveling as a part of the King's special forces that I may be days before finding a new home, but I would be able to find refuge once I fell upon a neighboring town. That only took me the equivalent of a daybreak and a sundown before I found a small town. Modest in size, the centerpiece of the town was a church reminiscent of the church that had housed the original orphanage that Ulf and I had resided in. Only a few doors down stood an inn offering rooms for rent for both short and long terms. I approached the main desk and asked if they had a need for labor. "I should be in town for several days and am in need of shelter and work."

The gentleman behind the main desk, a bit scruffy in general nature, looked at me with a suspicious eye. "I know not of one who has such a need, but I will keep you in mind in case something arises." He said this with a closed look, generally telling me that he had no intent to do any such thing.

With that I said, "Thank you for your consideration, kind sir." And then I went off into the dirt streets lined with intimate cottages and random establishments.

The bakery had no need for assistance.

The butcher said much the same.

I knocked on nearly every door to identify someone who may be in need of assistance of some kind until I landed on the street corner politely asking those passersby if they may have work or could spare a few coins.

Once I had a handful of money, I made my way back to the inn and purchased my first meal in what felt like days. I sipped the house-made mead, thankful for the drink, and ordered a plate of whatever the house special was for the evening meal. I showed the barkeep my coins which encouraged him to go into the back kitchen and return with a metal platter piled with mutton, roasted potatoes, and a rich and savory gravy. I swear I had not had such divine foods in my life and ate like I had not seen any kind of foods in months.

I chugged the mead in between bites and felt nearly euphoric. The inn's main dining area had been partially populated with those staying at the inn. I went out of my way not to interact with them. Since I did not have a sense of why they were in this intimate location, I did not know if any were individuals I could trust.

"Did you find work?" The innkeeper approached me and inquired.

"Not as of yet," I said. "I am open to anything that may be available." I finished off my drink and pushed the cup aside. "I am a quick learner."

Wiping down a pot, he nodded in affirmation. "I will keep that in mind." With those words, he slowly walked away and returned to the back.

I looked around the inn, acknowledging that all those present must have been in some type of transition. Heading from one place to somewhere else, this small town was not one to attract visitors for significant lengths of time. Realizing the hour for sleep slowly approached, I knew, without funds to cover an overnight stay, I would not be welcomed in this location. With that, I made my way back onto the streets and found a horse stable in which I opted to hide underneath the robust straw that filled the stalls, and among the horses I watched as the midnight moon climbed high in the sky and shone with the bright stars in the night sky. And with that, I found myself asleep.

Upon awakening, I knew that I needed to find something more long term. I needed a plan for how to move forward. I still had the book of spells that I had been gifted by Eric, so I could study them, but I needed more. I needed to find the Seeress or someone who was an equivalent to her in order to guide me through the next few months of my maturity.

I assumed that I was going through the equivalent of my teenage maturity and once I found someone who could guide me through this, then I would be able, not only control, but leverage my shapeshifting gifts at will. The key remained in finding the equivalent of the Seeress. Now although that may sound like a relatively simple task, the reality was that I had no idea how to find another Seeress. It felt like our finding the Seeress in the first place was pure happenstance so recreating this miracle seemed nearly impossible. I remained huddled in the corner of the horse stall and tried to figure out how best to go about this.

As the morning matured, I decided to make my way back to the inn and try to approach this in a relatively simple manner.

Just ask.

I did my best to brush off the remains of the hay from my clothes and then approached the gentleman who managed the stall regarding chores that I could perform to earn a wage that would at least get me fed for the day. Luckily, he was able to oblige and had me clean out the stalls and care for the horses which earned me enough coins to justify my return to the inn and earn my daytime meal.

Upon my return to the inn, the innkeeper's look of circumspection had diminished. He could have easily shown me the door and told me not to return, but instead, when I approached the main desk, he seemed to soften.

"Did you find work?" he asked.

"The stable owner kindly gave me some chores to fulfill this morning." I then showed him the coins that I had earned that morning. "Do you have a morning meal in which I can partake?" I asked this in the most polite and formal manner I could imagine. Without another word, the innkeeper motioned to the main seating area of the inn and disappeared into the back, only to return several moments later with a platter of breads, cheeses, and muesli, as well as a pint. I thanked him as he put the platter and pint before me.

"When you have a moment, I wondered if I could ask you for advice regarding the best individuals to approach locally for certain tasks?" I truly was not sure the best way to approach him regarding the topic of finding another Seeress. I was not even sure how to approach the topic of shapeshifters, so I did my best to approach the topics in a soft and careful manner. As I devoured the meal, he stopped by to seemingly check on me. At one point, he turned to me, "what is it that you would like to inquire about?"

I wiped my mouth and settled in the chair.

"I am in search of someone with specific gifts. One who is familiar with ancient rituals and rights. One who is familiar with a variety of beliefs and incantations."

He smirked. "You are speaking of one who believes in ancient ways?" He looked slyly around the inn as if others may be listening in on our dialogue.

"Yes, you could call them ancient ways."

"Ways of those other than the natives of the town?"

I perked up. The way he spoke, I had a feeling that he had been approached in a similar manner in the past. His hinting as to other creatures nearly caused me to pop out of my chair.

"Yes, far more ancient ways and beings." I said the last bit in a whisper. I did not want to start trouble or cause alarm if there were those in the inn who were not familiar.

He wiped down the table. "Are you of the special forces that work for the King?" His own voice reduced to that of a whisper. I leaned in to ensure that he was the primary individual to hear my inquiries. "I had been. I am now in search of one to assist me in maturing my skills." I looked him dead in the eye. Based on his return of my gaze, he understood what I referenced.

"I may be able to assist," he began. "There are those of the old ways who still reside nearby." He looked me up and down. "If they cannot directly assist you then they may be able to point you in the direction of those who can."

I nodded in acknowledgement and understanding. I did not want to seem too eager, but I felt like jumping up for joy since I never thought that I would be able to identify another Seeress or someone who was an equivalent so quickly. If anything, based on the challenges I had had over the last few years, I assumed I would have great difficulty.

In truth, I was a bit surprised that my hallucinations and nightmares had decreased—which only proved that my gut instinct was correct and for whatever reason residing in a place full of other shapeshifters who were in the same equivalent of puberty was only worsening my own transformations. And when others of the gift did not react in such a violent manner, it only proved they didn't have a similar need to move on from living in such close quarters.

"Here," he pulled forward a piece of paper and a quill with ink. "She had been away for quite some time, but has recently returned." He marked up the paper. "She is known for her gifts and her ability to help guide those of the special talents. You will want to approach her humbly since she is truly one of the rare ones." He noted. "But if she meets you and deems you to be one of special gifts, then she will be more than happy to assist you in your pursuits."

He placed the paper before me and I studied the runes and how they directed me to a home in what appeared to be the middle of the woods.

"It is at least a half day's walk from here," he said. "If you choose to approach her then you will want to leave soon."

I nodded and wrapped up the paper and put it in my waistband. "Thank you for your help," I said. "I will be sure to thank her for any assistance and guidance."

"She may expect more than thanks." With that the innkeeper cleaned the placemat before me and moved on to serve others within the dining area.

I took the opportunity to make my way out of the inn, out into the town, and then towards the cottage he had written directions for.

I made my way through the forest, following the directions, and simply kept my thoughts focused on what awaited me. I was insanely thankful that I had had a respite from the hallucinations and random transformations and prayed that I could continue in this manner for as long as humanly or inhumanly possible. My luck seemed to be quite high as I continued forward. After a handful of hours, I made it upon a clearing in which a small home, seemingly barely large enough for one, was anchored.

I gently knocked upon the door and put my head down, listening for footsteps or other sounds indicative of someone inside.

After several moments with my doubt as to whether anyone would answer the door swelling with each tick, I heard footsteps approach the door and the slide of a lock. "Who's there?" asked a soft and familiar voice.

"I am in search of one who has studied the ancient ways. One familiar with the old paths." With the last words, the door opened a bit more and I saw a glimpse of a face peek through the opening. "Birger?" said a woman's voice.

"Yes, I am Birger. Who art thou?" I asked.

The door flew open and before me stood The Seeress dressed in nearly identical cloak of years prior, I was in near disbelief.

"How did you find me?" she inquired.

I held up the paper that the innkeeper had provided. She studied it briefly and then waved me in and welcomed me. "Truly," she began. "How did you find me and where is Ulf? The last I saw you both had many learnings before you. I trust you have had quite the adventures."

The cottage was quite similar to the one in which she had resided so many years prior. So similar I took a double take in near disbelief. "We did as you had directed," I said. "We joined the King's special guard and were taught many lessons."

"And partook in many battles, I trust."

I looked at her, nodding slowly. "Yes."

15
2000S - LUNA

Once he had introduced me to the other instructors and walked me through the grounds, Birger spent the next few hours with me. At first we found a small room which had been sparsely populated with modest furniture in which to reperform the ritual and regain—if not stabilize—control of the Lycanthropic gifts. This was to ensure that my bestial state and transformations would be matters of expected routine, and not haphazard events of untimely change. I hoped that this would cover my bestial state both when I was consciously awake and also when I was in a dream state. Based on what he had said, this would do that, but a part of me was still a little anxious about it.

We performed it in the native Swedish first and then repeated it in English.

"Just in case," he said.

I understood that, I mean, heck, who knew what may have ended up being the most effective, so it definitely didn't hurt to repeat it a few times.

Once we were done, I definitely felt stronger, as if we had

reinforced my own spirit. I also felt grounded so I was betting that whatever it was that needed reinforcement had, in fact, been reinforced.

Thank goodness.

I could feel my anxiety level reduce tenfold. And interestingly, he also looked like his anxiety had gone down too.

With that, he took me into one of the classrooms and began. "We will need to start with the primary Swedish family lines. From there we can expand to the primary lines from other countries." Boy, was I glad I had a notepad and pen because he had a ton to cover.

He stood before an old school chalkboard and began reviewing my family line and his own. He even covered Chago's primary branches.

"These are the primary factions that came from the Swedish lines. Every country has family lines that are the dominant ones. Some are related, while others, at least as far as we are aware, have no relationship to one another."

"How do we know?" I asked.

He paused for a second, as if he was gathering his thoughts.

"Back in the eighth century we began recording the family lines to help us better understand the relationships. This is also when we started studying the family lines and the types of shapeshifters in case there were genetic correlations. There were instances when we discovered the different family line's genetic strengths during their training."

"The defense training or the spells stuff?" I genuinely was not sure. I guessed that he meant the spells, but every time I turned around there was something else I didn't understand.

"Both, really. It could be either. Typically it is during the spell training. It comes out when a maturing Lycanthrope discovers his or her breadth and depth of shifting abilities."

"Okay. Not to be dense, but what does that mean?" I asked.

He smiled. "Believe it or not, not all shapeshifters are were-wolves. We have shifters who can change into multiple forms including those once assumed to have been mythic."

"Like a phoenix or something?" I said facetiously.

"Yes, that is exactly correct," he said without a twinge of sarcasm.

"Wait, what? You're serious."

He nodded. "I am quite serious."

I felt my stomach drop. "So I had every right to be worried about what was happening when I was unconscious and dreaming about being in other forms."

"More than a right. We have had examples of maturing lycanthropes who completely lost control in what they thought were dream states and in reality they were in an alternate form. A form they could not control."

I didn't need to take notes on this. It was such a *holy-shit* moment that I felt like his words would be forever embedded in my mind.

"Were you planning on telling me about this, or was this going to stay a secret."

"You are the one who didn't come back to complete your initial training," he scolded. "But, I am telling you now." His voice softened. "And know that the more we dive into the lessons, then the more you will grow to understand how all of this is correlated." He pointed at me. "Because it is. Deeply correlated."

"Let me guess ... and the more powerful a shifter is, the more deeply correlated all the different aspects of this life turn out to be?"

He nodded. "Exactly."

"Is there a correlation between one who loses control of their abilities and how powerful they are?"

He pondered that for a minute and then replied. "In truth,

officially there is not." He pointed at me again. "That said, I would not be surprised if there was one. It is simply that we do not often encounter a Lycanthrope who can shift into the unnatural or mythological. In fact, it is most common for a Lycanthrope to be able to turn into a wolf solely. The next most common is a bear and then a raven. Of those shifters with the more extensive gifts, many of them you would be most familiar with because they have become known through fairy tales and what are thought to be myths. Humans do not call them shifters because most humans are unaware of our existence. That said, all countries, all human forms have fairy tales and mythology that reflects the existence of shapeshifters."

"And what about me? What bloodlines do I come from?"

"That we will confirm during your trainings. Once Hilda begins walking you through your various forms, then we will have a greater understanding of your gifts which will then point us to which family lines you come from. And some may even reveal themselves when Rune goes more deeply into your self defense and battle training."

"That sounds fair," I said. "And when do we start those lessons?"

He looked toward the doorway and tilted his head upwards. "After lunch, which we will break for in a moment. Then Hilda will come for you in the cafeteria. Both Hilda and Rune will spend the initial classes taking you through your paces to better understand your natural abilities."

He quickly broke for lunch and guided me back to the cafeteria. I was a little surprised that there weren't more students in the facilities. The place wasn't empty, but it seemed like there were more folks working there than there were individuals present for training and classes.

With our trays of sandwiches, we took a seat in a far corner. I was sure to sit across from him, eager to take this moment to have some of the more obscure questions answered.

"Why aren't there more students here?" I asked as I took a sip from my ice water.

"This is considered off season." He put his napkin on his lap. "Typically a class will consist of between twenty and thirty students but this happens to be the time when most students are home for holidays. You will most likely meet other students in the coming weeks as they return from the holiday break."

I pummeled Birger with questions, some he answered, others he politely ignored. He encouraged me to focus on my lunch, "Hilda will be returning for you shortly so you may want to finish up your lunch." He said this with a tinge of encouragement, making it clear that he was finished answering my questions.

I barely finished my chicken salad sandwich when I looked up to see Hilda in the doorway. Her arms crossed, she looked impatient, eager for me to finish up. I nodded in acknowledgement and quickly devoured my last few bites. "I'll be right there," I called out.

"I will see you once you and Hilda are done today. Best of luck," he said.

Thinking that sounded a bit ominous, I put my dishes away, used some hand sanitizer, and then obediently followed Hilda to her training room. Similar to the layout of a dance studio, mirrors lined the one wall where she already had a mat rolled out on the floor.

"Now to start, I'll need you to come over to this spot." She pointed to the center of the mat. "First I'll need you to kick off your shoes. We're going to begin in our stockinged feet."

"Okie doke." I tossed off my sneakers and took the place

before her. She went into the back and then returned with a dark blue robe which she put before me.

"Now don't be embarrassed," she nodded at the robe. "I'm going to leave the room for a few minutes to give you a chance to change. You'll want to be out of your street clothes when we begin running you through the basics."

"No problem," I said and started stripping out of my jeans and t-shirt. I got totally naked and then covered up with the robe which was surprisingly comfy.

A few minutes later, Hilda returned, also changed into a similar robe. She walked up to me and placed her hands on my shoulders.

"For us to begin, I'll need you to take a deep breath in and then a long breath out." She demonstrated the technique and then shook out her arms. "And then you'll need to shake out your arms and legs and close your eyes."

I did as instructed. Pretty much putting complete faith into her because, I admit, I had no idea what was about to happen. I heard her walk around me and then come up from behind.

"Now breathe in again and out." She did the exact same thing. "The purpose of our first exercises will be to get a better understanding of your capabilities."

I nodded. "Sounds good."

"From what Birger mentioned you've already demonstrated quite a few forms."

I didn't remember telling Birger about the paces that Chago walked me through when we were battling at the United Nations or what some of his minions had walked me through either, but I guess I had. "Yeah, there have been a couple."

"Good. To begin, I am going to ask you to clear your mind and try to transform."

With that direction, I did just that. I first shifted into a werewolf and then a wolf and then a bear and then back to my human form.

"Good," she said. "Now in order to explore other forms, I'm going to ask you to repeat after me. I'll be helping you in your transformations, but I want you to repeat the spells so you can learn the triggers and perform them without my guidance."

I nodded. "Sounds good to me."

She began with a spell that shifted me into a raven. I could feel my body changing. Similar to the dream state, I felt like the room had become blurry and it was as if I was looking down at my body in these alternate states through a third party's eyes. I watched as my skin sprouted jet black feathers and my arms expanded to wings, my feet to claws, and in the mirror I saw my face covered in feathers and my nose becoming a beak. Once the change to a raven had completed, I spread out my wings and let out a cry.

"And now for the werewolf," she said. With nearly no effort, my body shook and my wings shed the feathers, and then the underneath skin grew the wolf-type fur. My beak changed to that of a snout and my facial shape to that of a wolf. In the mirror I saw my tail come forward and fluff. I let out a howl in acknowledgement of the completed change. Honestly, I was surprised at how I had retained my consciousness. I must have really matured in the last few weeks.

Birger wasn't kidding when he said these were the most common forms. Next she went after the bear form and with that, my size doubled. She looked satisfied with that transition and then guided me through returning me to my human form. "Has anyone tried other forms on you yet? Beasts or, well … anything?" she asked.

I admitted to the times Chago had changed me and to what forms I was aware of. Admittedly, since those moments were unexpected I wasn't totally aware of what the beasts were. I simply knew that he was the one controlling the changing. She wrote these shapes down and seemed to be making notes regarding them. "Good. This will help in our next phase."

"I don't understand."

"We just walked through the most common forms. Next we will go through some of the less common. If you have the ability then I will be able to walk you through them. If you do not naturally have the abilities then your shape will remain the same. My question for you is, do you trust me?"

"I guess so," I shrugged.

"I ask because if you let me, then I can walk you through your other forms relatively quickly. It's easier if you allow me to do it versus if we have you try to walk through them one after another. In this manner we can discover your abilities a bit faster. Otherwise, this could be weeks, possibly months before we finish this initial stage."

I really wanted to get home as soon as possible, so this sounded like a great alternative. "Is there any drawback to it?" I asked.

"The only drawback is that I will be walking you through them versus you walking yourself through them. So you won't learn the triggers upfront. That said, by allowing me to walk you through them, it means that we will learn your abilities faster and focus on honing your skills."

"Based on that it sounds fine. Let's do it." I said with as upbeat a tone as I could muster. And that's when things got really weird.

Hilda stood directly behind me and, for a brief moment, she placed her hands on my waist. In the mirror I could see her close her eyes and she looked like she was in deep concentration—a deep focus. I heard her mumbling something, I still have no idea what, but it was definitely not English.

I felt my body beginning to vibrate and in the mirror I saw

my arms and legs shake. To be honest, I got scared because I didn't really understand what she was doing and I wasn't sure I wanted to see my body change into god-knows-what. So I closed my eyes and, boy, am I glad I did. I felt my body change in all kinds of ways. In ways I simply didn't understand at the time. And I could hear her chant something in a different language which was clearly what made me shift.

I briefly opened my eyes to see what looked like part dragon, part human, part lizard. At least, I think that's what it was. My shifting continued in such a manner and with such a rate that I closed my eyes again. At least it didn't hurt so far and I prayed it would continue in that manner. I controlled my breathing since I wasn't really sure what was going on and I didn't want to lose complete control of myself although, to be honest, I definitely was not the person in charge of my own body.

After what felt like an eternity, I realized the room had grown quiet and Hilda had taken her hands away from me.

"You can open your eyes now," she said. Her voice tinged with amazement.

"So?" I croaked, my voice rough and my eyes fluttering in the light.

Hilda wrote something down and then replied. "I need to talk to Birger. There are some things we need to discuss." She looked perplexed. "Meantime, go back to your room and rest. One of us will come for you in a little bit."

"Is there something wrong?" I asked.

She paused for a moment, looking me up and down. And then she replied, "I don't want to answer until I talk to Birger. But don't worry. We will come back shortly."

I gathered my things and then she directed me back to my room, closing my door behind me. This was definitely not what

I had expected for my first day of training. If anything, I wanted to call home.

I dialed Javier's phone, but he didn't answer. Not by his phone? Avoiding me? I didn't know. I didn't want to know.

Homesick and feeling isolated, I called Margarite. She didn't answer either.

The distance between what I knew and what I didn't was suddenly expansive, cold, and lonely.

I sat on my bed and impatiently waited for someone to return.

After several moments, I decided it was best to relax.

I had no idea how much time I had.

16

BIRGER'S - 10TH CENTURY

The newly resurrected queen Gyrid glared at her son as she sat atop the throne. He nearly glowed from the power that he had commanded. A power that he had stolen from his mother and her husband. Queen Gyrid called upon her fellow resurrected beings and planned out how they would take care of the mere child. At least a mere child compared to the age and experience of his parents.

Queen Gyrid brought forth her favorite reborn warriors. Those, who in life, would have been sent to eradicate a problem —for instance, the problem of a child King who needed to be taught a lesson. Those she would have sent to eliminate what stood between her and the throne that was rightfully hers.

The crowds of townspeople and royalty dissipated leaving the lone King on his throne as he glared over his lands. Alone, he simply sat in the darkness and waited for what he was not quite sure, but he knew that he waited for someone or something. He could feel it in his bones unlike any other foretelling he had sensed before. He knew that his battle for the throne and the kingdom was not over.

Within the secret passageways of the castle, Queen Gyrid made her way through the mazes with her followers. In near quietness, they worked their way through the shadows until they reached the open throne room. Once they had reached the darkness of that space, Queen Gyrid slowly stepped out from behind a column to reveal herself to her once seemingly obedient son.

"Just as your father's father and his father before him," she approached the throne that she had once dominated and that her husband had dominated before her. "You simply could not leave well enough alone."

The new King gazed out of the windows to the city below. With the sound of his mother's voice he turned. "I had a feeling you would find a way back." He leaned into his hands and dove towards her. The room filled with a hesitance, an uncertainty that radiated from the new King.

"I never went anywhere," she smiled. A sly, mischievous smile. "In your research of our family histories you seem to have forgotten a critical factor."

The new ruler raised his eyebrows. "Really? What might that be?"

"You forgot that my father and his father before him were from a lesser known tribe. One that our historians could not track."

He smirked. "So? What does that have to do with me?"

"Among the different blood lines of our people, we have much more than lycanthropes. Albeit your father was quite fascinated with the lycanthropic lines. Our families actually did quite a bit of experimentation to see what they could do with all of the different strains. They wanted to see what kind of powers they could unearth through cross-breeding—cross-pollinating."

"Oh?" The new King perked up. "And what might they have discovered?"

She stood before the new King. Her followers lined alongside her, to her left and her right. "My family line, my father's father, was very good at keeping secrets." She approached the throne. "And we have one secret that is especially dear to me."

The new King flung himself back into his chair. For a brief moment, the queen felt sorry for her son. His overconfidence truly filled the room. "Dear, please tell me, my mother."

Queen Gyrid leaned into the throne, her pale eyes cloudier than the last time the King had seen them. She got close enough so that she nearly touched his face. She looked him directly in the eyes and whispered, "Depending on how we die, if we die an especially traumatic death then our true nature comes forward."

They held each other's gaze for a moment. Just long enough for the new King to realize that he was in a bit of trouble.

At this juncture, the queen took one fingertip and placed the sharp end of her fingernail on his nose. "We are Draugr —vampires."

The next morning, the queen was found on the throne, where her son had been. When asked what had happened to her only child, she simply shrugged.

Some months later, the true King returned from his plan to conquer others in neighboring lands to find his wife, ashen pale, on the throne. Surprised by her appearance on the royal seat and dominance of the room, the King greeted his wife.

"I trust your travels found you well," the queen directed toward the King.

"We continue to rule over the neighboring lands and for those spaces previously unsupervised, they now are under the watchful eye of one of our key guards." He motioned to his lycanthropic guards as they stood only a few hundred feet away. The King motioned throughout the throne room. "Seems as though events here were lively."

The queen shrugged. "Nothing you did not prepare us for, my lord."

The King looked around the room, into the hallway, and down the alleys. In a slight panic he asked, "Where is our son?"

"Our son felt as though he was a better ruler and behaved as such." The queen looked around the room for motions of dissension and found none. Instead she only found a room filled with distant eyes that would not meet her gaze.

"What does that mean?" the King inquired.

Queen Gyrid again searched the room for a challenge, any voice of disagreement, and, instead, found looks of embarrassment and dissatisfaction. "It means our son decided that he would overthrow our royal court and rule this and neighboring lands."

The King stood still, quiet. "And?"

The queen continued, "And his efforts failed to bear fruit. I did not want to bother you with such topics so soon upon your return, but we must identify a new next-in-line."

The King stood stock still as the true meaning of his wife's statement sunk in. He took his place next to her on the throne and asked, "Who might you suggest?"

INTERLUDE 8

(800'S AD) BIRGER AND CHAGO

"Come and sit." The Seeress motioned me to a chair before the fireplace. "And with those battles came the mastering of your shapeshifting skills?"

"Not quite," I replied. She looked at me with a bit of confusion, so I took the opportunity to explain to her the past few years. How Ulf had come naturally to his shapeshifting abilities. How he had mastered at a rapid rate. How I fell upon my own abilities with clumsy inaccuracies, and how being around others of similar abilities triggered my skills in a way I had not anticipated.

"And I trust this means that you have become the head of the battalion."

"Why?"

She poured me a steaming cup of tea and herself one as well. "Your delay in gifts and subsequent triggering is a sign of the most gifted. Typically ones with this are also gifted with the ability to transform into multiple creatures and the mastery of said transformations."

I explained to her what had occurred. How I had transformed at seemingly random times and only in the last battle with my brother had I been able to control the shifting and my own level of consciousness during the shapeshifting.

"And Ulf, his gifts have stabilized, yes?"

I looked at her blankly. "I am sorry, I do not understand."

"Ulf's gifts were triggered at an early age and he showed a level of mastery that was rare, but that is also a sign that he would stabilize at a young age. At this point, he should have fully matured."

I did not understand what she meant by this, and, in truth, I would not understand for years. Still, I sat in silence absorbing what she had shared. With a sigh, she continued, "what brings you to me?"

I looked up at her and pondered what I should ask next. My mind swam with seemingly dozens of questions, all dying to be answered.

"I need your help," I began. "I need help in gaining control of my skills." I took a sip from the steaming mug. The drink was surprisingly fulfilling and nourishing.

She looked at me quizzically. "You should have been taught those skills by the instructors of the King's army. They are the most skilled and knowledgeable."

With her comment, I was forced to inform her of the last exchange I had with Ulf. Admittedly, I did not reveal his command for me to never return. I figured I would address that when or if needed.

"I see," she gazed into her own mug and then looked up at me. "And they did not leave you with a booklet of spells?"

I pulled out from my pant's waistband the booklet that Eric of the Fairhair Dynasty had provided and handed it to her. "This has been most helpful, but I fear it is not enough."

She studied the pages and then asked, "And this was given to you by Eric of the Fairhair Dynasty?"

"Yes," I replied.

"And you do not feel this is enough? This did not resolve your challenges?"

"No."

She gazed into the fireplace as if in deep reflection. I sat quietly, hopeful that her response would be one of affirmation and acknowledgement that she could—and would—assist.

"When was the last time you shifted?" she asked.

I sat back and pondered what I had remembered of the last several days. "Admittedly," I began. "I am not sure." And with that statement, I described to her my dreams and what I thought were, or what at least felt like, hallucinations. "The most recent occurred while I slept last night."

"And in that did you exchange with another of the gifts?"

I described the horse stall and my travels through the town. "But I do not remember another."

"When your mama had come to me before your birth she had worried about this type of occurrence."

"You knew my mama?"

She explained how my mama had sought her out while she was pregnant and had asked for the Seeress to teach me and my brother the basics of our people. "She worried that since your papa was no longer with us to teach you of the old ways, that you would have the challenges you are experiencing today," she said. "When I first saw how you and your brother were transforming and your types of gifts, I knew that I would only be able to teach you so much and that you would need the guidance of those of the skill level of the King's guards. I did not think that—" She folded the booklet into her lap.

"Please," I began. "I simply cannot do this alone."

"I cannot promise you anything," she said and tapped the

booklet. "There is another who may be able to assist. He is of similar gifts."

I thanked her profusely, unsure what this may have meant or how this person could help, but desperate to try anything.

"He goes by Chago," she said. "Return tomorrow and I will take you to him. We shall see what he can do."

17
LUNA'S - 2000S

For what felt like days, I forced myself to lay down on the bed and did my best to coax my muscles to release their tension. With that attempt at relaxation, the forceful shifting finally hit my muscles and they ached like I had been training for a marathon. I hoped it got easier the more I did it because this shapeshifting thing would really suck if I hurt like this on a regular basis.

"May I come in?" I heard Birger's voice at my door.

I must have fallen asleep from all of the exertion because I was completely unaware of him approaching my door. "Sure, come on in." I sat up.

I watched as the door slowly slid open and he made his way inside. We must have been in the same day because he was dressed in the same outfit as the last time I saw him. That said, he definitely had bags under his eyes like someone who had been up all night or who didn't get a good night's rest.

"What time is it?" I asked, curiosity getting the best of me.

"You have been resting for approximately twelve hours," he

looked at his watch and replied. "We are at the beginning of your second day of training."

"Wow, it's been that long? What's going on?" I asked.

He pulled out the chair at my desk and then pulled it up next to my bed. His seriousness reminded me of when I was a kid and me or Daniel did something bad enough for our dad to come in to reprimand us.

"We need to talk." The gravity in his voice definitely gave me cause for concern. I did my best not to freak out.

"Okay, sure. About what?"

I studied his body language to see if he would give anything away. Other than the fact that I was in some kind of trouble, this man was definitely a master at hiding his feelings.

"Hilda and I discussed your initial training classes."

"Yeah, she mentioned she was going to do that."

"Do you remember when I told you that based on our legacy and the initial abilities that you had demonstrated, you were unique?"

"Yeah, you said that a lot."

He ran his hands through his hair.

"Hilda's tests confirmed what we had assumed. In fact, she not only reinforced the assumptions, but she was able to prove beyond a shadow of a doubt as to your abilities. Both in terms of breadth and depth."

"What does this mean?" I blurted out.

He acted evasively like he didn't want to broach this topic, but I didn't come to Sweden just to have him run some spells on me and then jet. Not that I was against the idea of that. But after everything we'd been through, it was time to just tell me whatever the hell was going on.

Birger resettled in his chair and began. "Do you remember when I explained how there are different bloodlines and some bloodlines had greater abilities than others?"

"Yeah, so?"

"Based on what Hilda was able to delineate from the tests and what she could discover from the various forms that you are able to transform into and out of, as well as the ease in which you can transition, you seem to have the genetics of not only one of the familial lines, but all of them."

"So? That's good, right?"

He took a moment and stared at his hands before he continued. "I have never seen this before. In order for you to be able to transform into all of the beings that Hilda described, it means that you have the genetics from all of the strongest houses—worldwide."

"That sounds like a lot of bloodlines," I said with a smirk. I didn't know if I should take him seriously or not.

"I did not think this was physically possible. It would mean that you have the genetic traits of at least 343 houses." He looked up from his hands and made eye contact with me.

Instinctively, I replied, "wow, that's a lot." Suddenly I knew I needed to take him seriously.

Without a blink or a twinge, he continued, "it represents every single house of Lycanthropes that we are aware of and that are tracked by The Lycanthrope Society."

"Wait, what? Is that possible? I mean, that would mean that—"

"It means that somehow your ancestors congregated and procreated across all continents and all shapeshifter forms."

I did my best to absorb what he just said. "Ok, so then, based on that, what are are you telling me" What does it all mean?"

"It means that you can transform into any being, any creature known to man."

I laughed. He had to be joking. "Yeah, okay," I tapped him on the arm. "Now for real. What does that mean?"

He looked at me with a seriousness I never thought I would see. I mean, I never thought he could look more serious than he did on a normal day. This was way over the top. "You are sincere? You aren't kidding."

"In approximately the twelfth century, one of our most trusted geneticists had predicted that at some point, this would occur. At the time he predicted that without intervention this would most likely occur around the 25th century, but that this would most likely be sped up due to crossbreeding."

I stared at him. All of this sounded like something out of some weird science fiction book. Or maybe even some kind of horror novel. "Crossbreeding?"

He nodded. "At various points within history different world leaders realized the power of our kind. Some, when they made this realization, then decided to experiment to try to harness our powers. In those experiments, some chose to force breeding..." His voice trailed off.

I winced at the thought of it. "No need to explain. I understand." In all honesty, I didn't want him to explain. My imagination brought up images I truly did not want to have.

"What we believe happened is that when two different genetic lines cross bred, some of the offspring gained the capabilities of both lines and if that breeding happened frequently enough then eventually that meant that ... well."

He didn't need to continue. I knew what he was going to say. "This is why me and my brother were left at an orphanage?"

"You were probably the result of some of the later breeding. I do not honestly know what happened or why, but the tests are pretty clear in terms of the results."

I unconsciously kneaded my hands together. This was not the conversation I thought we were going to have. If anything I had assumed that he would tell me I could do lots of stuff. I never in a billion years imagined that he'd tell me I was the result of lots of raping and pillaging which was basically what he was telling me. "Now what?" I asked.

"Based on this, and your basic abilities, you are the most powerful, strongest Lycanthrope of our recorded history."

"That's really funny—" He had to be joking. I mean, I hadn't even gotten through the shapeshifter's equivalent of puberty and he was declaring me the most powerful of them all. That was just crazy talk.

"I am not kidding." He looked me dead in the eye. "We have never seen anyone with this much ability. Ever. And due to this, I have some concerns." He folded his hands in his lap as if he prepared for a whole 'nother round of conversations. "I need to make a proposal to you."

"Why do you look so grave?" I asked. I had never heard him provide so much preamble in the whole time I'd known him. Admittedly, considering he was probably over a thousand years old, I didn't know him very long, but still.

"I am concerned because we need to ensure that you are properly trained so that you can control and manage all of the different forms that you are capable of. And I am worried that we may not fully know what your true capabilities are."

"Okay," I shrugged. "So we find out, right?"

He nodded. "So, we find out and when we are done we will need to discuss how to best use these abilities."

"Okay? I don't know what that means, but sure."

"It means you are the most powerful shapeshifter known to man. And based on our laws and historic precedent ..." he paused as if he was trying to figure out if he should really do what he was about to do next. Then with a bit of a forthrightness, he looked up at me and said, "I need to ask you to lead us."

I stared at him because there was absolutely no way he was serious. "You have got to be shittin' me."

"I understand why you may be a bit in disbelief." He stood firm.

I laughed. "A lot more than 'a bit.'"

"I know you have only begun reading up on our history and I am happy to give you more time to do further research. That said, you need to understand that this is a critical time in our kind's history. We are in the midst of a battle of beliefs. A battle between The Lycanthrope Society and The Righteous Group which you may have also heard as TRG—Chago' group. One believes that humans and shapeshifters were meant to share the planet and allow one another to live in peace and harmony. Without one influencing or impacting the other. While the other has a very different perspective."

I smirked. "What? Like one take over the other? What is this, *Pinky and The Brain?*"

He simply stared at me.

"Holy shit, you're not kidding. You're telling me that The Righteous Group is trying to take over the world? That's insane!" I nearly squealed. How did everything get so bizarre so fast?

"You experienced it at the UN conference. It has been Chago's objective for more years than I can count. For longer than I would like to acknowledge."

"What do I have to do with it? You think he'll try to convert me to TRG to help him in his devious plans?" I said with a tinge of mockery.

"I do not just think that he will try to do so. I know that he will. He has done similar actions in the past with much less-gifted Lycanthropes. Based on that, he will definitely try to find ways to either convert you to TRG or to eliminate you as a threat."

I sat up even straighter in the bed. "Kill me? Just for existing?"

He nodded. "You saw what he is capable of. Chago has been trying to overturn the control that humans have had on much of the world for hundreds of years. Therefore, once he discovers your full abilities and that you are the physical representation of what was foretold quite a while ago, then he will seek you out and—"

"Either convert me or kill me."

He nodded. "Convert you or kill you."

"But what does that have to do with me leading either group."

"Part of The Lycanthrope Society's foretelling is that one day a lycanthrope will be born who represents all forms, all beings, and will choose to lead us into the next era. Lead us in peace with all creatures of the world."

"Admittedly, that whole live in peace thing sounds much more my speed."

"The legend continues to state that without you, or someone of similar gifts, the world could turn to chaos," he said. "And if you do not take on the role, then there's an increased likelihood that Chago will redouble his efforts to have The Righteous Group become the most prominent organization on the planet, and with that he will make himself the leader and their focus will change to ensure Lycanthropes dominate and enslave all humankind."

And with Birger's last words and the gravity of his tone, all I could say was, "Damn."

18

BIRGER'S — 10TH CENTURY

The queen pondered her husband's question. Since they no longer had their son to be named the King of their lands, they had decisions to make regarding naming a potential next in line.

"Of all those remaining of our family lines, if you and I are no longer available to lead these wondrous lands, then the greatest likelihood in terms of successor would be Harald, our nephew from your sister."

The King considered this. He looked across the royal court members and those present in the throne room. "Is he a bit young?" the King asked.

"Of the most immediate of our family lines, Harald is the one with the humility needed to be successful in this position of leadership. He has demonstrated common sense and a curiosity that will benefit him in the years to come."

The King thought on this.

"And based on your desires to expand our lands, he has the most natural ability in terms of political capabilities and the power to gain the trust of others to broaden our lands with the greatest ease."

The King raised his brow and tilted his head. He had never thought of his nephew in this capacity and yet the queen's points were well made. "Do you believe this is a function that he would be eager to take on? I do not anticipate that we will need him in such a manner anytime in the near future." He paused. Ready to deny his wife's suggestion, he looked out among the court and realized that he did not see a single eye that spoke to him as a natural ruler. And for the King, that was a concern. He turned to the queen, "But it is to our benefit to name our successor."

The queen looked across the members of the court for it had never occurred to her that her nephew would not be interested in being named the royal successor. "Do you have concerns regarding him being named in this fashion?" the queen replied.

"In truth, I had never considered him in this manner." Quietly he admitted to himself that he had not really thought of who might be the next in line since he did not anticipate that he or his queen would be pulled from their current standing anytime in the near future. He sighed. "Therefore, I had not thoroughly thought this through."

Concerned that he may make a decision in haste, the King then called upon his most trusted advisor among the royal court and asked his opinion as to who might be the best to be named the royal successor. The advisor bowed before the royal pair and replied.

"The queen makes excellent points, my lord," he began. "Naming Harald as the next in line also sets us to unify the lands of your sister and her husband, the Duke of Denmark. And with that unification your power grows exponentially and your influence with the neighboring countries grows as well."

"True," the King replied.

"This also enables us to ensure the long lineage stays within your natural bloodline," the queen continued the advisor's thoughts. "As well as influence in terms of who shall rule with him across Denmark and Sweden."

The advisor waited a moment to ensure that the queen had completed her thought and then continued. "My understanding is that he has already eyed marrying the duchess of the Iberian Kingdoms or that of the African Kingdoms. Naturally enabling an even more extensive expansion rather quickly."

The King smiled and then did his best to hide his giddiness at the thought of these political maneuvers. And yet, both the queen and the advisor smirked at his reactions.

"Your suggestions are well taken," the King said. "Let us call upon Harald to gain his perspective."

The King directed his orderly to call upon Harald, the Duke of Denmark. Within weeks, the duke made his appearance before the King and Queen of Sweden. He had been provided a heads up as to why he had been beckoned considering he had not been requested before the royal couple since his childhood.

"I assume you are aware as to why we called you before us?" the queen asked.

Harald, one of great desire to rule far beyond the immediate lands, responded, "I have been informed as to your desires."

"And what are your thoughts," the King questioned.

The duke bowed before his uncle and aunt. Knowing that in moments such as this, the more minimal of a response he provided, the better, with a softness and subtlety to his manner he replied, "Although I do not foresee a need for your desires to be executed in the near future, I am honored to be considered in this manner and to be named the royal successor." He knew better than to stand or make any gestures that could be perceived as dominant with this King. So he remained in a state of submissiveness before the royal pair.

The King, happy at the duke's subtle acknowledgement that this was a gift to be given by the royal couple, and internally elated at the thought of such expansion to his power base, he stated, "Then with that, we shall consider you the official royal successor." He then brought forward his royal sword and placed it against his nephew's shoulders declaring him the next in line. At ease beside her husband, on her royal throne, the queen subtly smiled and gave a slight nod.

INTERLUDE 9

BIRGER (800'S AD)

As commanded, I left the Seeress and hid in the same horse stalls eager to be out of the way of others. In the night, my dreams took me to shift into the creatures I had experienced in the past. This time I commanded myself to shift into alternate beings and shockingly, my body obeyed. I watched as my arms changed from that of a man to that of a wolf to that of a bear and then back again. The horses nearby whinnied in response as if they were acknowledging my happenings. I stayed as far away from them as I could without revealing myself to any potential nearby townspeople. I did not want them to become aware of my true nature since I did not know what they would think or how they would respond. I feared that they would attack or excommunicate me, and although I was trained in self defense and battle, I did not want to use those skills unless absolutely needed. With that I commanded myself to shift back and then lay back down to rest. In the morning, I was greeted by the horses who surprisingly seemed to welcome me like they had not done so before.

I approached the owner again to perform stall chores. Once

he saw the welcome of the horses, he requested that I perform the same chores that I had done in the previous morn. Without question I did so and once I had finished and gotten paid, I made my way to the inn for a day's meal.

"Did you get what you need?" the innkeeper asked the moment he saw me.

I placed the coins on the counter. "Yes. Thank you for your help," I said. "May I have a platter before I head out today?"

He nodded, cupped the coins into his palm and then made his way into the back. I looked around the room, noting the other patrons enjoying their morning meals and preparing for their days. The room was warm and comforting. I thanked the innkeeper when he returned with my meal. Doing my best to be unacknowledged, I ate my meal in peace and quiet.

Without additional fanfare, I left the inn and made my way back to the Seeress, anxious for her to take me to meet Chago. I did my best not to be overly excited, but much of myself was incredibly eager. The pieces of my puzzle were finally coming together.

When I reached her cottage I stood before her door, took a deep breath, and then knocked. Moments later she responded. The door opened a crack. "You cannot come in," the Seeress stated. "Go."

"I do not understand—"

"You have been flagged as a traitor."

"By whom?"

She glanced behind me as if she was in search of others. "The King has declared you a traitor. Anyone caught assisting you will be punished."

"But why?" This did not make sense to me since I was not among the preferred warriors of the King. I was the last among the special guards that he would care about. I doubted he even knew who I was. "This is impossible."

"You must leave." I could feel her fear radiate in her tone.

"What about the other?"

She tossed something towards me and slammed the door. When I looked down, I noted she had thrown instructions at me. I knocked on her door again, in the hopes that she would reconsider. I begged her to let me in, to not reject me so coldly. And yet she did not respond.

"Please, you are the only one I know who can help me."

"Go," she said through the sealed door. "Chago, he will guide you."

I knocked on her door again in the hopes that she would reconsider, but found no response. My only option was to follow her direction. Based on her note, this Chago resided at least two days away. Defeated by her tacit rejection, I began my trek to see him.

19

LUNA'S - 2000S

Birger continued to fill in the blanks of The Lycanthrope Society's legends.

"There was once a woman who had been known as The Seeress. She was considered the most powerful of spell casters. The one who had first identified the means for those of our kind to transform and use our skills. And in her time, she had foretold of someone like yourself." Birger motioned towards me. "Someone who had all of the primary bloodlines in her background. And when she made this prediction, she also stated that that descendent—you—would be made the head of The Lycanthrope Society and use that position to truly benefit our kind and teach the world the benefits of our kind as well."

"Okay. That's weird, but, sure."

"The key to the foretelling is not so much that you would exist because the odds demonstrate that at some point this would make sense," he continued. "What is truly the most significant point of her prediction is that you are destined to unify the opposing Lycanthropic societies. Something in your abilities, your nobility, your leadership with bring together the warring factions and we will finally unify after over eleven hundred years of battle."

"No pressure," I smirked.

He agreed. "No pressure."

Birger's words rang familiar. I thought I remembered Chago mentioning something similar. Something about unifying the two societies.

"Now what?" I asked. "If you ask me, I'd like to complete my training and then have the chance to make up my own mind."

"That is reasonable," he said. "We can continue forward with your sessions among myself, Hilda and Rune."

"How long do you think that'll take?"

"Based on our standard training classes, we are looking at approximately four weeks."

"Wow, that's a long time."

"That said, since we have never worked with someone of your abilities, it may take longer. I would say probably closer to six weeks."

"Six weeks? Isn't that kind of long?"

"It is not unreasonable considering ..."

"Considering ..." I trailed off. This was a lot to take in. "How about this ... why don't we go through the training and then see what happens."

"I will meet you here this evening. In the meantime, Rune is eagerly awaiting her first session with you."

"Let's do this."

20

BIRGER'S

Now that the King and Queen of Sweden had declared their successor, they refocused on stabilizing their lands. They wanted to be sure that their people felt they were in good hands with the current nobility.

They traveled across the towns and villages to meet with persons from all walks of life, sure to personally interact with the townspeople and local farmers, listening to their concerns. Hearing their joys, their sorrows, their worries. Discovering what all the people desired. They met with those who ruled on their behalf within each town and hamlet, ensuring that all knew and understood that the King and queen were there to represent and help all within their lands.

With these conversations they discovered from many that King Albert, the King of a neighboring country of Finns, had inferred that he intended to slowly take over the Swedish lands and rule as a monarch. At first the King and queen did not take these rumors seriously, but as they visited the towns and villages that bordered Finns, the rumors and concerns of the townsfolk increased.

"My King," the queen began. "This may be an opportunity for us to see Harald's skills as a leader."

The King perked up. He had been concerned about the rumors and had been trying to discern the best course of action.

She continued to suggest that they have Harald take a faction to represent them to King Albert. "If Albert does not agree to a peaceful neutrality between the countries, then we recommend that Harald overtake them."

The King immediately saw the advantage to this since it ensured that he remained in power and did not need to go directly into battle. He quietly agreed to the recommendation. He had his top-ranking general call upon Harald, explaining it was time to demonstrate his loyalty to the King and queen.

Unsure of the scope and full purpose of this visit, Harald strategically called upon a small faction of his special guards to travel with him to the Finns. He wanted to be sure he was prepared for—and protected from— whatever may come his way.

The day before Harald and his guards left, the queen appeared at his doorstep. In secret, she had arranged to meet with the young duke independent of her husband and their court.

Dressed in a cloak that masked her royal status and presented her as more of a random traveler, she entered Harald's domain. When she entered his court area, she meekly waited for her opportunity to speak to the duke. She listened as he heard members of his own kingdom bring forth grievances and suggestions. She noted his responses and noted upon whom among his own court he leaned. When the moment came for her to speak to the local ruler, she took one step and then another until she stood squarely before him. The duke, looking a bit disheveled after a full day of hearing one complaint after another, called the stranger forward with a wave of his hand.

The disguised queen slowly lowered her hood and raised her eyes to meet his, thus revealing her true identity. Though surprised at her presence, he still demonstrated the appropriate decorum and bowed before her. The queen smiled and beckoned him to rise.

"My queen, your visit is an honor." The words stumbled from his mouth.

Placing her fingers to his lips, she motioned for him to quiet. She whispered, "No need for such formalities. I am here on my own accord—to provide guidance," she said.

The duke stood and returned to his place of honor and had a court member bring forward a chair for the queen to sit. "A place to rest after your travels," he said.

She sat before him and took a moment to settle in and then she began. "I want to thank you for your loyalty to the court and to your agreement to represent us to the King of the Finns," she said.

The duke bowed his head in acknowledgement. "It is my honor."

"And this representation also gives you an even greater opportunity."

"How so, my queen?" Harald asked.

"Once King Albert is overthrown, and thereby Finns and Norway have been unified, then you are positioned to take over the lands of Sweden."

Harald, surprised by such words, paused. He took a moment before responding, unsure of the best way in which to reply. "I am sorry, my queen. I do not believe I understood you correctly."

The queen took a moment to refocus her thoughts. "It is

time for the royal family to finally be reigned by one of both lycanthropic and human blood. And that person is you." She motioned to him. "With the lands being unified under you, then it naturally unifies humans, Draugr, and shapeshifters. A long overdue joining of the various bloodlines."

Harald tilted his head as he pondered what the queen brought forward to him. All the queen proposed was not simply interesting, but also enticing. With that, he knew he needed to ask, "What about the current King?"

The queen had anticipated such a reaction and with a steady tone replied, "That too will be taken care of."

Their eyes met for a moment, long enough to clarify and reinforce what the queen suggested. Before Harald could continue the conversation, the queen stood from her chair and then placed her hood upon her head. She nodded to the duke, bowed before him, and then exited the room.

The following day, Harald had officially been given his orders by the King, graciously accepting the task, and made his trek to the Finns' castle. In seeming obedience.

Upon Harald's arrival at King Albert's court, to no one's surprise, Albert quite openly stated that he had every intention of unifying the lands, in his own way.

At this juncture, various records tell us different accounts of how Harald did as the royal couple had requested. Some letters state that he immediately launched into an attack and shoved a dagger into King Albert's heart, quickly killing the King, then many of his followers as well.

Other letters speak of Harald spending days negotiating with King Albert to see if he could come to some type of agreement. Only after Albert made it clear that he simply could not, or would not, acquiesce, then Harald waited for a night in which the moon provided guidance for him and his special guards to launch a lycanthropic and Draugr attack on the King.

So in the subsequent morn, all that remained were the bloody detritus of the former ruler and his modest court.

While still other letters spoke of days upon days of battles. Ones in which, at first, Harald followed the standard procedure of only warring in human form against human form. He even used the same types of swords and daggers as Albert and his men. They fought in the same style and with the same battle cries. Harald and his warriors even went so far as to end the fighting as soon as night fell and his opponents did not have the same ability to see in the darkness.

According to this series of letters, only after Harald had gotten tired of being fair and fighting with the same tools as his opponent (a technique that his trainers and mentors had insisted upon) did he advise his special guards that, "The time has come for us to finish this ludicrousness." The frustration in his voice made it clear to his guards. He need not say anything further.

His special guards, already trained in the battle arts of the Draugr and the lycanthrope, nodded in agreement. That evening, they crept upon King Albert's castle, leveraging their stealth-like forms, and covertly made their way to the King's chambers. With only the gifts of their natural weapons, those of fang and claw, did they leap upon their opponents. Harald slashed Albert's throat with a single efficient swipe of his claws and ripped Albert's head from his neck. The spewing of blood surprised no one.

This simple act thus ensured the King would not fulfill his threats of a monarchy.

During Harald's tour of the Finns' lands, the queen called upon her royal guards. In consideration of their natural talent, these guards had been put in place by the queen, and she personally ensured they had been given special treatment and special training. With little guidance, she directed them to jail her husband.

Without question, they waited until after their King had enjoyed a multicourse meal with his favorite foods of salmon soup, salted pork, black sausage, boiled potatoes, rich cheeses, and freshly baked rye breads. All accompanied with his most treasured Farmhouse ale. The queen sat across from him at their dining table and simply sipped upon her neat cup of Kvass, enjoying the sweet and sour balanced liquor. Once the King had sat back in his chair and rubbed his stomach, a clear sign that he was satiated, she motioned for the guards to enter.

Watching the special guards easily overtake the bloated King, she listened as he demanded that they cease their actions, then she commanded that they discontinue. They dragged him out of the dining room and into the hall towards the jail cells.

The King threatened his opponents with torture and then a lifetime in jail and then death. Those they passed in the halls knew better than to intervene, aware of the special guards abilities and their alignment to the queen. Once the King realized that they would not listen to him, he began flailing to get out of their grasp, screaming, "I am the King! I am *your* King!"

The queen quietly followed them through the halls, down the stairwell, and to the cell chambers.

Once they had reached the jail doors, the guards looked at the queen to confirm their final actions. To this, she simply nodded and motioned for them to toss the King inside. They did as instructed and slammed the door behind him, the sound of the lock clicking shut resonated throughout the chamber halls.

The King scrambled across the dirt floor of the cell, stood up, and grabbed the cell bars, as if he could somehow miraculously pull them open. He yanked at the bars screaming at the guards who simply stepped back and stood at attention.

"How can you do this?" the King shrieked.

From the shadows of the jail, the queen came forward, her voice as calm as her demeanor representing decades of royal blood. Without a single question in her stance or her manner, she simply stated, "It is time."

INTERLUDE 10

(800'S AD)

The journey was one of two days and two nights. I made sure to sleep along the riverbed and find foods within the wild to gain nourishment. I crossed the path of few travelers on my journey and when I did happen upon others, I was sure to duck out of sight, my fear increased based on the Seeress' response to my presence. I had no idea what I had done that would cause the King to declare me a traitor but I certainly did not want to attract additional attention.

By the time I reached the location specified by the Seeress, I had avoided the engagement of at least a half dozen parties. The spot turned out to be a cave on the side of a mountain. One that must have been in existence for centuries. I approached it, uncertain what I might find.

"Hello?" I called into the echoing cave structure. "Anyone here?" I asked. My voice reverberated through the walls and into the shadows. I carefully made my way inside and wandered throughout the cave, finding little evidence of others. "Is Chago here?" I asked.

With no response, I found a spot in which to rest and took

my place there. If I did not find this person, then what was I to do next? There was so much left unknown, so many questions to be answered and yet I had no idea how to go about gaining them.

I fell asleep in the chill of the cave, my dreams of shapeshifting returning, the shifting less random than previously although I felt an odd tingle that I had never experienced before. With the tingle that ran up the back of my neck and ending with a kind of twinge. I turned to find another, a creature in the darkness that seemed to nearly be a part of the shadows.

"Chago?" I said, hoping for a response. The being seemed to vibrate. With his vibration I felt my own tingling engage. "Hello?" I called out again.

With no verbal response, the being raised his hands as if commanding something, and then I could feel the tingling increase, my skin began to vibrate and seemed to call for an inner being—or beings—to come forward. My body transformed in ways I had never seen before. From the wolf to that of the part wolf, part bear, part human that I had become when in battle with my brother to the structure of a dragon to that of a horse. Horrified, I tried to regain control and only found that I was able to slow down the transformations. I tried to speak, but could not find my voice. I tried to question how—and why—this being did this to me and only found the growl of a bear as I was in that state. In my mind I commanded myself to return to the shape of a man and after some battle to regain control of myself, I finally found my way back to that form.

"Who are you? Why are you doing this?"

"You have many skills," he said. "And yet you still do not seem to have learned all of them."

"How do you know?"

I felt the back of my neck tingle once again and I struggled to maintain control of myself. With much effort and concentration, this time, I was able to do so.

"Yes, quite skilled," he came out from the shadows, revealing a part human and part wolf being. His face with the snout of a wolf and the eyes with the gleam of a beast. "Why have you come here?"

"I need your guidance," I began. "I was sent to you by The Seeress." With that he seemed to find comfort and shifted to his human self. A man of average height and long black hair. His clothes those of a townsman. "She said I should come to you for guidance. I need help in gaining control of my gifts."

"Why are you not with the King's guards?" he asked. "Or of similar groups?"

I briefly explained how I had been with the guards and the challenges I faced within the ranks. I spoke of my fear of how I had harmed others and how I wanted to learn how to control my abilities. "I want to use them to help others," I said. "Not harm them."

He physically relaxed, his shoulders softened. "And what do you bring of benefit?" he asked.

I had not thought of that. I did not anticipate that he would insist on me giving him something to help him. "What would you like?" I asked.

He beckoned me over and commanded me to sit. "I will teach you on one condition."

I nodded.

"You must assist me in saving the others of our kind who are in isolation."

"Others?"

He went on to explain how there were many of our kind who had been abandoned by the King and were in hiding. "If he found that they did not fulfill a need of his, then he declared them to be banished."

I suddenly understood my status in the King's realm, so without a moment's delay, I agreed. "Of course. I would be happy to help."

"It means that you will be of the excommunicated as well. All those who help the ones who were spurned by the King are declared traitors to the throne and treated as such."

I smirked. "I believe I have already been identified as a traitor."

He looked me up and down and nodded.

"And so we begin."

21
LUNA'S - 2000S

The next several weeks were truly amazing. I cannot explain or describe what it was like. I think Rune and Hilda learned as much as I did and I was the damned student!

Once done, I felt like I had finally gotten control of my various forms and if I hit a period when I wasn't in total control initially, then I could regain control through the spells and techniques they were teaching me. Birger admitted that he didn't think we had uncovered everything since every time we turned around there seemed to be another something-something that came up, but that was okay, he assured me, since we were able to manage it. And in all honesty, my biggest concern was to get into situations like I found myself before where I either didn't realize something was actually happening or where I was in a situation where I tried to regain control I couldn't.

That is what terrified me the most.

. . .

Knowing that I could claim ownership of my powers, I felt safe returning home. I packed my bags, called Margarite to let her know I'd be back soon, called my parents to check in and see if it was cool to stay with them when I get back (it was, but I had to do house chores), and took the off chance to call Javier in case he'd pick up.

He didn't.

With this, I thanked my instructors for their direction and guidance and then headed out. I didn't really want to stay around for the other students to return. I really just wanted to go back to the life that I knew before that fateful phone call from the mortician.

As I made my way out, Birger stopped me in the hallway. I figured he'd do as much, but I kind of hoped that I would miss him.

"You did very well these last few weeks," he said. He sounded as lighthearted as I had ever heard him, which wasn't necessarily saying much.

"Thank you. I appreciate all of your guidance. I could not have made it through these times without you. I have grown."

He gave a slight bow from his waist. "Have you taken additional consideration to the conversation we had at the beginning of your stay? The one regarding you taking a leadership role with The Lycanthrope Group?"

That was the question I wanted to avoid.

"In all honesty, I have not. I don't feel like I have the right to do so. I mean, what do I know? I barely got through six weeks of training. What gives me the right to be in charge of a group that's been around for hundreds, actually, thousands of years."

He grinned. "I understand. Know that you are not and would never be alone. We have an advisory board that would be here at your disposal for all decisions. In fact, you would not be able to make a decision without them."

"But what is it I would be doing?" I asked. "I mean I get that there's a whole community that relies on us, but I don't get what I would have the accountability or responsibility for."

"Now that is a bit more of a complex question," he rubbed his chin. "How about this ... let us meet with the key advisors and they can walk you through your regular duties and answer any questions you may have. How does that sound?"

I looked at my watch because, admittedly, I really wanted to go home.

"If you miss your flight then I will get you on the next available one. I will even upgrade your seat to first class."

With that, I couldn't very well say no. "That sounds fine," I said. "Show me the way."

He guided me through the hall and down to a room previously unvisited. He opened the door to reveal a U shaped table populated with a half dozen people who looked familiar, but who I am pretty sure I had never met before. They politely introduced themselves, and Birger pointed out a chair at the head of the table for me to sit at.

And then it began.

At first I was afraid of what they would say, but in the end the description of the society reminded me of the structure of a non-profit organization that's actually led by the person who is voted in by the board. They said it consisted of at least a two-year term, but most times the person fulfilled the role for at least six years, sometimes longer.

"Depends on what needs to be done," Birger said. "But you can keep with the two years and then withdraw from the board."

"What happened to the last person in charge?"

They looked at each other as if they were waiting for one another to speak up. This did not give me any warm fuzzies.

"The last person chose to move on," Birger said.

The others nodded in agreement, but I intuited that there was more to it than simply that.

"Luna, you are needed. We could use you not only for the reasons that I had already described, but we also could use the fresh perspective. And since you have never been on the board previously and you are still learning about our groups, we could all really benefit from you."

Some of the others looked like they agreed while others looked as if they didn't necessarily think that what he described was the wisest of choices.

Birger then turned to the other board members and asked if we could be excused. "Only for a few moments," he said.

They obliged, again, some looked a little reluctant, but what did they have to lose? After the last one had left the room and closed the door, Birger made sure that it was locked, and then turned to me.

"In truth, Chago is rather old school. He will not talk to me or the other board members and at this juncture we are doing our best to unify The Lycanthrope Society and The Righteous Group. We cannot do that unless we can at least be on speaking terms with Chago."

"Wait, Chago is back? I thought he had passed away after our last encounter?"

Birger sighed. "I can see why you may have assumed as such, but in truth there are many survival techniques that he has at his disposal that most are not privy to."

"What makes you say he's back, anyway?"

"There have been some events that revealed his return."

"Like?" I hated when Birger was evasive like this. Sometimes I wish he'd just come out with it.

"The previous head of our society disappeared several nights after the exchange at the United Nations and then came back several nights later under the direction of none other than Chago."

Before I could continue pummeling him with questions, he finally decided to fess up. "It seems as though Chago convinced him to join The Righteous Group and help guide the organization in their endeavors."

"That sounds pretty significant."

"It is not only significant, but it puts us at a distinct disadvantage considering that leader had been in charge for over a decade and had been our backbone for quite some time."

"I don't get it. How or why would he make such a dramatic change? And how did Chago return from seemingly being dead?"

"Those questions I cannot answer. Only through our continued discussions with The Righteous Group will we be able to infer their answers. Their most recent engagements with us have involved Chago demanding that unless we come forward with a true leader. One of the most dominant bloodlines then they will take over, beginning by invading and taking control of our home bases.

"And that's why you assume he'll talk to me? Because of my assumed bloodlines."

"Correct," Birger replied.

"I'm the only person with these traits? No one else on the board. No other members? Only me?"

He nodded. "In truth? Yes, you are the only one I am aware of who fulfills the predictions and demonstrates the vast numbers of family lines."

"Which is why he would also go out of his way to speak to me as well."

Birger looked surprised. "Has he?"

"Well, not recently, but considering all that I have read and everything you have told me, if he wanted to, then he could have had me murdered long before now. He didn't need to actually battle me at the United Nations. He never had to talk to me at all. With his amount of power he could have taken care of me long before now."

"Unfortunately, that is true."

I took a seat again. This was not the conversation that I had anticipated. "In reality, it's only to my benefit to join the society." They could provide levels of protection and knowledge that I would be unable to obtain anywhere else, other than possibly The Righteous Group and I wasn't really into their purpose for existing.

"You would have our protection either way," he said. "But, yes, it would be to your benefit."

"Right." I sighed and looked down at the ground. "Then with that," I looked up and made eye contact with him, "count me in."

22

BIRGER'S - 10TH CENTURY

The King was imprisoned in the bowels of the castle's jail, so the queen placed some of her most trusted guards to stand watch. She returned to the throne room and took her place perched atop her chair next to the empty throne of her husband and presided over the court. She politely welcomed the visitors and listened to the complaints and concerns of the town folks. All without acknowledging her husband's disappearance.

On the ninth day, Harald returned, exhausted, from his travels. His clothes in tatters, he was clearly in recovery from a battle, he bowed before the queen. "My lady, we have returned from the Finns and discussions with the former King."

"Former?" she replied.

"Yes, my queen. After discussions and some physical exchanges, the King of Finns is no more. The lands are now under my stewardship."

The queen smiled and nodded in acknowledgement. "Well done, my nephew. Well done."

"May I ask where your husband, the King, has gone?" He motioned towards the empty chair beside her.

The queen looked over her shoulder and feigning sadness, replied, "the King has died." And with those words the queen actually shed several tears, encouraging her court members to respectfully share their fondest memories of the newly passed royal, followed by moments of silence.

At first, the court members feared asking what had happened to him. They shared their most pleasant remembrances and spoke of the deep sadness they had with his passing.

Only after several hours did the second in command ask, "My queen, my deepest condolences on the loss of our most beloved leader."

The queen wiped tears from her eyes and nodded in agreement.

"We will forever be thankful for all that he has done for each and every member of our kingdom." Harald politely bowed before her. "May I ask, what had occurred? The last I saw the good King had been sitting beside you on the throne. It is truly shocking to hear of his passing."

The queen lowered her eyes and folded her hands before her. "The good King elected to go off into a last minute battle and in that fight we lost him," she said. She glanced at Harald to see if he would give away anything from their previous conversation and instead she noted that he kept his eyes downward.

An advisor to the queen paused for a moment and then continued with his words of sadness and mourning. When he finished the queen said, "We must have a ceremony so that all of the kingdoms may pay their respects. We must bring forward a statue replicating the mighty King at his height of power and strength. And then have the head of the church give a ceremony to speak of the benefits of our good King. Then followed by an opportunity for each and every member of our kingdoms to be granted the chance to place flowers and gifts of remembrance before the statue. Only afterwards can we declare him to be peacefully at rest."

"As you wish, my queen," the advisor replied. With that he exited the throne room and executed the queen's commands. Queen Gyrid silently watched as all that she had declared was made reality and as the Duke Harald stood by and simply remained among the other royal court members, keeping his thoughts to himself.

Only after all had been granted a chance to bid their well wishes to the representation of the King; only after the queen had publicly displayed her own moments of mourning before all present; only after all had shown their respects and left gifts to acknowledge how the King had been loved and admired; only after objects to help the King in the afterlife had been left with the physical representation of the good King; only after all of this had been done and the King had been declared happily in the afterlife, did Queen Gyrid convene the royal court and bring Harald forward.

"With the King's passing and considering my own state," she looked down at her gray and ashen limbs and referenced her gaunt cheeks, "I would like to declare Duke Harald the new overseeing King of all of our kingdoms."

The royal court members silently agree to the queen's commands. Along the edges of the royal court, the King's special guards stood nearby to protect the queen and the newly declared King. Among those special guards stood Ulf waiting to see what would be declared next. And under cloaks to hide their presence stood Birger and Chago.

Birger was fearful of what would happen next, considering all that the last King had done to those in the kingdom, and also considering the amount of uncertainty that came with the changes of the crown.

Chago was eager to see what would happen next for he believed that with every change in royalty came an opportunity for his own personal plans to be executed.

As Harald kneeled before the queen and she officially declared him the new King across the Finns, Sweden, and Norway, both Chago and Birger slipped out of a side passage ready to renew their services to the downtrodden of the lands.

And Chago prepared to do even more.

Much, much more.

INTERLUDE 11

(800'S OR 900'S AD)

We began without delay. He had lived in the cave by himself, but made had converted it to be a comfortable place for me to dwell as well. We also had a place where he typically built fires for our meals and warmth, and he had cleared a section that he used to train in the arts of our forefathers and foremothers.

By day, Chago taught me spells and what he called "the old ways." Surprised that he had not written these guidelines down, I secretly began recording everything from spells to historical events to mythology to where to find individuals within the different Lycanthropic houses. Even if I did not fully understand what he shared, I wrote it down, figuring one day I would look back on it with a deeper understanding and be able to expand upon those things with a richer clarity not available at the time of the telling.

By night we wandered the streets and neighboring forests to find those downtrodden. Before this, I had not realized how many had been dejected. The numbers were staggering. So many with physical ailments like a disability from being permanently injured during a fight. Those typically needed assistance in nursing their wounds and caring for themselves. We brought them food and dressings for their ailments and medicines. We found them in the dark recesses of the back-streets of the towns typically hiding in alleys and stalls. I admit that I felt fulfilled by being able to help so many who were in such pain and could not help themselves.

But the most depressing were those who suffered from mental illness. The ones who hallucinated and spoke to beings not present. With those, I took Chago's lead and did exactly as he directed. It was clearly based on his response to them that he had been treating many of them for a significant period of time. He understood exactly how to and how not to approach them for there were times when one would become violent and in that violent state would shift into creatures intended to attack. I admit, when this occurred, I could see why the King may have excommunicated them, but at the same time, I considered the cruelty it took to treat them unfairly and not provide care for them. Instead, the King had sent them off on their own. That truly disheartened me.

We sheltered in the cave afterwards, finding food and cleaning up before we would go to bed. Each time, part of me felt lost and saddened after interacting with so many who were unable to support themselves.

"What did they do before?" I asked Chago after we had completed a round of treatments.

"What do you mean?" he asked.

"Before anyone came out to help them with their injuries. Before anyone gave them shelter and food. How did they survive?"

Without looking at me, he whispered. "They did not."

. . .

Chago awakened me early one morning so we could continue our training and assist those shapeshifters who had been abandoned by the King and shunned by society. We were blessed that there were others who had befriended Chago and had gained an understanding and appreciation for the work that we did to help those less fortunate. This is how we gathered food, clothing, and medicines to help the ones who had been abandoned to the streets. This is also how we were able to give those who had been abandoned by the normal society a new purpose.

Some who had been injured, once they had regained their strength, joined us in our efforts. Others used their renewed abilities to seek out others of lesser fortune. Within their renewals, I also found my own strength and purpose redoubling far beyond simply gaining a better understanding of my own skills. Although that was of significant benefit. Chago's teachings and charity gave me the true meaning that I had starved for since before I could remember. I used it as a means of catapulting my own reason for being into something of greater depth. Others joined us in our cave and Chago used this as a way to round out our simple day teachings of spells and self-defense to be more like the formal training that could be found among the King's special guards. Together, we discovered our abilities. Chago's guidance was reminiscent of the head of the King's guards and his training. I felt comfort in this, with the familiar, and even more in the finding of others while growing a small band of shapeshifters who existed to help and save others.

Finding that purpose that made the world have meaning.

At least for a time.

23
LUNA'S - 2000S

We let the other board members back into the conference room.

"I have agreed to take on the role. That said," I began, "I truly want to understand what our goals are. What are we trying to accomplish? What are you most concerned about?" I glanced at Birger. "And yes, I understand that means I'm definitely going to miss my flight and it'll take a little bit of time." I smirked.

He held out his hand and shook mine. "For that we are grateful."

I put my luggage in a corner and sat down, making myself comfortable. "Who wants to start? Tell me whatever you want. I want to be sure that I'm representing each and every member to the best of my ability."

And with that, each board member took their turn to walk me through their concerns, what they felt we were doing well, what we were doing poorly, and where they felt we should be going. All aligned to the overarching mission of The Lycanthropic Society to ensure that shapeshifters lived in harmony with humans and other creatures.

"We are not here to disrupt or harm other species," said one board member, "but rather to ensure that we all live in harmony, and if there is any way we can help other species in their own pursuits, then we do so."

"That sounds noble," I said.

"It has been the core of our beings since time immemorial."

Birger and I were left by ourselves in the room. I hadn't asked him for his thoughts in the larger quorum, yet I was eager to get his read on the information. I passed all my notes by him and then asked a simple question.

"What do you think?"

He had listened intently to the board members, and now gave me the opportunity to repeat anything of note from each individual. Although none sounded questionable necessarily or in conflict, it seemed like they were more so focused on their own wishes and desires.

"I thought we were supposed to exist to help all shapeshifters, right?" I asked Birger.

"Yes, our purpose is to help all shapeshifters and ensure that we live in harmony with all creatures."

"Then why are so many focused on benefiting themselves or undoing something someone had implemented in the past. What does that have to do with helping all shapeshifters and ensuring we live in harmony?"

With that question, Birger simply stared at me, then rubbed his hands against his pant-legs like a thoughtless act of anxiety. "Those are excellent questions," he said. "In some cases, I believe it would be best for you to finish the notes I provided. The ones that record the initial centuries of The Lycanthrope

Society and The Righteous Group. Once you have completed those notes then I think I can better answer your questions."

"You can't summarize it?" I asked. "Those were a lot of notes."

He thought for a second. "I think it is best if you read them all and then we'll reconvene. Otherwise the answers could be over simplified and it is best to understand our history in all of its complexity."

I glanced at my luggage and envisioned the stacks of papers within it. "If you say so, but that means we're going to be here a while."

"With that it is best if I return you to your room so you can continue your studying." He stood up and secured my luggage, rolling it back down the hallway, leading me to my room.

Before he could leave me to my own devices, I let him know that I needed to get back to the states within the next few days. "I'd already promised that I would be back soon."

He looked disappointed. "Is there any reason that I need to physically be here in person?" I asked. "Can we continue this work by video conference and stuff like that?"

I could tell based on his delay that he had never really thought about it before. I'm guessing that this was an unusual request.

"We can accommodate this," he said. "I only ask that we continue to chat each night, similar to what we had done before, and if you are needed to return that we quickly make those arrangements."

I honestly couldn't think of a single reason that I had to stay there. Based on my conversations with Rune and Hilda, they both could continue their training by video. Rune was even willing to find someone local to teach me self defense techniques.

"Sure, I can agree to that," I said.

"Good, then I will make your flight arrangements later tonight and make sure that they are executed within the next twenty-four hours. Good?" He asked.

"Perfect," I perked up. This was the best news I had heard all day. "And don't forget, you promised first class."

Birger smiled, nodded in agreement, and then turned to leave. But he paused. "Oh, one more thing," he said. "It is tradition that the person in command names a successor. So consider who you would like to be your next in line."

"Sounds like you'd be the best selection. Actually, sounds like you'd be the best leader."

"Although I am honored by your sentiment, I ask that you select another from our group. Being in the role of the librarian, my focus is on keeping records of our kind and our history. I cannot be designated as the leader of our society. I must do my best to remain in a more neutral role because I am representing all of our kind. Make sense?" he said.

I understood the intent of what he had stated, but I still felt like he would be the best individual to oversee our kind. I shrugged. "Sure, if you prefer it that way."

Just as he was exiting, I stopped him. "Out of curiosity, has there ever been anyone else in the role of the librarian?"

He turned and asked, "Truly?"

"Truly," I said.

"I am the first and, similar to the role of the head of our group, I too had to name a successor in the event that something occurs to me."

"Are you concerned that it might happen?" I could tell that what I asked didn't quite resonate, so I clarified. "I mean, are you ever worried that either someone will purposefully seek to replace you or that you may be requested to be replaced?"

"Ah," he began. "Things of this nature happen all the time. It depends on who is in charge of our society, what the goals of the board are, and what is happening within our kind." He paused for a moment. "In all honesty, due to these same reasons, each and every one of us has been asked to be replaced at some point. In some cases, members gladly give up their function. In other cases, the individual making the request is replaced because by making this request they reveal their own true intents."

"I'm guessing some of these examples are in the historical records that I am currently reading? Including why and how the last leader moved on."

He smirked. "Oh, you have no idea."

24

BIRGER'S - 10TH CENTURY

"Why another King?" asked the Duke of Shirvia. He stood between the queen and Duke Harald as she initiated the crowning of him to become King Harald of Sweden, Norway, the Finns and all other neighboring lands.

The Duke of Shirvia had come to pay his respects to the recently deceased King and the newly widowed queen. "In the invitation to come to the royal court, there was no mention of a declaration of a new King. This is not what I had agreed to," he said.

"To what are you referring?" asked the queen. She did her best to respond with little to no conflict in her voice, but admittedly, she was a bit annoyed by this impetuous behavior.

"My queen, the rulers of your lands came these days to pay homage to the recently deceased King and to you, our queen. We did not agree to name a new ruler so quickly. We have not had an opportunity to meet with the proposed ruler. In times past, we were given an opportunity to provide our seals of approval."

"This is true," said the second in command. "Our historic

records reflect that if the King and the queen are unable to fulfill their roles and there is no natural successor to rule the lands, then the royalty from each of the towns and lands will have a chance to place a bid on the royal throne and with that bid will also be given the chance to vote on the rightful successor."

The queen looked around the throne room and noted that several of the royal court had perked up in a way that implied they were ready for battle.

"How dare you question the desires of the King!" the queen blurted out. "This had been agreed upon well before his disappearance." With these words she stood up and stretched her arms outward as if she was preparing for flight. Her eyes glittered with anger. She outstretched her arms, her body seemed to grow in size as she reached outward. "This is the will of the King!"

"Disappearance?" The Duke of Shirvia pulled out his sword and motioned for other warriors. They flanked him on both sides, hands on the hilt of their swords. "And this is the will of the people," said the Duke of Shirvia. "And the people will have what they desire."

INTERLUDE 12

(800'S OR 900'S AD)

C hago, myself, and the other shifters who had elected to join in on our efforts, spent our days studying the ancient ways and I did my best to record all that we discussed and discovered. In the evenings, we continued to assist those who were of lesser means.

We had been told that the King had died in battle and to properly pay our respects, the queen had arranged for a week-long ceremony of mourning for all from the lands to honor the King.

Surprised by this news, I wondered how this would affect our people and the ways of others within the lands. Chago looked euphoric.

"We must go," he said. "We must pay our respects and see what the queen has planned."

It was the last part that I knew was what Chago was truly focused on. I could tell based on his reaction that he wanted to confirm the passing of the King. Especially since he had dedicated his life to the saving of so many of our kind due to the cruelty of the King.

It took us several days to travel back to the royal castle. When we arrived we found legions of others from across the lands present to pay their respects. Some of the King's people, others from neighboring lands, and still others from tribes I had never seen or heard of before.

We got in line with our gifts for the King to assist him in his passing to the other side. Both Chago and I spent much of this time listening in on conversations of those around us. Some truly mourned the death of the King. Others seemed grateful for his passing. Still others seemed resentful for they had been beckoned—commanded—to give honor to the King.

"We have spent our lives doing what this greedy, selfish man desired. For what? So that we can barely feed our own people? And now we are being told that we must give even more to this selfish bastard in his afterlife?" Someone only a few feet away from me complained.

"With this we will finally be able to have our own will," his friend replied. "We simply must get through these days, and then our will becomes our own."

"Our will has never been and never will be our own. You are delusional if you believe this would ever be the case," the first man scoffed.

"What about when the queen had been the ruler? Our lands were much more at peace."

"Our lands were at peace for some, yes. But for others, they were forced to care for and look after daemons. Who is to say that we will not return to those behaviors?"

"At least we all had food and shelter then."

"What makes you believe that?" said the other. "All she did was cover up the bad behaviors of years prior and then gave shelter to those who were not of our kind." He said the last bit with a bitterness I had rarely heard.

I was sure to hide underneath my cloak's hood and noted

that Chago did as well. It was clear that we both deduced that these men were fearful of our kind and referenced how, at least for a brief period, those of our kind received aid from the queen and her royal court members. Their resentment dripped from their pores.

We continued forward in line to give our respects, hiding our true selves among this wide variety of persons from different clans, tribes, and forms. The closer we got to the ceremony honoring the King, the angrier and more resentful those around us became.

We made it to the stand and then I led Chago down a side passage that took us directly to the main royal throne room. We remained near the back of the courtroom and listened to the discussions of the queen and her court. This is when we discovered the intent to declare the Duke of Norway, Harald, the new King of the Finns, Norway, and Sweden. Chago glanced at me and smiled.

"Good," he whispered. He looked up at the queen and I swore for a second that they had made eye contact albeit only for a second. "This will finally put one of our kind in charge," Chago said.

"Wait, what? The duke is a lycanthrope?" I asked.

"The duke is half shapeshifter and half human," he replied. "In truth the queen is also of multiple bloodlines, but she can only be in this role for so long. In her transformed state of a Draugr, she will slowly degrade, causing her to need to feed more frequently and with that need she will not be able to control her hungers." He said this matter-of-factly. "Come, we have discovered what we needed to know," Chago said. "Let us return to our cave."

With that we slid back out the lesser known passageway and began our travels home.

25
LUNA'S

Thankfully, Birger kept his word and put me on the next flight back to New Jersey. I admit, I had never been on a first class flight and this was pretty killer. Lots of room and the service was spectacular. I swear it was as if the stewardess knew what I wanted well before I even thought of it. What was even better was that it was the perfect environment to really focus on all of the reading I had to do. Finding out that Chago was still alive was one thing, but it was a totally different level to find out that the previous leader of The Lycanthrope Society decided to join The Righteous Group and at Chago's encouragement. And then to discover that Chago was preparing to take over The Lycanthropic Society if we didn't come forward with a leader and one that he was willing to talk to. I mean, all of this was a bit much, in my opinion.

That said, the more I read up on the origins of The Righteous Group and The Lycanthrope Society, the more I understood how much they were intertwined even if from a distance they seemed to have polar opposite purposes. I continued my studying and starting making plans in my head to meet with

Chago and at least begin our discussions. I called Birger from the airplane and asked him to set up the meeting. He said he would try to contact Chago, and would call be back to verify the arrangements.

On a short layover in Munich, Birger called. It was all set.

I safely landed back at Philadelphia International Airport and my parents generously picked me up.

"How were your travels?" my mama asked.

"I don't even know how to begin," I hugged her, thankful to see her after so long.

By the time we got back to their home, I only had a few hours to prepare for the initial conversations between The Lycanthrope Society and The Righteous Group. I took a quick shower, unpacked, and went over my notes again to see what might be the best approach.

Chago picked up on the video call right on time. He looked pretty much the same as the last time I saw him at the United Nations. It was interesting to me that he didn't seem surprised that I had accepted the role. I mean, I had no idea this was going to happen but he seemed like this was just another day.

"Good to see you," he started. "Let us begin."

I was a little unnerved at his calm demeanor—the last time I saw him, he had tried to kill me.

He dove right into the purpose of the call. "My expectation is that we will rejoin forces," he said. "The question is when."

"Actually, isn't the question, how?" I asked. "Based on all that I've read and heard, the two organizations have not been in agreement as to overall purposes in quite a long time."

"Mere trifles," he smiled. "We have always meant to be united."

I sat back and listened to his perspectives. Although what

he said made sense and his arguments for the two parties to become one were completely logical, something in his vibe told me not to trust him. Everything he said contradicted all that I knew of him and all that I knew that he had done.

After a few hours of conversations, with me asking leading questions and listening, I came forward with the following proposal. "May I suggest," I began. "That we agree to disagree and continue our negotiations to potentially join forces?"

Chago looked as if he pondered my suggestion. "Simply agree to disagree?" he asked.

"Correct."

"And you will not interfere with our activities?"

I had to think on that one. He was implying that if he renewed his activities to dominate humans then we would stay out of it.

"We will respect your belief systems as you will respect ours."

He sat back and folded his hands in his lap. "You did not answer my question," he said.

"I can promise that we will acknowledge your beliefs and we will continue negotiations to potentially join forces."

"How do I know you will not interfere?" he asked.

"The same way I know you will not try to invade and take over The Lycanthropic Society."

He smirked. "Fine," he said. "I will agree. For now."

26
BIRGER'S - 10TH CENTURY

The queen outstretched her arms, her body seemed to grow in size as she reached outward. "This is the will of the King!"

The Duke of Shirvia pulled out his sword and motioned the other warriors forward. They flanked both his right and left sides, hands on the hilt of their swords, and stood at a combat ready position. "And this is the will of the people," said the Duke of Shirvia. "And the people will have what they desire."

Without delay, the warriors unsheathed their swords and surged forward to take the queen and her nephew with force. Immediately, the queen began to change into a raven, her favorite form, which shocked those in the court. She had spent her lifetime hiding her own abilities from those within her husband's will.

Meanwhile her nephew transformed to the werewolf form that he had been known for within his own kingdoms, but he had been careful not to advertise since he had first been beckoned to the court of his uncle and aunt.

They had changed with the anticipation that between the

surprise of being shapeshifters and their own physical prowess that they would be able to overtake the court members and regain control. What they had not anticipated was the Shirvian guards being more than ready for their actions and with a speed rarely seen, the guards changed into their strongest forms— some of wolf, some of bear, others of raven, falcon, and hawk— easily overtaking the queen and her nephew and forcing them into custody.

Queen Gyrid and Duke Harald reluctantly changed back into their human selves, the court members holding them under cover of their swords, the Duke of Shirvia leading the pack.

"And with this, you shall come into custody."

"You do not have the right," the queen said under her breath. "Who gives you this right?"

The Duke of Shirvia smirked, "The people give us this right and the people will decide upon who will lead these lands. You were not named the monarch. You were not named the ruler. You will not behave as such."

He motioned the queen and duke to get up and directed the queen's special guards to show them to the lower chambers and the jail cells. They first hesitated, but knives to the throats of their queen and their newly appointed King made them reconsider and comply.

Fearful that they would find her husband—very much alive and well— the queen was shocked when they reached the cells to discover them empty. Realizing that someone or something had released her husband and that he must have been wandering the lands, preparing for his return, she quietly took a spot within one of the cells. She looked to her nephew who seemed not to be surprised to find the cells empty.

"What do you think you will do?" the queen asked the Duke of Shirvia.

He locked the cell doors behind the queen and Duke

Harald. "We will do as what had been agreed upon for centuries." He let the click of the lock resonate through the nearly empty room. "We will pull together the leaders from these lands and the neighboring kingdoms and come to agreement upon who shall oversee this kingdom. Once that decision is made then it will be the will of that ruler as to how you shall both be punished."

Keeping to his word, the Duke of Smiria took the court members and visited the lands to identify who would become the replacement to the King. In reality, he used this time to demonstrate his own knowledge and how he would provide benefits to the people. How, unlike the previous King, he would focus on empowering those of the lands and how he would partner with the neighboring leaders, not spend his time in trying to take over as many countries as possible. Because of this approach, he was secretly nicknamed the Peasant King.

By the time the royal court and others who may have had interest in becoming the new ruler had finished their tour, the murmurs were that if the Duke of Shirvia could simply get the buy-in of one more neighboring ruler, then he would be named the King.

With this, the Duke of Shirvia spoke with his advisors regarding who would be the best neighboring ruler to become aligned to. "There is no question," an elderly advisor stated. "King Donnchad of Scotland."

The Peasant King nodded in agreement and then declared, "we will have one more visit to complete. And only then will we vote and decide upon who will be the new King."

. . .

The Peasant King continued forward to Scotland with remaining court members and those who would have a say in the next in line.

The travel was hectic considering the amount of time that had passed since they had had stable leadership. The Duke of Shirvia sensed that they needed to come to a conclusion soon otherwise there was a high likelihood that one of the other neighboring leaders would simply overtake the lands of Sweden, Norway, and the Finns.

He entered the royal court chambers of King Donnchad unsurprised as to their sheer size. The room was triple that of the royal court of Sweden and quadruple that of the Duke of Shirvia's own chambers.

The King welcomed his visitors. "I assume you have traveled for several days and must be tired." The King with long dark brown hair, pointed beard, and hooked nose motioned to his visitors. "You are welcomed to recuperate in our guest chambers before we dine this evening."

The Duke of Shirvia bowed and thanked the King for his generosity.

That evening, the King greeted his visitors with a feast of wild boar and venison. "I assume you come to discuss the recent changes in royalty among the neighboring lands?" the King stated and bit into a generous piece of boar. The juices dripped from his mouth, down his beard, and onto his jacket of royal colors.

"We are here to see if we may have your agreement on who may be the next to rule the Swedish, Norwegian, and Finns."

"I see," the King replied. "And who may you be presenting for this role?"

The duke resettled in his chair and smoothed his napkin into his lap. "It has been proposed that the joining of my lands and those that had already been under the rule of the King of

Sweden would be of benefit to the neighboring rulers and the people."

The King took a deep drink of his ale, washing down his bites of meat. "And why would I not simply rule those lands myself."

The duke paused, aware that he must move forward with care. He knew he needed to offer the King something that he would find beneficial for his own rulership. The duke drank from his own pail of ale and then replied, "A joining of the lands would be of great benefit to all."

"How so?"

"My daughter is of marrying age. Along with a gentle dowry then I believe we could come to an agreement."

INTERLUDE 13

(800'S OR 900'S AD)

We returned to our cave ready to renew our endeavors. Our followers were eager for Chago and me to share stories of our travels to which we told of the ceremonies and gifts, and such. I still vibrated from the knowledge that the King who had ruled for so long and done so much to both benefit and harm our kind was no longer. I had tried to broach the topic of what this meant to us and our undertakings during our travels home, but Chago did not seem open to it. He was more focused on our reuniting with our people and renewing all that we had put in place. As we informed our people of the events of the last several days, I noted that Chago did not speak of the additional tales we overheard while we waited to pay our respects, therefore I took his lead and did the same.

Continuing our visits to those less fortunate, we split up so that we could cover more ground in less time. The sheer numbers of downtrodden had increased in the previous months. Even with all of our efforts and with the increased number of shapeshifters who had joined forces with us to assist those less fortunate, the number in need and the amount of time it took to care for them had definitely grown.

I took a handful of our followers along with supplies including medicines and foods and led them to the opposite part of town from where Chago headed.

"We shall reconvene in our place of residence once we have finished for the night," he said.

With eagerness, I guided them down the alleys feeding and giving medicine to those in need. Near the end of our chores, exhausted, I looked forward to returning to our residence when I came upon a familiar face. In the doorway of an inn, within the wee hours of morning, a cloaked woman curled in to rest. As we approached, she raised her head.

"Seeress?" I said. I could not believe it. I did not think that I would happen upon her again.

"Birger?" she replied. Her face brightened. "You look well."

I kneeled beside her and gave her a hug. "How are you?" I observed how she moved, to see if she was in need of treatment.

"I am well," she smiled and sat up, her entire stance seemed to brighten. "I am traveling back to my home and needed a quick place to rest for a few hours before moving forward. Unfortunately, the inn was completely booked, and so I took the chance to take quick shelter here." She looked up and at the main entry of the inn somewhat disgusted and then changed the topic. "What brings you here at such an hour?"

I told her of how I had found Chago at her recommendation and the agreement he and I had made. "That he would teach me in our ways as long as I would assist him in the care of those less fortunate among the Lycanthrope." I then found myself blathering about the sheer numbers we had discovered in our endeavors and how we were able to bring so many back to health. "There is so much to learn and know," I continued. "I found myself recording these tales from our kind's past and doing my best to share this information with others we happened upon." I smirked. "I am so proud of the numbers who have chosen to join us. They could have simply moved on once they had returned to health and were in positions in which they were self-sufficient. And yet so many have chosen to join our efforts." I could feel myself glow with pride at the knowledge that we not only helped them, but they elected to help others as well. "I admit that some of this I simply do not understand," I continued. "I would have thought that with our humanitarian efforts we would see less among those in need, but the numbers simply continue to grow."

She did not look surprised by my statements. Instead she nodded in acknowledgement.

"Are you aware of the changes within the kingdom?" I asked.

With a look of concern, she shook her head and tilted her head with curiosity. "Did you see your brother?" she asked.

I admitted that I had not seen him in our visit to the royal castle.

"He has been newly appointed the head of the royal special guard," she said.

This truly shocked me. "How can that be?"

"In the last several endeavors of the King and then of the queen, he proved to be quite a natural leader." She abruptly stopped and said no more, which allowed me to infer what I wanted from her statement.

I related to her how this seemed ironic considering all of the work that Chago and I had been performing and how it was counter to what Ulf was doing on behalf of the royal court. "As we do our best to save and unite, Ulf seems to be dividing and destroying."

This combined with the last words my brother had spoken to me made me feel even more distant from him and that the man he had become was one I had no desire to engage with. I longed for the brother I had once known. The one who cared for others and looked out for so many beyond himself.

She placed her hand on me. "You must not look at things in such a black and white manner. For they are anything but straightforward."

I scoffed at her warning. "You do not know what I have seen," I said.

To this she renewed her concerns. "Birger, I have heard from those within the realm of your great works as well as what your brother has been made accountable for. And I respect the perspective that you provide." She shook her head. "I do not discount what you have witnessed. I can only imagine the gravity of it all. But please be careful in your engagements with Chago. He has been around for quite a long time and his true intent may not be the most obvious."

"I do not understand. You sent me to him. He clearly has done much, knows much, and is the most powerful and thoughtful and considerate of our kind."

"And because of this, you must be careful," she said. "All I ask is that you approach his proposals and engagements with caution."

I looked her in the eyes and saw her deep concern. I nodded. "I understand."

I placed my hand over hers and acknowledged her current state of homelessness. I asked if she needed anything.

"I am headed home and will be fine," she began, "The best thing you can do is continue your focus on education and recording the vast history of the Lycanthrope. These are areas that have been sorely lacking and to have someone finally take the time to not only focus on them but also to share and teach others is the greatest gift you can give."

I thanked her for her guidance and wisdom and promised I

would do my best. Not willing to simply leave her there, alone and without, I gave her a care package to tide her over as she renewed her travels home.

Upon my return to our cave, I ensured my team of humanitarians had all that they needed before they rested. Chago and his group came shortly thereafter to find me writing down all that I could remember from the previous day.

"We must continue," Chago said. "With all that has occurred, we must continue in our teachings and efforts."

I agreed.

"And with all that we have found, we must see how else we can assist our kind."

"Of course," I said. "Always."

He motioned to the portion of our cave in which we typically slept. "Now, let us rest. Tomorrow we will continue our teachings. We have much to teach and much to learn."

I could never have anticipated the subsequent days. We worked diligently at teaching our kind in terms of understanding and leveraging their gifts. Chago reinforced the fact that we needed to also know how to protect ourselves. "Simply because you have these abilities does not mean that you are prepared for battle," he said. "We must continue in our physical training so that no matter what state we are in, we can defend ourselves."

He continued to lead our instructions in managing and learning our gifts as well as our self-defense training. He had even guided others to act as the primary trainers on his behalf. Even though I was physically exhausted from our daily training, I simply knew that we needed to continue in our recordings of our kind's history and humanitarian efforts. I not only recorded the tales that Chago told, but I also used the nightly outings as an opportunity to interview those who were less

fortunate. So many had been either witness to or had partici-
pated in events of note that I simply could not give up the
chance. By the time I had finished each night, I simply fell into
bed, yet eager to begin another day. Never in my life had I ever
felt like I had been of so much value nor had I ever given so
much to so many. With our actions I knew my true purpose in
life and eagerly awaited each moment.

Several nights passed and during our meal, many congregated to discuss how else we could help those in need. My
fellow humanitarians shared the stories they had heard during
our travels and what they themselves had experienced. They
spoke of fights and those of our kind being enslaved by those in
power. They shared stories of mistreatments including beatings
and spoke about how some would be left out in the streets like
lesser beings.

"And with all of this, there have been even more fights
across the lands," Chago said. "So many have shared about the
destruction being caused. The homelessness, the mistreatments, leaving those for dead."

He shared the stories that he had been privy to during our
nightly endeavors, causing others to redouble their tales. Many
of these stories I had heard as well and had recorded. All
making me ponder what we could do to help one another.

"There must be more we can do," he stated.

I agreed. "But who is initiating these fights?" I asked potentially with greater innocence than I had any right to vocalize. In
my heart I knew.

"The battles do not begin with us," he said with disgust.
"We are simply the playthings of those in power." Others
among us agreed as theiranger increased with each statement.
Chago piggybacked off of the words of our fellow shapeshifters.
He shared how the ruling factions continued to use our kind to
perform their acts of greed. "With each fight, more are left for

dead, while others are glorified to the royal court. Our kind are made to sound like royalty but in reality are simply playthings!"

He continued to talk with passion and anger of how our people were simply being used and how we were worth so much more. My fellow followers chanted in agreement. Their passions growing with each word. "We should not be at others' whims!" he demanded. "If anything they should be at ours!"

Our followers pumped their arms in the air and roared in agreement. Their passion continued. I winced at the last statement and moved to a position so I was not in the center of this. I understood his sentiment, but we were not the only ones who were harmed by the acts of those in power. Many were negatively impacted by the battles and the decisions. The laws that were put in place by the ruling parties harmed our kind and made them have less rights than those in power and they also did the same for those of other kinds who were not descendants or related to the royal families. Should we not look for ways to help all?

He continued his sentiments, further enraging our people, causing them to be even more impassioned. Pointing out, "We have the power! We can fight any war! We are mightier than those in power!" He spoke of how with our knowledge, our gifts, our training we could take over anyone. "They have no right to treat us like lesser beings!"

I simply listened and nodded, careful not to show signs of disagreement. For with these words, I feared what lay ahead.

By the end of the evening, a subset of our people had agreed to move forward with the beginning efforts to take over small neighboring lands.

27
LUNA'S - 2000S

"How was your initial discussion?" Birger asked. He looked a bit hesitant.

Thankfully, I had the chance to grab a bite with my parents before getting back on a video chat to catch up with Birger.

"It took a while," I said. "I mean, there was a point I wasn't sure if we were going to finish, but we did." I looked over my notes.

"And?"

"He agreed to both parties staying out of each other's way."

"Wait, what? Why would you agree to that, Luna?" Birger looked anxious.

"Well our choices were A, we stay out of each other's ways; B, they try to take us over or eliminate all of us; C, we try to take them over and from what the board had described I did not think that C was a desired outcome."

"It definitely is not a preferred outcome," he agreed.

"This definitely isn't the end though," I said. "I still need to pick a second in command. Someone who can take over in case anything happens to me or if I ditch." I sighed.

"It sounds like you think this is an opportunity of some sort."

"Well, if both parties are trying to influence one another, may I make a suggestion?"

Birger looked at me quizzically.

"If I need to name a next in line then why don't we select someone from their organization and have them select someone from our organization to be next in line for Chago. That way both parties have leverage over one another."

I would be surprised if Birger had never thought of this, and since he sat there for a moment and seemed to be pondering the suggestion but without a lot of fervor, I'm guessing I was right.

"Do you have anyone in mind?" he asked.

"In truth, I don't know enough people. I'm guessing it would make sense to name either Chago or the previous head of The Lycanthrope Society to be next in line and maybe name you or one of the other board members to be next in line for The Righteous Group."

"Have you lost your mind!" he blurted out. "Do you know what that would mean?"

"Yeah, it would mean that they would have leverage with us and we would have leverage with them."

"It would give them an even bigger impetus to try and eradicate you."

"Well, I guess you could think of it that way." I paused for a moment. I was too tired to keep talking about this. I really just wanted to rest, go to the bakery, get my bake on, and spend some time not having to think about all this stuff. "I'll tell you what ... why don't we take a few days to think about this and our other options and then make a decision."

"Considering you are clearly not thinking correctly, I think that is the best option."

I ignored his sarcasm and hung up. Thankful for a night off.

My next morning I spent in the bakery getting caught up on all that I had missed. Margarite arrived with my favorite latte in hand and all smiles. "It's good to see you, *mi amiga*," she said. "You've been gone a while."

I eagerly accepted the cup and took a sip. "Ah, I've missed this," I said. "What's happened?"

She led me over to the pages of orders that had come in over the previous weeks and glowed about the great work Alfina had done. "You did good training her," she said. "But I must admit that we all missed you quite a bit."

The rest of the day I gloried in getting back into the grind. Reviewing special orders, meeting with some of my favorite customers and catching up on their needs. It felt so good to get my hands back into the batter, measuring the ingredients, guiding my assistant in her efforts.

This, this truly felt like where I belonged. I glowed with the joy of it all.

I came home to find a message from Birger, "Please call."

I looked at my mom. "When did this come in?" I asked.

She shrugged. "A few hours ago. He sounded eager," she said. In mom-speak that meant he was in a panic.

I cleaned up and then gave him a buzz.

"I thought over your suggestion and I understand it," he said. "I still do not necessarily agree with it, but I understand it. Let us put it before the rest of the board and get their advice?"

"Really?" I didn't think he would come back with that. If anything I figured he'd taken it totally off the table. I mean, who was I to make a suggestion like that? I was just a baker from a small town in no-where's-ville.

"Really. I will convene everyone shortly and then we can vote on it," he looked at his watch.

"That's sounding like I wouldn't be present."

He laughed. "Correct. Per our rules, you would not be a part of the vote. You will be informed afterwards of the board's decision and of any commentary that is provided."

"Sounds good to me," I said. I really just looked forward to not having to be a part of it although I was super curious as to what the board members would say.

We hung up. I left my bedroom to find my mama in the hallway. "That was fast," she said.

"Yeah, he just wanted to tell me about something that's going to go down in a little bit."

"Want to share?"

I thought for a second. "Not yet," I told her. "Maybe soon but not yet."

His return call was surprisingly fast. He even looked surprised.

"So?"

He ran his hands through his hair. "They agreed."

"Wait, what?"

"The board agreed that the best path forward to ensure that we keep out of each other's way would be to name their first in command to be your successor and vice versa. Either both groups will continuously try to murder each other or it will cause us to stay out of each other's way."

"And they agreed to that?"

"Well, if we do not, then the other most likely happening is that we will continue warring and everyone is at risk of being murdered."

"Oh great. So they like it because it's my butt on the line."

"They concurred that it is the better of the options," he smirked. "Plus you were the one making the suggestion. So since you made the recommendation they figured you were most likely into the idea."

"The idea of being murdered. Nope, not really. That said, now that we have agreement, what happens?"

He looked over some notes and then responded. "We will notify Chago and his board of the recommendation and then place guards on your watch. Just in case."

"Just in case."

28

BIRGER'S - 10TH CENTURY

King Donnchad leaned into his cup of ale. "You propose your daughter's hand?"

The Duke of Shirviagave a slight smile. "I propose that to demonstrate our partnership, I offer my daughter's hand."

"What kind of dowry would be part of this agreement?" the King questioned. He did not want to chance other possible engagements that he could have if this did not show a benefit to him of another kind.

The Duke of Shirvia acknowledged the King's wishes. "How about we present the islands of Orkney and Shetland as a dowry? This will also be a physical representation of the joining of our kingdoms."

The King showed a moment of pondering before he placed his cup of ale before him.

"Agreed."

The Duke of Shirvia and his party eagerly left the King's residence with the knowledge that they had his backing and the duke had the additional benefit knowing that his daughter had a prestigious man prepared to marry her.

Upon their return to the King of Sweden's castle, he re-initiated the discussions regarding who would take over the throne. Under the guise of being democratic and fair, he sent servants of the court to each of the ruling parties of the countries of Norway, Sweden, and the Finns as well as to their neighboring rulers to obtain their votes.

To little surprise, the servants returned with an overwhelming majority stating that they preferred the Duke of Shirvia to take over the crown. In addition, the people of the lands to be ruled, gave their majority vote for the Duke of Smiria. With confidence and a bit of arrogance, the duke accepted the proposed title and launched a multi-day celebration inviting the court members, the neighboring rulers, and even the peoples of his lands.

To much surprise, several weeks later the King of Scotland, Donnchad, arrived at the new King's residence. The King of Scotland looking a bit perturbed and with knights and warriors in tow.

"What brings you to these lands?" the new King asked.

"We had an agreement," the King of Scotland stated. "And that agreement has yet to be fulfilled."

The King looked surprised. "That cannot be," he began. "My daughter has been sent to you. Her hand already brought forward in marriage. Is this not what we agreed?"

"It is the lands," King Donnchad said. "They have yet to be delivered. Without the required dowry, we have no deal. And without a deal, these greater lands shall fall under my rule."

The warriors encircled the castle, battle gear raised, ready for the fight.

"This cannot be so," the King said. "I sent along the proper papers declaring that the island of Orkney and Shetland to be gifted to you as a dowry."

The King of Scotland motioned to his parties to move forward, preparing to overtake the King's parties, knowing full well that his warriors completely outnumbered the new ruler. "Then we were both betrayed. And with that, I claim the larger lands." With those words, the warriors moved in and overtook the castle and the castle's respective guards. Excited at the prospect of expanding his dominance to include not one, but three countries, King Donnchad eagerly encouraged his best to fall upon the special guards of the new King, fully aware that the special guard's allegiance most likely did not lay with the new King but rather remained with the previous court.

King Donnchad came forward and climbed the stairs to the royal court, making his way upward to the King's throne. Fully aware that this act, along with the act of imprisoning the new King's based on the lack of fulfillment of their agreed upon partnership, based on the old rules of how lands were declared, would make him the official King across all of these remarkable lands. Just as he readied to take seat on the good King's throne a voice came from the main hall.

"I believe that is mine."

King Donnchad of Scotland turned to find a rather filthy and weathered man, the true King of Sweden, Norway, and the Finns. The man assumed to have been killed based on the words of Queen Gyrid stood before the King of Scotland. His favorite warriors of the special guards, including Ulf, flanked him.

"It is time that I reclaim my throne," said the King.

"How can this be?" the King of Scotland questioned.

"After some confusion and much effort, my good warriors were able to bring me out of the place of imprisonment and return me to where I belong."

He swept his arms across the royal court.

"Here."

INTERLUDE 14

(800'S OR 900'S AD)

O ur group's neighboring invasions proved quite successful. After each attack, Chago was sure to provide speeches of encouragement, pointing out to our people all they had achieved, all they had overcome, and all they were capable of.

And we fought.

That is the best way I have to state it. After each battle, I listened to our people and recorded their tales of the fights. Of the wins and losses. Of the pains and glories. And Chago and I fought over what should be done with these wins. He believed we should increase our invasions and take over the royal houses of each area. I believed we should be using all of the great work that we had done to date and recruit more of our kind and more of the humans whom we had helped to unify and elevate us all.

I pointed out how so many of the humankind had helped us in the past and how they all deserved to be treated well.

"The humans deserve to be treated as equals," I said.

To which he scoffed and restated how our kind had been treated as lesser beings for far too long.

"It is time we take our rightful place of power."
His words dripped with hunger, anger, and passion.

29

LUNA'S - 2000S

I must admit that I was just as surprised as anyone else that The Lycanthrope Society's board agreed to the proposition to have me named as the rightful successor to the leader of The Righteous Group and the leader of The Righteous Group to be named the rightful successor to me, the leader of The Lycanthropic Society, but I was even more amazed when Chago agreed as well. He could have easily seen it as not putting him in a position of advantage, actually putting him in the same danger I had been placed in, and simply declined the offer thereby declaring an immediate end to our truce. But he did not.

Instead, Chago—perhaps alleviating some of the danger— agreed to the change and then immediately had the previous ruler of The Lycanthrope Society named the new leader of The Righteous Group. He seemed rather in awe of taking on this leadership position. It was definitely an unforeseen change. With seeming glee, he agreed to not only take on the role but also to the agreements between the two lycanthrope communities. I have no idea what went through his head, maybe he thought this put him in a position to take over both groups. Maybe he thought this meant that he was now in a much more significant position of power or something else, but he definitely seemed to think that he was a raging rockstar based on the amount of glee he brought into the role.

But of course, things couldn't end there. I had spent a few weeks getting everything set at the bakery and preparing Alfina to take on even more responsibility. Margarite had been talking about expanding the bakery by opening more stores in other areas. Maybe in Philadelphia or New York or Boston, which sounded like a lot of fun to me. And it would give Alfina a chance to possibly take on the lead baker role at one of the new locations. Again, super cool.

With all those conversations in play, I also began talks with the new head of TRG to see how else we could possibly unite the two organizations. I figured we could get together at some place neutral in Philly. Like maybe a coffee shop or something, and then take it from there when I got a call saying he couldn't make it.

"I must inform you that he has gone missing," said his assistant. "I was preparing his travel arrangements when I tried to call him to just check on a few things when he didn't answer. When he didn't answer several times, I finally went to his place to check on him and found his place fully locked up and he was nowhere to be found."

"Where do you think he went? Is there something I can do to help?" I asked.

"Not at this time," his assistant said. "I have asked some of our people to see if they could find him. Once we have an update, I will be sure to reach out to you."

With those words, I hung up the phone, my sixth sense telling me that this may be a bit more than him simply going out for a walk. I hoped I was wrong.

I closed the bakery that night and as I locked the door, my cell phone rang. "Hello?" I answered.

An unexpected voice answered. "I have unanticipated news," said Chago.

I sighed, leaned against the exterior of the bakery, and cut him off, "Yes, I know. I got a call about it earlier today."

"We found him," Chago replied coldly. "He is dead."

30

BIRGER'S - 10TH CENTURY

Surprised, the King of Scotland at first questioned the statement that this man was the rightful ruler of the lands. For he had no reason to believe this to be true.

"How can you prove what you claim?" King Donnchad proclaimed.

From the former King's side came a general of the court. "I can validate that this is truly the King Otto, the rightful leader of Sweden, Norway, and The Finns."

The King of Scotland scoffed. "One voice does not make this true."

And with that statement others from the royal court came forward and reiterated the general's declaration. As did the leaders of the special guard, including Ulf. "He is the one who has led us to many lands, to many victories." The good King Otto nodded in acknowledgement of those who proclaimed his rightful place.

Realizing his claim to the throne and the agreements he had made with the old Duke of Shirvia were nullified with the return of the true King, King Donnchad, reluctantly stepped down.

INTERLUDE 15

(800'S OR 900'S AD)

The next events are ones that I should have seen coming. After myself and a small group of our people had returned from a night of caring for those on the streets and had provided physical treatments to those who had been injured in battle, we fell to sleep in exhaustion.

We awoke to the footfalls of others entering our cave, followed by the sounds of their battle cries. I opened my eyes to see those of various forms—wolf, werewolf, bear, and part human, part beast, invading our home. They launched at our people as they laid in rest, teeth bare, claws drawn, swords and knives unsheathed. Those who awoke before they were taken down, ripped into mere pools of blood and flesh, were able to defend themselves from the attack. I launched deeper into the bowels of the cave to avoid the engagement. Yes, I had been trained how to fight, but I did not want to harm others if I did not need to.

I transformed into the shape of a bear, hoping that the size would assist me in defense, and hid only to be sought out by a werewolf who launched at me with barren teeth, eager to tear at my flesh. To which I parried, slamming my paw against the werewolf's skull, causing him to fly towards the cave wall and get knocked out. I went over to look at him and as he transformed back to his regular human form I realized that this was none other than my brother, Ulf.

I placed my hand on his head to see how badly I had injured him. This was the last thing I had ever wanted to do, and yet I could think of nothing else that I could have done. I looked up to find Chago standing over both of us. He shifted out of his form of a werewolf and back to his own human form.

"I am sorry," he said. "I know this is not what you had wanted."

I did not know how to respond. "What should we do?" I asked. I looked up to see the other invaders taking off, leaving those who were harmed behind. So many bodies. So many ripped and torn and left for dead. Nothing of this seemed right.

Chago called upon some of our other warriors and guided them to take care of those left behind. "We will not kill them," he said. "But we cannot leave them out here like this as well."

They gathered those injured and placed them in a space that they quickly made a makeshift cell. At the direction of Chago, they began treating their injuries.

"I know you did not want this for your brother," he said to me. "But we cannot keep him here."

I wanted to ask him not to kill Ulf. I wanted to tell him of all the benefits that Ulf had provided to our people. Of all he had done for me. But I also knew that much of this Chago already knew.

With these thoughts, I saw the flash of lightning and heard the crash of thunder. Chago looked out towards the exterior of our cave.

"I will move him on," he said. "He will be cared for."

31

LUNA'S - 2000S

"I'm sorry, say that again?" I said into the phone. I couldn't believe it.

"We found him. His body had been shoved behind a line of dumpsters in a lot near his home."

"*Fuck*," I whispered.

"We will investigate what occurred. In the meantime I will take over the lead role for TRG, at least until we find another party to do so."

"I'm guessing this means our meet and greet is canceled."

He smirked. "That would be an accurate and apt assumption."

I don't know what I expected for him to say at this point but what came next was not it.

"I think it would be best if we wait to continue our negotiations until after we have identified the true nature of how his death occurred and who may have been the instigator. Especially considering it is unlikely that he shoved his own body behind a dumpster."

I slid down the wall and sat, knees up, onto the sidewalk. I sighed. "That sounds like an accurate assumption and a good choice in terms of next steps."

We hung up without further discussion. I looked out across the horizon and admired the sun as it went down. I couldn't believe all that had already happened in such a short period of time. So much change, so much mystery, so much pain. I stared at my phone pondering who I could call next when all I really wanted to do was make my way back to my old apartment and snuggle with Javier but at this point I doubted he would greet me, let alone snuggle. But damn, snuggles sounded good.

I reached out to Birger and told him about what had happened with the leader of The Righteous Group and Chago's response.

"Dear god," he said. "Based on everything that's happened in the last few months, it could be anyone from anywhere."

"You took the words right out of my mouth," I responded. Considering all that he had done and all that he had been through, so many could have considered him a traitor while others could see an advantage to their own position with his demise. Still others could have killed him just to end the agreement we had made between the two parties. "The Righteous Group and The Lycanthropic Society have been in opposition for so long, I am sure that there are dozens, if not more, who would want to see him gone for a hundred different reasons."

Birger nodded in agreement.

'Now what?" I asked.

"Did Chago continue with the truce?"

"Yes, he said he still agreed to it, but he did not want to meet or do anything further until we discovered the cause and nature of his death. Or as he put it, 'considering it is unlikely that he shoved his own body behind a dumpster.'"

"That is a reasonable request." Birger smirked.

"That's what I said. But now what do we do?"

"We have a long history," Birger said. "And many engagements and decisions in our past. Which is part of the reason why I elect not to be in the leadership role of TLS. Plus I am most effective in the role of librarian and teacher."

"Okay, but what does that have to do with this?"

"I think it is best if we call upon our board members and ask for their thoughts as well," he said. "Each will come with their own perspective, their own history, and their own biases. Just as I do." He said the last words in a near whisper. "And although I would like to claim to be completely unbiased in this, I do not feel it is of the best decision for our organization's primary perspective on these most recent events to come from me. By the agreement, you are now the leader of the TRG."

I was a little surprised by his statement. If anything, I would have thought that he would want to have primary say as to our next steps. That said, all of the points that he made were good ones. "Okay, then with that, let's call a special convening and get their thoughts."

"I am scheduling the meeting as we speak."

With that, I pulled myself together and made my way to my parents. I was surprised by my mama greeting me with homemade pollo guisado, a one pot chicken stew with adobo, sofrito, achiote, garlic, cilantro, oregano and mama's secret spices along with a side of fried plantains. I was in freaking heaven.

"What's the special occasion?" I asked as I shoved a piece of plantain in my mouth. Seasoned just right with light on the salt and again her special seasoning. I must admit, I definitely came by my love of homemade foods honestly.

"We are thrilled to have our girl home," she gave me a hug and kissed me on the cheek. "We know you need to grow up, but that doesn't mean we don't love it when you are here."

"Alright, what gives?" I asked. "Not that I don't believe you, but there must be something up for all this fabulousness."

Mama laughed. "Enjoy your dinner," she said and then walked back into the kitchen.

If it wasn't Mama with something going on, then it was definitely my pops. That said, I was willing to go along with whatever this was and simply enjoy the feast.

Close to the end of the meal, Papa finally came home and sat across from me. Mama came in with a bowl full of stew and a side of plantains with fresh baked rolls just like Papa liked it.

"How was your day?" I asked him as I took another bite of plantain.

He scoffed. "More of the same. People around here have gone crazy." He cursed some in Puerto Rican slang, words I would rather not repeat, and then dove into his meal. After a few bites, he continued. "You know your *titi* from downtown? The one with the daycare?"

"You mean Titi Ariana? Yeah. What's up?"

"She called today. Mentioned she has a party she needs help with."

"Ah," so this is what the fancy dinner was about.

"She insisted that your *mami* help with the luncheon meals."

"Okay. So?"

He glanced towards the kitchen. "Of course she agreed. We cannot say no to family," he said.

"And?"

He sighed. "And what glowed about the cupcakes you had made for her last year. The ones to celebrate her birthday."

"She wants more?" I asked.

"She wanted to know if you would make double the number of last year and a cake or two."

I shrugged. "Sure, we can do that."

"And she wants them for Saturday."

"Two days?"

"Two days."

"That's not so bad," I said.

"And she insisted that it be you to make them. She says you have a gift like no other." I could tell he tried to say this with charm and even a little enthusiasm, but he sounded annoyed. He hated asking for favors. It was simply not in his makeup.

"Let me guess," I continued his thought, "you mean for free."

He dipped his bread into his stew and sopped up a good amount of the gravy. "I see you know your *titi* well."

I popped a plantain into my mouth. "It's fine, Papa. I'll take care of it."

"Are you sure?" he asked. "You know your *titi*. This means she wants it for a lunch party."

I shrugged. "Considering the type of day I've had, no this doesn't surprise me. Tell her I'll be happy to get her them."

He brightened.

"I cannot promise I'll be the one to make everything. I'm going to need help considering the numbers she wants and how fast she wants them."

He waved it off. "I'll tell her, I'll tell her." He came around the table and kissed me on the cheek. "Thank you, *mi nina*."

"It's fine, Papi. All good." I excused myself from the table and made my way back to my bedroom. I texted Margarite and gave her a heads up that we had a special request from my *titi* and I'd need to knock it out between tomorrow and Saturday morning to which she gave me a thumbs up. "All good, family comes first," she texted back.

At least that was easily resolved, I thought.

32
BIRGER'S - 10TH CENTURY

King Donnchad stood at the head of the throne and looked out over the bevy of people crowding the space. Royal court members, King Otto, his special guards, and others shoved themselves into the room shoulder to shoulder. He considered telling King Otto that his claim to the royal throne had passed, and it had become that of himself, the King of Scotland. He considered stating that because he had married the Duke of Sirvia's daughter and had a rightful dowry that his claim to the throne took precedence to any other claim. But he knew that this was barely arguable. He considered calling upon his own warriors and duking it out. For he had always wanted to expand his lands.

All of these options seemed like potential responses, but he knew that none were very strong. And although he had a history of overtaking lands and making choices that were not necessarily considered the most viable ones, he decided that he would rather wait and follow up on this claim for another day. So, reluctantly, he stepped down from the throne, prepared to return to his own lands, and readied to fight for the expansion on another day.

"It is yours," he said to King Otto, bowed, and motioned to the throne. "All yours."

INTERLUDE 16

(800'S OR 900'S AD)

I could not simply leave him. Chago had encouraged me to do so, just to make it easier, but he was still my brother. I accompanied them as they traversed through the storm as it raged onward. Surprisingly, Ulf remained unconscious. I hoped that during our fight I had not inadvertently injured him significantly.

Along the road, we found a spot to the side. They placed him gently down, at Chago's direction, and backed off, returning to our residence. I stayed. As the storm raged on, the thunder clapped, the lightning brightened the darkened sky, I hid across from his spot on the open road and waited. Thankfully, I did not wait long for another to appear. In a brief moment of reprieve from the raging rain, a young woman appeared. She looked upon my brother with eyes of concern. She checked his body for significant injuries and when she found none, she took him with her to shelter.

I stayed far enough behind so that she would not see me but close enough so that I could ascertain where they went. She took him to a modest home along that same road.

Knowing that my brother was safe, I moved on, returning to my own place of shelter.

Upon my return, I found that those of the invading group who had been injured had been placed in a makeshift cell, isolating them from the others. My own group recuperated as they huddled around fire pits. The fire brought warmth and healing.

I found a spot of refuge near a fire pit and proceeded to find comfort in it. One of my fellow humanitarians handed me a cup of broth for which I was quite grateful.

"This is not done," Chago stated, his voice low, his tone resolute. "It cannot be done."

Others of our tribe nodded in agreement. Their murmurs of concession began to fill the cave.

"The King cannot treat us this way. We are not second class citizens. We are not beings to be played with and eliminated at his whim."

Others concurred. Their own unhappiness was evident in their tones.

"We must show him that treating us in this manner is unacceptable. We must show our force!" Chago stood at the height of the firepit and raised his arms, fists pumped into the air, his might evident in his stance.

"Aye!" others proclaimed.

He went on to describe how we must physically show our power through the injured warriors whom they had left behind. I observed our fellows as they reenergized with the statements.

As they grew in their anger, I could not simply stand by. "You are proclaiming that we should harm those who we have spent our lives trying to save," I stood. My own stance was one of evident dissatisfaction. "You want us to harm, no, murder, those of our kind simply to make a statement."

"They have come to murder us!" Chago retorted. "They are the killers. They are the ones who have disgrace on themselves!"

"This does not make retaliating in kind right. There are other ways to show our might. It does not need to be with bloodshed."

Thankfully, some of our tribe muttered in agreement. For a few moments, I feared that I was the only one who believed in such behaviors, the way the majority followed Chago in his beliefs made me question much of what we had been doing in the last years.

We fought. I cannot say that our fighting was without raised voices. I wish I could say that we simply agreed to disagree, but instead, the arguments continued with Chago restating his previous sentiments that shapeshifters were meant to be in charge and should no longer be treated like slaves. "It is time for us to conquer! Humans are weak and only the lycanthrope are the righteous ones!" At this point he changed to a creature of mythology rarely seen, a three headed oversized beast with a body of a hound and heads of a hound, ox, and serpent. His heads burst forward with fury and rage. He blocked the entry to the makeshift cell holding the injured King's guards, making it clear that we were no longer welcomed.

33

2000S

While Birger has scheduled the special board meeting, something in this situation didn't sit well with me. I know this sounds weird, but based on everything I had been reading about the history of the groups and the different fights, something told me that I may want to reach out to each board member individually. I give Birger a lot of credit for sharing these documents with me. I mean, they covered a ton of information that he may not really want others to know about. If I was him, I wouldn't want anyone else to know about them. But instead he gave them to me and asked me regularly if there was anything I needed or wanted or didn't understand. Still, some of the dissension gave me the gut reaction that these guys didn't really trust each other, so it was better for me to reach out to them individually.

Oh, boy, was that enlightening. At first most sounded like they were just going along with whatever I said, but I think once they realized that I wasn't there for any private gain, other than getting these guys to stop fighting so I could go back to my own life full time, they started opening up about the groups and Birger and Chago and why the groups were necessary. I must admit I hadn't thought of that before. I just figured that it was like the Girl Scouts or Masons. I didn't think that these groups were actually needed.

"How else do you think we learn of our kind?" one board member asked me. "How do you think we were able to get through our maturation? How would we learn of our abilities? How would we learn of each other?" All great questions that were raised to me, which I again had never thought of. I just assumed we all looked out for each other because it seemed like the right thing to do.

Anyway, I had gotten everyone's thoughts and walked them through what I was thinking, to stay with the game plan and act as partners with The Righteous Group on identifying new leaders of each group moving forward so that we all knew and were in agreement, reducing the amount of conflict. The majority seemed open to this approach and minimally agreed to consider it.

Meanwhile, I continued my head baker duties including pulling together the orders from my *titi*. Admittedly, I didn't do all the baking, as she had insisted, but she didn't need to know that. All she needed to know was that everything came from our bakery.

Birger scheduled the board meeting for Saturday evening, the Saturday of the daycare's celebration, which turned out to be perfect timing for me.

My parents volunteered to join me in delivering the delectables to the party which I really appreciated because I had lots of stuff to bring over.

The daycare was a modest one story building which was part of a community center used for the daycare, an elder care community, and for any local neighborhood meetings. On a

Saturday, they typically hosted some community gatherings including birthday parties, so I was not surprised that as we approached the main entrance, there were already quite a few families present. Some for the daycare party and others for their own get-togethers. My *titi* greeted us at the main entrance and opened the doors for us. Dressed in her favorite stretch jeans and oversized sweater, she glowed when she saw us.

"Luna!" she exclaimed. "So good to see you!" She hugged me and took the boxes from my grip, allowing me to take other packages from my mama and papi.

We set everything out on the folding tables that had been set up for the buffet. My mami had gone out of her way to make extra special hand sandwiches, corn fritters, plantains, and empanadas. *Man*, she must really love these kids because this was a super special feast! As we laid everything out, I snuck a few bites of plantains, admittedly my favorites, and prepared to head back out. My parents planned to stay and help my *titi* out but I had let them know that I needed to head back out to take care of some things.

I hugged my parents and my *titi*, letting them know, "If you need help in tearing things down afterwards, just text me. I'll come out."

I made my way back to my car and immediately noticed an unusual presence. Someone who definitely did not fit into our 'hood sat in his car across the way. I had noticed him before but figured if he didn't do anything wicked then I would leave it alone. That said, I was a little worried considering we were at a daycare. I made a mental note to mention this to Birger. I know he had said he was going to appoint a guard to stay with me, but something in the way this guy behaved, no eye contact, no acknowledgement, but definitely not from this neighborhood, made me concerned that this was not the guard.

Back home, I snuck a plate of treats that mami had left behind and prepared for the board meeting.

I looked out my bedroom window and confirmed that, *yep, the guy was definitely following me.* I took a quick cell phone picture and messaged it to Birger asking if he was with us.

Moments later he confirmed my suspicions that, *no, this guy was not one of us.*

Crap.

"Do not worry," Birger texted back. "I will take care of it."

I'm not sure that's really what I wanted to hear. I mean, yes, I was happy that he responded so quickly, but "taking care of it" had lots of different implications.

Within the hour, two guys in street clothes came up to the vehicle and had a rather intimate conversation with the gentleman. They then guided him away from my home. I guess this was a good thing. All of this happened in time for the board meeting.

All members appeared, right on time. Each on video, which was nice to be able to see everyone. Birger forewarned them that since this was an official meeting it would be recorded. The looks of distaste, but agreement, let me know that my choice of chatting with everyone on the side was the right one.

I sensed that many were on guard, hesitant to share their true feelings and thoughts.

Understandable.

Birger guided us through the conversation, recapped the events of the last several days, including the questionable passing of the head of The Righteous Group.

"Considering our current truce with TRG, I ask that we agree to any requests associated with their investigation into what had happened."

None seemed surprised although all seemed hesitant. I don't think anyone had been in a position like this in years, potentially centuries.

I brought forward my proposal. "I believe this truce between The Lycanthrope Society and The Righteous Group is of benefit to both. I also think that this enables us to influence the decisions and actions of each other."

"You want to take them over?" one of the board members asked.

"No, I mean that by each of us having a say in who leads the other's organization then we are influencing what one another focuses on, how the group is led, and hopefully it implies that there will be less hostility between the two groups."

"Interesting," said Birger. "And what if the organizations cannot agree on their new leaders?"

"I guess we will simply need to enforce the agreement to do so," I said. "To our benefit, it would point us to what direction the other organization wants to go into and enable us to respond accordingly."

The board members murmured in response. Nothing of clear agreement or disagreement. More like an acknowledgement that this was a potential outcome.

Birger looked at the time. "Okay, let us adjourn for the time being. We can reconvene in the coming days once we have had an opportunity to fully consider the proposal."

I headed back out and helped my parents and *titi* in the clean up. I truly missed being around the family members and celebrations like this one. I loved watching the kids play and their pure joy.

The more I watched the kids, the more I reflected on my

conversations with the board members and the guy who had
been following me around. I was not comfortable with the idea
of being near children. I felt like I put them at risk of being
hurt. The more I thought about it, the more I questioned what I
wanted to do. I understood the influence I could have over the
future of the societies, heck, on the world. And I also truly
started to understand the impact this would have on my daily
life. Change that, how my daily life could never, ever be the
same. Is that something I wanted?

I contacted Birger and voiced my concerns. "You got what you
wanted. You wanted a truce. We got that. Or we'll get it shortly.
Once we put forward the proposal for how to select the head of
each group moving forward. No matter how TRG responds.
Then that goal is reached."

"What are you trying to say?"

"I'm not sure if I should continue. I mean, look at what's
already happened. How do we know I can make a difference?"

The silence on the line made me think he had dropped off.
And then he sighed. "There's more, Luna," he said. "There's a
reason I had you read the archives. It's more than simply understanding our history."

"Okay." *Of course.* I wondered where this was going.

"It's understanding your history and how you can make a
similar impact as your lineage. You are more than a
lycanthrope."

"It is an interesting proposal," Chago said. We had gathered
both organizations on a video call. "One that I would like an
opportunity for our leaders to discuss amongst ourselves."

"May I suggest that each comes back with a response within the coming days?" I said. "I believe we would gain benefit from hearing the pros and cons from each party."

Chago bowed his head slightly and then folded his hands before him. "To that, we can agree."

Meanwhile, the investigators from TRG moved forward with their investigation of their leader's demise. To no surprise, they interviewed the most prominent members including those who seemed to have no ties to the deceased. I wondered what they would discover and hoped that whomever had committed the crime and for whatever reason, that it had nothing to do with this decades long disagreement—or worse, with the most recent agreement I had made with TRG.

Birger called an emergency gathering of our leaders. A bit surprised, I agreed to the session. "What's up?" I said, as light-heartedly as I could muster.

"We have received a listing of concerns and benefits of the proposal from TRG. Since they have a need to identify a new leader sooner rather than later, they have requested that we review and respond in kind as quickly as possible. Respecting their needs and wishes, I agreed."

The others joined the call in different states of disarray. Birger displayed the note that he had received from TRG and walked us through them.

By the end we had agreed to the points and all had agreed to the means of selecting a new leader. With that, TRG had brought forward several potential names to be put at the helm. To everyone's surprise, Chago's name was not at the top of the list provided for our consideration. The front-runner was named Lin and had been with the organization for years. Originally a member of the Philipine faction, her efforts had taken her all over the globe and gave her a unique understanding of both organizations and their efforts. We felt as though we had selected the best candidate to drive both organizations forward.

34

BIRGER'S - 10TH CENTURY

"It is yours," King Donnchad of Scotland said to King Otto, acknowledging the true King's rightful place, removed himself from the stage, bowed to King Otto, motioned to his own people to follow him, and then looked at King Otto, and motioned to the throne.

"All yours."

King Otto returned the bow, physically in disarray, still in need of a bath, fresh clothes, and rest, elected to instead regain his seat and declare his royal court. "For as our ways have been for hundreds of years, we must ensure that those who will be of greatest benefit to our people should be at the helm."

His chief advisor came forward and acknowledged the King's wishes.

"My lord," he began. "In truth there has been much discord in recent years. May I suggest that we take our time in making additional changes that affect our lands and our people?"

The rightful King Otto repositioned himself on his throne. "We shall do so, but first there are those who have caused much of the chaos who need to be acknowledged."

King Otto motioned towards the entry of the throne room which signaled his special guards to bring forward Queen Gyrid, Duke Harald, and the Duke of Shirvia.

"Unfortunately, I had trusted them with my lands and my life only to be repaid with malice."

The crowds within the room gasped in surprise and murmured with wonder.

"You cannot do this!" Queen Gyrid demanded. "You have brought pain and discord to these lands long before our acts which enabled the people to live better lives. Nothing like the horrors of before."

"*HUSH!*" King Otto exclaimed. "You have no rights. You are long past the living and will be treated as such." He beckoned his special guards who transformed to their most mythic of creatures from Kraken to werewolves to Draugr to Fenrir. They flanked the queen as her true nature of Draugr was brought forward by her own angers. After she lashed out, they countered, and a fierce battle ensued until she was finally kept at bay. The two dukes who had previously been aligned to the good queen looked on in horror. Realizing that they were outnumbered, they both backed away from the fight.

King Otto came down from his throne with his sword drawn and raised.

"And with this needful act, we will bring our lands back to stability."

He motioned for his guards to hold her down, while with a force rarely seen, he removed the queen's head with a mighty blow.

The dukes realized that they were next and attempted to escape. With a simple hand motion, the King had the guards hold them back.

And then with a few simple blows followed by decapitation for good measure, the King eliminated his enemies of note.

INTERLUDE 17

(800'S OR 900'S AD)

With Chago's transformation and several of our tribe following suit, I exited. This was not what I wanted. I did not want to fight. I did not want this discord. I simply wanted peace.

At the time I was not sure who would follow me, but I was heartened to find that several of our members did so.

We made our way out of the cave and into the neighboring forests. We had performed enough travels that we were familiar with places of refuge that were available to us.

Once settled in our shelter by the river, we discussed what to do next.

"I truly am not sure," I acknowledged. "We have always been one with Chago and although I agree with much of his proclamations in theory, I do not believe anyone has the right to harm another." In truth I felt guilty about how I had left it with my brother, Ulf. And that I had been the cause of his injuries, even though what I had done was because of his own actions against me. "That said, we must protect one another. Physically, emotionally, spiritually. We must continue our efforts for generations to come."

The others agreed. "We grew up with nothing. Only through our own actions can we ensure that ourselves and future generations will have safety, will have comfort, will have truth."

"But how?" One of the followers asked. "How do we ensure this will be true?"

"We will dedicate our lives to allow shapeshifters, lycan-thropes, humans, all beings to live side-by-side," Birger said. "We will do this with The Lycanthrope Society. Our official name for all of us who stand by these beliefs."

He looked across the group before him. All looked forward at him. "All in favor?" He asked.

In unison, they proclaimed, "Aye".

"All opposed?"

None replied and with this exchange, The Lycanthrope Society was born.

35
LUNA'S - 2000S

A few days after the initial board call, I figured I could refocus on my normal life, at least for a little while. I knew I had a lot more work to do with the societies and a lot more to learn from the archives and from Birger. But at least for a few days, I could enjoy the quiet of a normal-ish life.

With glee, I returned to my favorite bakery. For the first time in more nights than I could remember, I slept with no disturbances and awakened in the morning to my alarm. I slept so soundly I felt like I had a hangover. Not a bad one, but more like one you get when your body had been through a lot and then had hours to recuperate.

I stretched, went for a quick run in the neighborhood, and then came home to shower and head out to work.

Per our usual, Margarite arrived with hands full of lattes and a bag of special orders. Our first customer was a long timer who I sensed within seconds of his entry. "Hello Double Chocolate With Coconut Icing, how ya doing?" I greeted him.

He laughed. "Good to see you too."

"How can we help you?"

Of course, he ordered a double chocolate with coconut icing (I was never wrong), picked up a few items from the display case, and then headed out. Slowly the typical Sunday morning breakfast and brunch line formed, curling around the corner. Margarite and I switched off taking care of the walk-ins and knocking out the pre-orders. I hadn't seen Margarite so happy in ages and I must admit I felt the same. By the time we closed for the day, we must have served a few hundred folks, taken just as many orders, and prepped a ton for Monday. It was glorious.

The subsequent days continued much the same. Margarite and I discussed the opening of the coming shop and our best approach to move forward. Alfina, although eager for the new place to open, seemed a little hesitant to take on the head baker role.

"Are you sure?" she asked. "I mean, I've only been at this for a little while."

"But you came from the same school as me, you've been taught by both me and Margarite, and you've definitely got the chops," I said. "Plus we're always here." I knew where much of her hesitation came from. She had also been alone much of her life. Her family had been small and when she was young, her father had lost his job, leaving her family homeless. Thankfully, that didn't last more than six months, but those times definitely formed much of her beliefs in herself and her own abilities. The only reason she had even tried for the cooking school was at the behest of her home economics teacher in high school who saw her natural abilities and recommended she go for the scholarship. Knowing that she wouldn't be able to afford the advanced school without it, that same instructor secretly wrote a letter of recommendation and encouraged other instructors to do the same, which is what got her the funding and the courage to go for it.

With my last bit of reinforcement, reminding her that we weren't going anywhere, she seemed to get a bit more at ease with it.

"Thanks," she said. "I appreciate it."

She had done so incredibly well in the last several months, we couldn't have been prouder.

At night, on my way home from work, I drove by the apartment I had once shared with Javier. Part of me hoped that I would see him either leaving or coming home. Of all the things I wished I could change from the last few years, at the top of my list was all I had done that tore us apart. If only I hadn't been so selfish. If only I had been more honest with him, just like he had been with me.

His car wasn't even in the parking lot.

I made my way home to a plate of leftovers, pork chops and paella. "You know we love you, right?" Mami said. Any conversation that started with "you know we love you" is destined to be a nasty one.

"Yeah?" I replied. "What's going on?" I bit into the pork chop. Yet again, Mami had outdone herself. Some of the most flavorful, tender, juicy pork chops I had ever had.

She poured me a glass of home brewed iced tea.

"Your papi and I have been talking and we think it's time you found a new place. Some place you can settle."

I figured this was coming. I mean my parents loved me and all, but I'm sure they wanted to enjoy their retirement without the disturbance of me coming in and out on a daily basis.

I took a sip from the tea. "Thank you, Mami," I said. "Not a problem. I'll start looking for a new place, tomorrow. That work?"

She nodded. "Perfect." She headed into the kitchen. "Oh and you got a phone call." She looked at her notes next to the kitchen wall phone. "Birger?"

The board meeting had only been a few days ago. He had absolutely no reason to call me, which means something was up. *Dammit.*

"Are you sure he said his name was Birger?" I asked.

"Absolutely. Said you should call soon. He sounded concerned about something, *mi nina.*"

Double dammit.

"Sorry to bother you," he began. I had called him on the video phone, figuring he might prefer this over a telephone.

"No worries," I said. "What's up?"

"We have received some news that you may find interesting and of which we may need your assistance."

"This can't be good." Especially if he started the conversation off like this, it definitely was not warm fuzzies.

"After a thorough investigation, we have discovered the means in which the former leader of TRG died." He paused. "It seems as though this person had been secretly meeting with him ever since he had resigned from TLS. They had been in discussions regarding our kind. According to the notes, the former leader had initiated an argument with him that resulted in a physical battle in which both shifted. Based on the injuries, he had been killed by one of the perpetrator's more powerful forms."

"Oh no," I had a bad feeling about this. "Who was it?"

He sighed. "Chago," he said. "He is claiming that he had lost consciousness in his most powerful state and does not remember what had occurred. To be candid, I do not believe he lost control of his abilities. He is too powerful and considered one of the masters."

I could feel a combination of anger and resentment rise within me. Why did everything evil always point to Chago?

How did he always become the center of anything nasty? I took a deep breath and asked, "what do you believe happened?"

Birger studied his notes for a minute and responded, "Well, that is what makes this especially difficult. It is the reason he stated that they were fighting."

He paused.

"According to Chago, they were trying to find means of joining the warring factions. Similar to what we had done by looking to the legends in order to identify the strongest potential ruler. They had concluded that it would be the one with the strongest shapeshifting abilities and the one who could best represent all of the families. He had stated that he made the most sense, considering he had also already led TLS and was the current leader for TRG."

"This was before we made the propositions we made?" I asked.

"Correct," he said. "But, unfortunately there is more. According to Chago, the former TRG leader had concluded that the natural ruler or as he put it 'the rightful savior' was himself."

"Oh shit."

"Chago felt as though he did not need to share their exchange. Only after he had been approached by both organizations' investigators did he come clean."

"Now what do we do?" I asked.

"Chago claims that the former leader had demanded that we all bow down to him and then demonstrate our allegiance by eliminating all lycanthropes who were in disagreement."

"So he went bat-shit?"

"You could describe it that way, yes."

"Based on that, it does sound like Chago saved us, I guess. Now what?" I asked.

"Once he had explained what occurred, the investigators

tried to bring him into custody. Let us say he did not go willingly. It seems as though after he had been presented with the evidence and it was demonstrated that there was no evidence that this was an accident, Chago overpowered the investigators. He is currently in hiding."

"Oh no. Have we pulled anyone in to help find him? To me, him taking off demonstrates that this wasn't an accident."

"There are others who are in agreement with you."

"And?" This felt like there was more.

"And now we must find him before he can cause further harm. We must leverage your other abilities."

36
BIRGER'S

With a few simple blows followed by decapitation for good measure, King Otto eliminated his enemies of note. Previously among those he had trusted the most, the King looked at the bodies, their blank eyes stared into the air, with no acknowledgement of the world around them, and he mourned the people they had once been.

Quietly, members of his nobility made their way out of the royal chamber. They had realized that King Otto would continue his cleanse of the factions within his court and they did not want to be among them.

Once transformed, King Otto commanded his special guards to take the bodies and dispose of them, "In proper form." The heads to be burned, each in its own firepit, the bodies to be slashed and fed to the royal beasts, ensuring that the traitors of King Otto would never return.

He then called upon Ulf, "You have one small task to perform."

"Yes, my lord," replied Ulf.

"I need you to take our best and eliminate those who have been secretly growing a legion against us. They live among the caves beyond the rivers. They need to be taught of your might. They need to be taught their proper place."

Ulf bowed. "Yes, my lord."

3 7

LUNA 2000'S

Birger continued to explain what evidence the investigators had found and what they had done to date to bring Chago back in.

"They have narrowed down the potential hiding locations to three. One in New York, one in the Philippines, and one in Finland."

"Why don't they just go get him?" At this point I was getting a little confused. I mean, I understood the need to contact me and fill me in on everything but I did not understand why they didn't take care of it. What was I going to do that they couldn't?

"We want to be sure that whomever is sent to retrieve him will have the greatest likelihood of success. Considering Chago's natural abilities and strengths, that greatly limits the number of individuals who can accomplish this."

"Let me guess ... the top name on the list is mine."

He smirked. "Your bloodline and already demonstrated skills make you the natural choice."

I shifted in my chair. I wasn't really comfortable with

where this was going, but I couldn't argue what he said. Especially after the months of training and all that I had learned about our kind. That said, I definitely had a lot more to learn.

"Okay. Where do we start?"

By the time we had finished our conversation, Birger had been given the green light that Chago was definitely in New York. Within the hour, my train ticket had been purchased and we had identified the best of the special guards to accompany me.

The train to New York wasn't as bad as I thought it would be. Amtrak definitely set things up so that commuters were as comfortable as possible. Sitting in Business Class, I had plenty of leg room and they even provided snacks! I know I shouldn't get so excited for a snack box of pretzels, peanuts, and chocolates but heck, I was always up for a treat. Plus lounging on the train gave me a chance to do a little more homework on what I could expect in New York, what the investigators had found, and the best approaches to bringing Chago back.

I found the lull of the trainride relaxing. The soothing hum of the engines and the cushiness of the seat made me want to curl up and rest. Once I had finished going over everything I needed to, I took a quick nap. Just long enough to refresh before I reached Penn Station in New York.

Upon arrival, the hectic and chaotic nature of Penn Station nearly overpowered my senses. Travelers scurried everywhere in a mad dash rush to wherever they were going. You'd think that since I grew up in the inner city I'd be used to this kind of action, but for some reason, it hit me in the face. I took a deep breath and sought my special guard members to take me to our destination.

To no surprise, it was a high end condo within walking distance of the United Nations. He must have used this as his residence while he plotted and executed the events that had pulled me into the TRG and TLS.

Using a back entrance, myself and a handful of my guards, took the delivery elevator up several flights to the floor where Chago's condo could be found. I left a few guys at the main entrance, just in case we needed backup. We made our way down the long, empty and somewhat eerie hall. We had identified Chago's condo as being the one at the end of the hall. I sensed his presence within moments of stepping foot in the corridor, but I was distracted by another figure – a familiar figure.

It was Eddie, my assistant from the bakery. What was he doing there?

"Eddie?" I said, surprising myself that I even said it out loud.

He stopped and turned around, verifying I was not seeing things. He smiled, waved, and then he did something I did not expect. He *transformed*. Not into a wolf, a bear, a raven, or any animal shape. No! He transformed into...into *Javier*!

"What the..." I started, squinting to make sure I was actually seeing what I thought I saw.

Then Javier – Eddie – transformed back into the form of my assistant, and said, "There are still many things you don't understand or know, Luna."

. . .

"What are you talking about Eddie?" I asked and made sure I called him by his name to validate what – and who – I was seeing.

"I'm talking about Javier, a note on a door, and maybe even a meeting where you explained more than you really wanted to," Eddie replied. He smiled again and turned away.

I wanted to follow him, but my reason for being in that corridor was quickly and powerfully reinforced by a strong sense of Chago's presence. It was an intense feeling, and considering all that we had been through with the lycanthrope and my own training to gain greater understanding of my abilities, I knew that if I sensed him, then he definitely knew my buttocks was nearby. This was one instance in which my heightened powers were both an advantage and a disadvantage.

I sensed his awareness and his emotional shift from one of safety, complexity, clarity and cleverness to self protection, focus, anger and a bit of fear.

That last one, fear, surprised me. Here was a guy who had been alive for more years than I could count and he had anxiety? I tried to hone in on it and felt him block me. *Damn.* He definitely knew we were here.

I had to let my encounter with Eddie – and all the questions it raised – go ... for now.

I forced myself to refocus on the task at hand and motioned for the guards to take their positions. As we made our way down the hallway I felt vulnerable. There was nowhere to hide, nowhere to go. I looked up to find security cameras. Again, no surprise, but definitely did not give me any warm fuzzies considering Chago's ability to influence others. I wouldn't be surprised if he was tapped into the cameras and knew our exact positions.

No one said this would be easy.

I stood before his front door and sensed him right behind it. Screw it. May as well bring it full force.

"Chago, I know you are there. I know you are waiting for us." My cohorts looked surprised. I guess they had expected him to run for it. I'm glad Birger had explained to me a bit more about my abilities. I hadn't understood before that not everyone had these heightened senses. My guards' reactions reinforced this knowledge. "We just want to have you come with us so we can talk through this."

I sensed his cynicism grow and his anger turn to something more sinister. Something that let me know he wanted a fight. *Fuck.* If I could sense him, then he wanted me to feel what he felt.

I detected him shifting. That was the sinisterness, the evil, the horror. I felt his more animalistic self come forward. The depths of his ancient self that refused to be dominated.

I quickly motioned for my guards to turn so that they were ready for what would come next. Little did I know that Chago had already planned this out.

Within seconds, the front door blew open. The flying debris barely missed me as I was shielding my head and face with my forearms. When I looked up, I saw Chago standing within the doorway to reveal one of his more ancient forms. One of a bear with horns sprouting from his head. His claws extended and powerful. He let out a roar that shook the walls. He quickly swiped at me and I ducked out of his reach and then scooted behind my guards to buy myself a few moments to shift into a being that could at least match his force. Thanks to my training, I had learned how to control the pain that came with the shifting and to refocus on what I needed to become. I allowed my instincts to guide me as I turned to a larger were-wolf. One of force and height. I let out my own demonic howl.

Two of my guards, already in their wolf forms, lashed out jointly against Chago. One leveraged the strength and fierceness of his legs while the other went after Chago with his extended claws.

Clearly, Chago had experience at being in battle with two at the same time since he stomped on the one guard's legs and moved out of the way of the other's reach. Readying to join the fight, I mentally took note of these simple yet stellar moves.

In my head I heard his words of threat. "It is time for you to learn who the true ruler is!"

Oh, yay. He'd gone apeshit. That explained a lot. This should be fun. *Note the sarcastic tone.*

I had learned enough in my training not to reply to his projection, but rather respond. I dove to his legs and punched at his knees, one of the most vulnerable areas, and forced his enormous self down to the ground. He let out a howl letting us know that he definitely didn't expect that one. I guess he didn't realize I had been trained by some of the best since we had last battled.

I felt my paws begin to shake and realized that he initiated the incantation that he had used on me when we had battled at the United Nations previously.

Oh, *hell no.* He's not going to get away with it this time.

Similar to our last encounter, my paws shook, not like someone with Parkinson's Disease or with a nervous tic, but rather like someone shedding her skin. I could feel him trying to force me to transform into a smaller being. Transform me into a creature he could easily dominate. That made me so furious that I focused even more on retaining my form and controlling my transformations.

I countered by ensuring I was centered on my form and pushed his attempts out of my head. I deflected by leveling up and changing into a griffin, an ancient being with the head and wings of an eagle and the body, tail, and hind legs of a lion.

If he wanted to play, then let's play.

Similar to before, I knew this couldn't simply be a physical fight. This was a mental battle, a spiritual battle. I focused on my internal self and hoped that my guards would continue forward to neutralize this demon.

I extended my wings that filled the width of the hallway and immediately shot my beak out. I aimed for his throat figuring it was the best way to neutralize him faster. He had taken the opportunity of my own changing to shift his own form so by the time I went for it, he had nearly finished his transformation so I missed his throat and instead caught his shoulder.

He quickly finished his change into something that resembled a dragon mashed with a fur covered giant. I had never seen anything like it. He had to duck in order to fit in the room. Later Birger surmised that he had shifted to the legendary Grendel from Beowolf. At the moment, all I cared about was getting this dude under control.

With that thought, he responded, "you will not and cannot dominate me."

Before I could respond with a thought or action of my own, I felt him push forward like a bullet which was a shift that took me by surprise. I figured he would have physically gone after me, but as I said before, this was clearly a mental, physical, and spiritual battle. His latest maneuver was to attack me physically and mentally.

Quietly, I prayed that I would live through this predicament. I closed my eyes and simply allowed the pain of the shifts to take hold. It ran through my limbs and throbbed through each muscle. The agony was so great that at times I wanted to scream out loud. My amazing training taught me how to use the torture to recenter my focus.

Unlike before, when I had used my thoughts and emotions to ignore the pain, this time I envisioned gathering each bit of torment and pulling it out of my body and into a ball of energy that I held in my hands. A sphere the size of a basketball. With a clear mental focus, I shot that ball of torture, anger, and hate right at Chago.

His eyes widened with surprise. I'm sure this wasn't what he had anticipated. His stance of confidence and superiority weakened. I'm sure he had anticipated that I would shift into whatever weaker form he had projected, one that he could easily overpower. He tumbled backwards from the force of the energy sphere.

I used that moment of surprise to shift back to my favorite form of a werewolf and leapt at Chago as I released a howl. This time I put my full strength behind it. I was tired of this. I wanted his evilness, his trickster behavior to stop.

My impact was far more savage and powerful than he seemed to have expected. I drove him even farther back so that he pummeled backwards. Right behind me, two of my guards dove for him as well, taking him down even faster. He slammed down on the ground. His sheer mass landed with a crash that shook the floor.

I revealed my fangs as my guards lengthened Chago's head from his shoulders, making his throat vulnerable. As Birger had instructed, I knew not to simply slash at his throat unless I wanted him to return in another more sinister form. If I truly wanted to end this, I needed to sever his head from his body. I never thought I would be eager to kill another being, but the combination of the bloodlust from the battle and the frustration from all of his epic blackhearted actions, made me crave his ending.

Just as I dove forward, with a growl Chago renewed in his own savagery, his own passion for power, and thrust his arms forward and chest out which forced my guards off of him. Within seconds he revealed his own fangs and went for my throat. He snarled as his sharp teeth nearly sunk into my skin. "And with this, I will end your foolishness," these words vibrated through my mind.

I felt the fear rise within me. I thought he had truly had me. With that thought of defeat, a guard came forward and pushed me out of the way, taking the brunt of Chago's deadly bite.

"No!" I cried as I saw one of my own be taken down by the evil creature. Without thought I reciprocated and lunged after Chago, taking him down with my curved and elongated claws. With a simple swipe, his throat burst open and his veins spewed forward his own essence.

He screamed in surprise and pain, slashing randomly at anything in his path.

I tumbled backwards and scurried out of the way. I shoved my remaining guards so they would be out of his path as well. There had been enough agony and death on this day.

Torn among the intoxicating scent of Chago's blood, the mourning for my fellow soldiers, and the burst of adrenaline that came with the fight, I forced myself to refocus on the battle at hand. I looked up to see the form of Chago continue to wildly thrash his arms and legs, he screeched from the agony of his wounds. It was time to eliminate his pains and end the fight.

I stood and unsheathed a lone dagger from its place at my side.

"With this," I stated. "I end this."

EPILOGUE

In the pit of night as they fulfilled their obligations, several members of the special guard discussed the most recent happenings. "We have lost much," said one member. "Between the royal benefactor and our own leader."

Others nodded in acknowledgement, knowing that she referenced the queen who was a royal and a shapeshifter as well as Ulf who they had lost in the last mission commanded by King Otto.

"The queen has done much for us." They looked upon their scars and pondered what they had left.

"You still have much," said a voice. A familiar, dark, deep voice. "You still have your powers and one another."

"But what does that truly provide?" one responded.

In the shadows, the owner of the voice came forward, revealing himself in the light of the fire.

"It provides all that we need. Join me."

AUTHOR BIO

Kali Metis is the pen name for Lisa Diane Kastner. Lisa was born in Camden, NJ which was one of the most dangerous cities in America. In high school, she was a dancer and co-host on *Dance Party USA*. At the age of 20 she came home to find her house had burned down and she was suddenly homeless. She spent the next several years rebuilding and obtained her Bachelors, MBA, and MFA. While fulfilling an amazing corporate career, she began Running Wild, LLC which consists of Running Wild Press where they publish great stories that don't fit neatly in a box and RIZE Press where they publish great genre stories written by people of color and other underrepresented groups. Running Wild has been honored with two best of 2019 and two best of 2020 books according to Kirkus Reviews as well as several starred reviews and additional acclaim. Lisa was named to Yahoo Finance's Top 10 Entrepreneurs to Watch in 2021 and nominated to FORBES NEXT 1000, a list of American self-funded entrepreneurs who continue to strive during the challenging times of COVID. She was named to New York Weekly's Top Ten Females to Watch in 2021, LA Wire's Top 10 Businesses to Watch in 2021, and was featured in the August/September 2021 edition of FORBES magazine. She resides in Los Angeles, California with her husband.

ACKNOWLEDGMENTS

To everyone who supported us throughout the making of this book, we thank you.

To the wondrous people at Horror Writers Association, Pennwriters, San Diego Writers Association, Sewanee Writers Conference, Squaw Valley Writers Conference, Writers Coffeehouse, Yale Writers Workshop, Breadloaf Writers Conference, thank you for creating homes for the writing souls that come to you for nourishment.

To my husband for always listening to my wild tales, crazy stories, and next-level ideas.

To my amazing friends for being there to talk, whine, imbibe, party, act stoopid, and so much more - I love you more than words - Barbara, Peter, Ben, Mona, Nicole, Jeff, Taylor, Jonathan, David, Inez, Martina, Josefa, Alex, Lee, Sona, Shahzad, Doug, Eric, Andre, Alexis, Tihi, Alicia, Heather, Derrick, Lisa, Christopher, Kimberly, Evangeline, Lara, Joelle, Ed, Nina, Lisa, .

And to you for taking a chance on this little known author. I hope you enjoyed the ride.

Running Wild Press publishes stories that cross genres with great stories and writing. RIZE publishes great genre stories written by people of color and by authors who identify with other marginalized groups. Our team consists of:

Lisa Diane Kastner, Founder and Executive Editor
Cody Cisco, Acquisitions Editor, Editor, RIZE
Benjamin White, Acquisitions Editor, Editor, Running Wild Press
Peter A. Wright, Acquisitions Editor, Editor, Running Wild Press
Lara Macaione, Head of Marketing
Joelle Mitchell, Head of Licensing and Content
Rebecca Dimyan, Editor
Andrew DiPrinzio, Editor
Cecilia Kennedy, Editor
Barbara Lockwood, Editor
Cody Sisco, Editor
Chih Wang, Editor
Pulp Art Studios, Cover Design
Standout Books, Interior Design
Polgarus Studios, Interior Design
Kimberly , Production Manager
Evangeline , Production Manager

Learn more about us and our stories at
www.runningwildpublishing.com

Learn more about Lisa at
www.lisadkastner.com

Loved these stories and want more? Follow us at www.runningwildpublishing.com, www.facebook.com/runningwildpress, on Twitter @lisadkastner @RunWildBooks @RizeRwp